"The sexiest series I've ever read."
—Carly Phillips, *New York Times* bestselling author

PRAISE FOR

HOT FINISH

"Sizzling hot, jam-packed with snappy dialogue, emotional intensity, and racing fun." —Carly Phillips

HARD AND FAST

"*Hard and Fast* hit me like a ton of bricks and didn't let up until I finished the last word . . . A great second installment from Erin McCarthy! I was captivated and completely enamored of both characters and the love they shared."
—*Romance Junkies*

"McCarthy has done it again! This follow-up to *Flat-Out Sexy* is a thrill ride that's unexpectedly funny, sentimental, and thoroughly entertaining. It's full of real women and sexy men, and these authentic characters, their unexpected love, and a few twists will make you a stock car racing fan."
—*Romantic Times*

"A wild ride. This delightful tale entices the reader from page one . . . The passion is as hot as a firecracker . . . Buckle up, ladies, this is one fun read."
—*Romance Reviews Today*

"This is Erin McCarthy at her best. She is fabulous with smoking-hot romances! *Hard and Fast* is witty, charming, and incredibly sexy." —*The Romance Readers Connection*

"Author Erin McCarthy has written another fun, sexy, and humorous story that engages readers from the first page to the last . . . The sensuality between these two will have the readers fanning themselves as they race through the story eager to cross the finish line." —*Fallen Angel Reviews*

continued . . .

"This book had my heart racing with passion, laughter, and happiness for these characters from start to finish. Erin McCarthy has the magic touch when it comes to contemporary romance!"
—*A Romance Review*

FLAT-OUT SEXY

"Readers won't be able to resist McCarthy's sweetly sexy and sentimental tale of true love at the track." —*Booklist*

"A steamy romance . . . Fast paced and red hot."
—*Publishers Weekly*

"This is one smart, sassy, steamy, and flat-out sexy read. McCarthy will have you giggling on page one, fanning yourself by page twenty-five, and rooting for the hero and heroine the whole way through. Buckle your seat belt and hold on—this is a fast and fun ride." —*Romantic Times*

"A new series that sizzles both on and off the field."
—*Romance Junkies*

"The searing passion between these two is explosive, and the action starts on page one and doesn't stop until the last page. Erin McCarthy has written a fun, sexy read. The love scenes are sizzling, and the characters are memorable."
—*Romance Reviews Today*

"A runaway winner! Ms. McCarthy has created a fun, sexy, and hilarious story that holds you spellbound from start to finish . . . A must-have book for your bookshelf!"
—*Fallen Angel Reviews*

HEIRESS FOR HIRE

"If you are looking to read a romance that will leave you all warm inside, then *Heiress for Hire* is a must read."
—*Romance Junkies*

"McCarthy transforms what could have been a run-of-the-mill romance with standout characterizations that turn an unlikable girl and a boring guy into two enjoyable, empathetic people who make this romance shine." —*Booklist*

"Amusing paranormal contemporary romance . . . Fans will appreciate Erin McCarthy's delightful pennies-from-heaven tale of opposites in love pushed together by a needy child and an even needier ghost." —*The Best Reviews*

"One of McCarthy's best books to date . . . *Heiress for Hire* offers characters you will care about, a story that will make you laugh and cry, and a book you won't soon forget. As Amanda would say: It's priceless." . —*The Romance Reader* (5 hearts)

"A keeper. I'm giving it four of Cupid's five arrows."
—*BellaOnline*

"An alluring tale." —*A Romance Review* (5 roses)

"The perfect blend of sentiment and silly, heat and heart . . . Priceless!" —*Romantic Times* (Top Pick, 4½ stars)

continued . . .

A DATE WITH THE OTHER SIDE

"Do yourself a favor and make a date with the other side."
—Bestselling author Rachel Gibson

"One of the romance-writing industry's brightest stars . . . Ms. McCarthy spins a fascinating tale that deftly blends a paranormal story with a blistering romance . . . Funny, charming, and very entertaining, *A Date with the Other Side* is sure to leave you with a pleased smile on your face."
—*Romance Reviews Today*

"If you're looking for a steamy read that will keep you laughing while you turn the pages as quickly as you can, *A Date with the Other Side* is for you. Very highly recommended!"
—*Romance Junkies*

"Fans will appreciate this otherworldly romance and want a sequel."
—*Midwest Book Review*

"Just the right amount of humor interspersed with romance."
—*Love Romances*

"Ghostly matchmakers add a fun flair to this warmhearted and delightful tale . . . An amusing and sexy charmer sure to bring a smile to your face."
—*Romantic Times*

"Offers readers quite a few chuckles, some face-fanning moments, and one heck of a love story. Surprises await those who expect a 'sophisticated city boy meets country girl' romance. Ms. McCarthy delivers much more."

—*A Romance Review*

"Fascinating." —*Huntress Book Reviews*

PRAISE FOR THE OTHER NOVELS
BY ERIN MCCARTHY

"Will have your toes curling and your pulse racing."

—*Arabella*

"The sparks fly." —*Publishers Weekly*

"Erin McCarthy writes this story with emotion and spirit, as well as humor." —*Fallen Angel Reviews*

"Both naughty and nice . . . Sure to charm readers."

—*Booklist*

HOT FINISH

erin mccarthy

BERKLEY SENSATION, NEW YORK

THE BERKLEY PUBLISHING GROUP
Published by the Penguin Group
Penguin Group (USA) Inc.
375 Hudson Street, New York, New York 10014, USA

Penguin Group (Canada), 90 Eglinton Avenue East, Suite 700, Toronto, Ontario M4P 2Y3, Canada
(a division of Pearson Penguin Canada Inc.)
Penguin Books Ltd., 80 Strand, London WC2R 0RL, England
Penguin Group Ireland, 25 St. Stephen's Green, Dublin 2, Ireland (a division of Penguin Books Ltd.)
Penguin Group (Australia), 250 Camberwell Road, Camberwell, Victoria 3124, Australia
(a division of Pearson Australia Group Pty. Ltd.)
Penguin Books India Pvt. Ltd., 11 Community Centre, Panchsheel Park, New Delhi—110 017, India
Penguin Group (NZ), 67 Apollo Drive, Rosedale, North Shore 0632, New Zealand
(a division of Pearson New Zealand Ltd.)
Penguin Books (South Africa) (Pty.) Ltd., 24 Sturdee Avenue, Rosebank, Johannesburg 2196,
South Africa

Penguin Books Ltd., Registered Offices: 80 Strand, London WC2R 0RL, England

This is a work of fiction. Names, characters, places, and incidents either are the product of the author's imagination or are used fictitiously, and any resemblance to actual persons, living or dead, business establishments, events, or locales is entirely coincidental. The publisher does not have any control over and does not assume any responsibility for author or third-party websites or their content.

HOT FINISH

A Berkley Sensation Book / published by arrangement with the author

PRINTING HISTORY
Berkley Sensation mass-market edition / August 2010

Copyright © 2010 by Erin McCarthy.
Excerpt from *The Chase* by Erin McCarthy copyright © by Erin McCarthy.
Cover art by Craig White.
Cover design by Rita Frangie.
Interior text design by Kristin del Rosario.

ISBN: 978-0-425-23594-2

BERKLEY® SENSATION
Berkley Sensation Books are published by The Berkley Publishing Group,
a division of Penguin Group (USA) Inc.,
375 Hudson Street, New York, New York 10014.
BERKLEY® SENSATION and the "B" design are trademarks of Penguin Group (USA) Inc.

PRINTED IN THE UNITED STATES OF AMERICA

10 9 8 7 6 5 4 3 2 1

To Jen Dengler and Adrienne Fowler.
Thanks for being awesome friends
and for a great weekend at the racetrack!

ACKNOWLEDGMENTS

I would like to thank my fabulous editor, Cindy Hwang, for always supporting my ideas, especially this series.

Special thanks as always to Kathy, Barbara, Christy, Eddie, Jamie, Kristine, Mary Ann, Rhonda, and Susannah, awesome friends, and my writing support system.

CHAPTER
ONE

"I banged the bride. I feel a little funny about standing up for her husband at their wedding."

Ryder Jefferson almost shot beer out of his nose at his friend Ty's words. Swallowing hard, choking on the liquid and his laughter, he said, "Well, it's not like you slept with her after they started dating, so who cares? In fact, as I recall, she was still dating you when she started sleeping with him. So yeah, actually, I guess you're right. That is awkward, McCordle, since you got tossed over."

Not that he would ever rib his friend about that if his heart had been involved, but Ryder knew Ty had been half-heartedly dating Nikki Borden at best. It had been a relief to all parties involved when Nikki had trysted with Jonas Strickland and gotten engaged.

Which made the whole thing damned funny now that she had asked Ty to be a groomsman in her upcoming nuptials.

"Screw you," Ty told him, lifting his bottle to his lips, his head propped up on the worn bar with his hand.

"None of us want to be in this wedding," Elec Monroe said, on Ryder's right side, tossing peanut after peanut in his mouth. "But at least we can all hang out with each other at the reception."

"This is your fault," Ty told him, pointing a finger at him. "You're the one who was friends with Jonas first. You're the one who invited him to your party, where he met Nikki."

"And that's when you first starting dating your fiancée," Ryder reminded him. "So I can't see how you're figuring it's a bad thing, because if Nikki hadn't met Jonas, you'd still be with her instead of Imogen. Do you want to be dating Nikki 'Where's My Brain' Borden?"

Ty's face contorted in horror and he gave a mock shudder. "Point taken. But it's still weird as hell."

"Nobody's arguing with that." None of them were close to Strickland, yet all of them had been invited to participate in his circus of a wedding.

"I don't mean to be a dick or anything," Evan Monroe, Elec's brother, piped up from down on the end, "but doesn't Strickland have real friends? It's not like any of us are really all that tight with him."

"I'm sure he does," Elec said. "But the truth is, Nikki's pulling the strings here and she wants a splashy media wedding. She has half the top ten drivers in stock car racing in her wedding party. Talk about a photo op."

Ryder had already figured out that was her motivation. He didn't really care all that much, but he did have better things to do than waste a whole weekend wearing a monkey suit. Like watching TV and tossing a load of laundry in. And other stuff, none of which he could think of at the moment. But the truth was, he would do it, and not for Nikki or Jonas.

"Well, I for one feel cheapened and used," he said, amused by the whole situation. He also had a nice beer buzz going, which made him feel much more prosaic about the whole thing.

"You know what? I'm not doing it," Evan declared. "I hate wearing a tux and I always get stuck with the married bridesmaid, so there's no chance of even scoring post-reception sex."

"I'm not doing it either," Ty said, slapping his fist down on the bar. "I mean, what the hell? It's like incestuous or something for me to be standing there, in church, with Nikki and Jonas, and my fiancée sitting on the bench behind us . . . I'm not doing it. Screw it. No one can make me."

"Well, if you all aren't going to be there, I'm out, too." Elec rattled the peanuts around in his hand and wrinkled his nose. "I hate having my picture taken."

"That's because you're ugly," Evan told him, with all the love and affection only a brother can have.

"So it's settled, then." Ty sat up and adjusted his ball cap. "We all bail."

Ryder hated to break up this antiwedding sit-in, but he was going to have to own it. "Not me, guys. I can't bail."

"What? Why the hell not?" Ty asked.

"Because of Suzanne. She's the wedding planner for this crazy-ass mockery of marriage, and I have to do it. I've gotta support her." He did. He had to support Suzanne whatever way he could since his ex-wife had refused further alimony from him.

He had been busted up about that for weeks, worrying

about Suz. She was stubborn to the point that she made the mule look like a pansy-boy.

If she wouldn't take any money directly from him, he was going to do whatever he could to ensure her fledging wedding-planning business got off to a solid start. Even if that meant he had to suffer through a whole day of watching Nikki and Jonas delude themselves into thinking their marriage would last forever.

"Sorry, boys, I have to be there."

His friends and fellow stock car drivers gave him various expressions of understanding, overlaid with obvious irritation that he wasn't falling in line with their plan.

"Damn it," Ty said. "Truth is, I have to go, too. Imogen says if I back out, it's going to look like I still have feelings for Nikki or something. She's probably right, isn't she?"

Ty's fiancée Imogen was a brainiac and Ryder didn't doubt for a minute that when it came to matters of logic, Imogen reigned supreme over four guys in a bar at four in the afternoon. "She's probably got a point. If you're in the wedding, no one's going to think for a minute you're busted up about Nikki. If you bail, it might look like hurt feelings."

"Well, I sure in the hell don't want anyone thinking that. Guess I'm going to have to do it, too."

Elec gave a monumental sigh. "If you two are in, I've got no excuse for not being there. Jonas is a buddy of mine, and I can't hold it against the guy that he's marrying a woman whose voice is like a cheese grater on my nuts. He's got to be in love, he must be happy, and I should be there to help him celebrate that."

"He's not happy!" Evan said, gesturing to the bartender

for another beer. "Have you lost your mind? The man is drowning in a haze of endorphins, that's all. He's going to wake up in six months from his sex cloud and wonder what the hell he was thinking."

"You're such a romantic," Elec told him. "I can see why your love life is such a success."

"Screw you." Evan threw a balled-up napkin at his brother.

"There's nothing wrong with marriage," Ryder said, the words slipping out before he could stop them.

Suddenly all eyes were on him.

"Yeah?" Ty asked, looking at him funny.

"Yeah." Ryder put his bottle to his lip so he didn't expand on his statement. He didn't want to get into it, didn't want anyone to know he was thinking a lot about his ex these days and wondering what exactly had gone wrong.

Evan said, "I still don't want to be in this wedding."

"Guess you don't have to," Elec told him. "But it looks like the rest of us are in."

"What time is it?" Ryder asked, feeling his pocket for his cell phone. "We have to be at that wedding party–planning meeting thing at five."

Ty glanced at his watch. "It's quarter 'til."

"We need to head out then. Should we all ride together? Elec, you can drive since you only had one beer and you've been nursing it for two hours."

"That's cool," Elec said. "We're all going to need a beer after this anyway, so we might as well leave your cars here. Evan, you going or not?"

Ryder settled his bar tab and stood up, hoping they weren't going to be late. Bitching and whining while belly up to the bar had eaten up more time than he had expected and he didn't want to disappoint Suzanne. Or more accurately, he didn't want to listen to her reaming him.

"I'll go," Evan said begrudgingly. "I'll look like a total ass if I don't."

"True." Ryder clapped him on the shoulder. "Would it make you feel better if we let you plan the bachelor party?"

Evan perked up. "Hey, I wouldn't mind that. I could do that."

As they headed to the front door, Ryder wished that it were that easy to please himself these days. Something was missing in his life, and he was afraid he knew exactly what it was.

Or who, to be more accurate.

"YOU want fifteen groomsmen and fifteen bridesmaids?" Was she flippin' serious? Suzanne Jefferson looked at her client, Nikki Borden, who arguably had cotton candy floating where she should have brains, and knew the girl was one hundred percent serious.

"Uh-huh." Nikki nodded with a big smile. "My big day should be, well, big."

Right.

Nikki's thin, toned, and tanned arms went flailing out, a beatific smile on her youthful face. "Big like the Eiffel Tower. Big like elephants. Big like . . ." She paused, clearly at a loss for more large and lame metaphors.

"Big like the national debt?" Suzanne asked, shifting in her chair at her dining room table, unable to resist.

Nikki blinked. "Huh? What's that?"

Suzanne bit her cheek and squeezed her lips together in the hope she wouldn't laugh out loud and have Nikki guessing she thought the blonde had bacon for brains. Why the hell Suzanne thought she could go back to being a wedding planner when she'd never been able to hide her emotions worth a damn was beyond her. Oh, wait. She was dead broke, that's why she was pasting on a big old fake smile and listening to the likes of Nikki natter on and on about her perfect man and her perfect proposal and her perfect wedding.

At one time, before her own marriage and divorce, Suzanne had enjoyed the challenge of wedding planning, making sure every last teeny tiny detail was taken care of, and taking pride in the joy on a bride's face on her big day. There had been annoying aspects, sure, but they had rolled off her less cynical back a little easier in those days.

But since she'd spent the past four years working as a volunteer on the board of a charity that funded children's cancer research, she was having a hard time seeing the value in picking the perfect shade of pink for bridesmaid's dresses or suggesting the happy couple spend thousands of dollars on a cake that would disappear in under four hours.

Not that there was any point in whining about it. This was life, and she had to deal. The full-time position the charity had been promising her had disappeared with the budget cuts, and she had found herself without alimony or income. So she was going to squeeze the shit out of these lemons and force them into lemonade. Suzanne made a notation on her notepad. *Fifteen big-ass bridesmaids.*

Then she added a dollar sign on the end.

That made her feel a little better. She could cash in on

Nikki's enthusiasm for excess. "Well, that's perfectly understandable, Nikki. You want to share your wedding with those most important to you, and it's very difficult to cut anyone out." Though from the sound of it, Nikki was planning to ask every cousin, friend, and sorority sister she'd ever had, plus the saleswoman who'd sold her shoes at a discount and the yahoo who changed her oil to be in her bridal party.

Nikki nodded. "Exactly."

"But normally wedding parties run four to six bridesmaids and groomsmen. For a wedding party of thirty, plus your flower girl and ring bearer, that requires a lot of additional planning and coordinating. I'm going to have to increase my fee if that's what you choose to do."

"I understand." Nikki just stared at her serenely.

"By double."

"Sure." Now a smug smile crossed the blonde's face. "Jonas is paying."

"The deposit? Do you have it?"

A check signed by Jonas Strickland passed from Nikki's hand to hers and a glance down at it showed it was written for the entire original amount Suzanne had quoted Nikki.

"This is more than the deposit."

"Jonas doesn't like to be in debt. He said to just pay up front. I can get the rest to you in a day or two I'm sure."

Nikki might claim to love Jonas, but at the moment, Suzanne really did. He had just padded her checking account substantially. Her smile to Nikki was very genuine. "That's excellent, thank you. Now you said Jonas was going to be here, right? What time are you expecting him?

We can go ahead discussing venues and colors, or we can wait for him."

"He should be here any minute. And I think everyone from the wedding party said they could make it, too."

Suzanne tugged at her red sweater, adjusting her cleavage. Surely she had heard Nikki wrong. "Excuse me? The wedding party is coming, too?"

"Yeah, I thought that would be fun! They can help us make choices." Nikki beamed at Suzanne, clearly proud of herself.

Turning her dining room into sample central was working fairly well. She had access to all her books and menus and fabric samples, but there was no way in hell she could squeeze thirty people into her whole condo, let alone her dining room. There was really only room for her, Nikki, and a fat Chihuahua around this table.

Then again, she glanced down at the check on the table in front of her. For that kind of money, she'd let the best man sit on her lap. They'd shove people wherever for thirty minutes, throw some bridal magazines at them, then she'd get rid of them.

"I'm not good with decisions," Nikki said.

Yet she'd decided to marry a man she'd been dating for six weeks. Huh. That was promising. "No problem. That's what I'm here for, to guide you through the choices. Now let's talk overall tone of the wedding. Do you want it formal? Casual? Is there a certain location that appeals to you?"

"I want a *Gone with the Wind* theme."

Suzanne's pen paused over her paper, horrific images of hoopskirts, parasols, and skinny faux mustaches popping into her head. "How literal do you want to take that concept?"

Nikki's brow furrowed. "What do you mean?"

"You were thinking like maybe doing the wedding outside on the lawn at an antebellum home? But then simple elegance for the décor?"

"Oh, yeah. That's what I mean. Just like it really was during the Civil War. That was the Civil War, wasn't it? Anyway, whatever. Plus I want the big dresses they wore in the movie, and the guys in those long coats, and horses, and curled hair, and, well . . . all of it." Nikki beamed.

Maybe she'd like cannons, poverty, and runaway inflation in her wedding as well.

The doorbell rang, praise the Lord. Suzanne had nothing to say at the moment, which was damn near a first for her.

But how in the hell could she slap her name and wedding-planning reputation behind a Civil War–theme wedding? She'd be stuck doing theme weddings for the next decade, and everyone who knew her was aware that her well of patience wasn't very deep.

"I'll get that. Excuse me just a sec, Nikki."

Suzanne hustled to the door and opened it. She blinked to see Elec and Evan Monroe, Ty McCordle, and right in front, her gorgeous and annoying ex-husband, Ryder Jefferson.

"Hey guys, what's up? I'm kind of busy at the moment."

"We're here for the wedding-planning thing," Ty told her.

Oh, no. That meant that Nikki's fiancé Jonas had asked them . . .

"We're the groomsmen."

Damn. Just what she needed. None of them would listen or take her seriously. She'd lose control of the whole situation.

Ryder brushed past her, dropping a soft kiss on her cheek, his familiar cologne wafting up her nostrils and acting like a sexual trigger. She smelled Ryder, her nipples got hard. They were just trained that way.

"Good to see you, babe. And lucky me, I'm the best man in this wedding."

Suzanne fought the urge to grimace. Good God, this fiasco just got more and more ludicrous. Now she was going to have to spend a fair amount of time around Ryder for the next month, and she just couldn't deal with that on top of all her worrying about her future. He made her crazy, plain and simple.

And there was no way this best man was sitting on her lap.

Ryder handed her a manila envelope. "Oh, and this came addressed to both of us. It's from our divorce lawyer."

Suzanne looked at it blankly. It did have their divorce attorney's name on the envelope, and it was addressed to Mr. and Mrs. Ryder and Suzanne Jefferson. Ouch. It had been a long time since she'd seen her name linked with his, and damn it, it still hurt, which pissed her off. It didn't matter anymore, shouldn't matter. "What is it?"

"I don't know. I didn't open it. Figured you'd want it." He moved past her and the other guys did likewise.

Jonas Strickland was coming up her walk and there was a gaggle of Nikki clones behind him, women in their early twenties, tanned and thin and indistinguishable from one another except for the color of their various sweaters. There was red and yellow and aqua and two in white.

"Hi, come on in. I'm Suzanne," she said absently. "Nikki's in the dining room."

Curiosity killing her, Suzanne ripped open the envelope as she walked behind them, their giggles and chatter a buzzing backdrop. There was a pile of papers that looked like their divorce decree. Okay. She read the cover letter from the lawyer.

And stopped halfway down her hallway, the words blurring in front of her.

Oh. My. God.

She was going to kill Ryder. She was going to rip his arm off and beat him with the bloody stump.

This paper was telling her she and Ryder were not divorced.

They were still married.

"Ryder!" she screamed, aware that her voice sounded like a fair approximation of a banshee.

Everyone in the room looked up at her.

"You know," Nikki said, "I had a thought. I'm blond."

Elec let out a crack of laughter and Ty elbowed him.

"What?" Suzanne looked at the twit in front of her and didn't bother to hide her irritation.

"I can't do a *Gone with the Wind* theme. Scarlett O'Hara was a brunette." Nikki pointed to her head. "And I'm blond."

Jesus. "Good point," Suzanne managed. "Now would you all excuse Ryder and I for just one teensy minute?"

Ryder gave her an uneasy look, and the guys looked curious, but she didn't care. She had to discuss this with him immediately before her head exploded off her shoulders.

"What's up, babe?" he asked her, moving in really close to her, his hand landing on the small of her back as he guided her into the next room. "If we're going to fight, maybe we should be out of earshot."

Suzanne got two feet into her kitchen then couldn't hold back. She whirled and smacked the envelope and stack of papers against his chest. "This says we're still married!"

Ryder's eyebrows shot up. "No shit? Does that mean we can have guilt-free sex then?"

Oh, yeah. She was going to kill him.

CHAPTER
TWO

RYDER always knew when Suzanne was mad at him because of the way her face took on the look of that chick in *The Exorcist* right before the green stuff came flying out. This was one of those moments. And while so far in the six years he'd known her, nothing like pea soup had ever ejected from her mouth, you never knew. He could make Suzanne that mad without even meaning to.

Okay, so maybe he shouldn't have made a joke—not that he would turn sex down if she offered it—but hell, what was he supposed to say? They were still married? That was a shocker, to say the least.

She still wasn't speaking, she was just breathing hard and clenching and unclenching her fists on his chest.

"I guess that's a no on the sex."

Now she actually gritted her teeth and made a sound that was sort of like a snarl.

Damn. "Okay, well, this is unexpected, but it can't be that big of a deal, right? Does it really matter?"

"Yes, it matters! It's just . . . wrong to still be married when we're not supposed to be married. And this is all your fault, as usual."

Ryder bristled. "How is this my fault?" He'd heard that so many times when they were married, it was the one phrase guaranteed to make him defensive.

"It says you never showed up for your court appearance. You were supposed to give the lawyer power of attorney to appear for you or you were supposed to do it. And you never did."

Searching his memory back two years, Ryder shifted uneasily, wishing Suzanne's kitchen were a little wider. He suddenly felt the need to back up a little. Out of swinging distance. "I can't say that I remember one way or the other. I seem to recall signing a lot of papers."

But he definitely didn't remember ever going to court. She might be right on that one. Damn it. He hated it when Suzanne was right.

"Well, you obviously didn't sign the right papers. God!" Suzanne yanked the papers back off his chest and threw her hands up in total exasperation.

Ty's head poked around the corner. "Is everything okay in here?"

"Yes," Ryder said.

"No," Suzanne said.

"Maybe you could do this another time? You've got a lot of women in the other room with short attention spans. The blondes are getting restless."

Ryder said, "Thanks, we'll be there in a second."

Ty paused, like he wasn't sure if leaving them alone

would result in the need to call 911, but he went back into the dining room, a frown on his face.

Holding his hand out for the packet, Ryder said in as calm of a voice as he could muster, "I'll call the lawyer and take care of it. No big deal."

Suz held the packet tighter against her chest, the papers crumpling over her breasts. Momentarily distracted by the way her curves were nicely displayed in her sweater, Ryder didn't realize for a second she wasn't handing him the packet.

"I need the stuff," he told her, when he finally recovered from the unexpected blast of horniness.

"Like I'm stupid enough to give you the papers. You'll lose them or forget to call and in another two years I'll find out we're still married! Can you imagine what this had done to my taxes?"

Nope. It had never once occurred to him. And truthfully, he didn't care. So you filed some paperwork and had your accountant sort it out. No big deal.

But he knew Suzanne worried about money. A lot. First off, because she didn't have much, and secondly, because she was proud. Too proud to take his help. So if he had screwed up her taxes, he was going to have to fix it, and that was going to be a fight. But that was Round Two. First was getting the damn papers away from her.

"Give me the papers. I'll take care of it." Ryder lunged for them, but she anticipated his move.

Suzanne shoved the packet up her sweater, giving him a flash of taut tummy flesh and the bottom of her red bra. He narrowed his eyes, suddenly very much turned on. "You think *that's* going to stop me?"

She feigned indignation, but Ryder knew her well

enough to know her thoughts had gone in exactly the same direction his had. The light of desire had sparked in her eyes, and he took a step toward her, intending to get those papers back one way or another, while enjoying every minute of the persuading.

But Suzanne squawked, turned tail, and ran. "This conversation is not over," she called over her shoulder firmly, like she hadn't just been the one to back down.

"No, it's not," he told her, hanging back to appreciate the way her ass looked in her narrow skirt. She had some curves, and he loved every single one.

It had been a long time since he'd seen Suzanne naked, but he remembered every inch of her body, every delicious nook and cranny.

They were still married.

Huh.

For whatever reason, he couldn't bring himself to be all that worked up about that odd little fact.

SUZANNE was trying to hold it together. More people had shown up, cramming into her tiny condo, including her friend Tammy Briggs-Monroe, Elec's wife, who had been sucked into this circus of a wedding herself as a bridesmaid.

"Are you okay?" Tammy asked her quietly, under the guise of leaning down to pick up a dropped bridal magazine.

"Not really," Suzanne said. "But I'll be okay. It's not a big deal."

That's what Ryder had said, more than once. It wasn't

a big deal. So they were still legally married . . . that was just a piece of paper.

But it felt like a big deal. It felt like someone had reached into her chest and peeled out her heart with an ice cream scoop. The truth was, she wasn't entirely over the bastard.

Which she didn't exactly understand or appreciate and now was not the time to be reminded of it.

"If you want to talk about it later, give me a call," Tammy told her, her expression concerned.

"Thanks." Then knowing she needed to get her act together or potentially lose Nikki as a client and have to give back that beautiful fat check resting in her wallet already, Suzanne fixed a smile on her face.

"Nikki, are any of these bride or bridesmaid gowns appealing to you? Sometimes just seeing a dress you love can help us build your wedding around it." At a loss as to what to do with the guys, Suzanne had Jonas writing a guest list for his family and the rest of them competing to see who could download better bridal shower games on their BlackBerrys.

Nikki's bridesmaids were flipping through bridal magazines, their voices high-pitched and excited, silky in tone, stupid in content. If Suzanne heard one more of the twigs claim she couldn't wear such-and-such dress because it would make her look fat, Suzanne was going to smack her with a fudge brownie.

"I think I should pick my theme first," Nikki said, biting her bottom lip, then realizing what she was doing and caressing her lip like she could fix the damage with a little love.

"What about *Star Trek*?" Evan said, shooting a wink at Suzanne.

Funny.

"Eew!" was Nikki's opinion.

"What about a race car theme?" one of the brides-maids, whose name Suzanne would never remember, suggested.

"I can't," Nikki said, sniffing in irritation at the Monroes. "Elec and Tamara did that already for their wedding."

"We didn't do a race car theme," Elec protested. "We just had my car there. It wasn't a *theme*."

"It doesn't matter. I don't want a used wedding theme," Nikki said, looking to her fiancé for support. He just shrugged, chewing the cap of the pen she'd given him.

"How about Elvis?" Ryder said with a grin. "Everybody knows there's nothing as classy as a wedding with the King."

Cute. Not. Suzanne would have kicked him under the table but there were too many legs in the way.

"Oh, my God!" Nikki squealed. "You know what would be a great idea, not to get married by a fake Elvis, which is so tacky, but to do Elvis's wedding. You know, when he married what's-her-face."

"Priscilla?" Ryder said. "Yeah, that wedding had style."

"I love it!" Nikki turned and grabbed Jonas's arm, causing the wet pen cap to drop onto the table. "Honey, isn't that a great idea? You could be Elvis and I could be Priscilla!"

"I've always wanted to be the King. Thank you. Thank you very much," Jonas said in a suck-ass Elvis imitation.

Suzanne watched as a dull roar of enthusiasm went up from bridesmaids at the table. Was Nikki ser—

She stopped herself. Of course Nikki was serious. There was no point in further questioning that.

But she had the golden ticket to put the brakes on this Hunka Hunka Burning Crap wedding idea. "But Nikki, Priscilla had jet black hair when she married Elvis. And as you pointed out earlier, you're definitely blond."

Instead of Nikki's face falling in disappointment like she expected, her eyes lit up and her finger rose in the air. "But, the thing is, Priscilla didn't really have black hair. She dyed it! So I can just dye mine. I *love* this idea. Thanks, Ryder!"

"Yeah, thanks, Ryder," Suzanne echoed with a lot less sincerity than Nikki. Just how she wanted to launch her wedding planning business—with faux beehives and Graceland in fondant.

The doorbell rang before she could leap over the table and strangle him. God, who else was still absent from this debacle? There couldn't possibly be more bridesmaids. Or maybe this was the flower girl arriving on her bedazzled scooter to offer her two cents on hiring Miley Cyrus for the reception.

"I'll get it," Ryder said, springing up. "It's probably the pizza."

"What pizza?"

"I ordered some pizzas and beer for everybody," he said, holding up his phone. "Gotta love online ordering."

It was obvious she had zero control of this meeting.

Of her life.

And she couldn't even bitch about who was paying for those pizzas because she had no doubt Ryder had already prepaid with his credit card. There was nothing cheap about the man, there never had been. Which was annoying because it just stole an awesome reason to complain right away from her.

"Where did Elvis and Priscilla get married?" Nikki asked.

"At Aladdin's Hotel in Vegas," Suzanne said, not the least bit surprised she knew that. Her granny had been the King's biggest fan and the little house she'd grown up in with her grandparents had vibrated with his songs nearly as violently as his hips had swiveled onstage. Granny had saved clippings of Elvis from the newspapers and tucked them in a recipe book, including a wedding shot with Elvis and Priscilla in front of a fake genie lamp.

Suzanne reminded herself of that chubby check in her wallet. She needed the moral support to get her through the thought of decorating a wedding reception with multiple knockoffs of Aladdin's lamp.

"We should just go to Vegas then," Jonas told her. "We could elope."

Oh, pity the man who said that to his hell-bent-on-having-the-biggest-wedding-of-the-decade bride.

As Ryder returned from the door with a stack of six pizzas and two cases of beer, Nikki burst into tears.

"Don't you want to have a big wedding?" she wailed.

Suzanne realized Nikki's eyes weren't producing any actual liquid, though she was managing a hefty volume. She was fake crying, the little drama queen. Her friends all competed to pat her rubber band–thin arms while Jonas blustered.

"Of course I do! I want whatever you want. Truth is, Nikki, all that matters to me is you. I just want you."

The bullshit sobs disappeared, her distress vacuumed right out of the air by Jonas's words. Suzanne had to give the big lug credit. He knew how to appease her, which would be handy for the one or two years they managed to stay married.

Not that she was a cynic or anything.

While Nikki made googly eyes at her fiancé and he whispered things that were probably yucky back to her, Suzanne contemplated how to steer this Elvis theme to a less literal interpretation. With Nikki nice and calm and gooey over her man's attention, it was perfect timing to suggest that perhaps they go with a classic vintage look for the wedding.

Ryder, who had been passing around pizza and beer, waved the box in front of Nikki's face. "Pizza?"

"Oh." Nikki reached for a slice absently then recoiled when she suddenly realized what she was doing. "Oh, my God, get that away from me! I can't *eat*. I'm getting married in five weeks! I can't be faaaattt!"

So much for a calm bride.

Ryder looked bemused, the pizza box just dangling in the air in front of Nikki. "It's pepperoni. Protein is good for you."

Suzanne was about to grab it out of his hands, visions of her check being torn up, when Nikki turned and purposely punched the bottom of the box, knocking it to the floor. Where the entire pizza landed greasy side down on Suzanne's beige carpet.

"I'm starving . . . don't make me smell it!"

And while Suzanne was grateful to know that Nikki didn't actually enjoy subsisting purely on iceberg lettuce, she wasn't too thrilled with the pizza sauce and grease stains that were never going to budge from her carpet without professional cleaning.

"Uhhh . . ." Ryder said, looking stunned.

"Sorry, Suzanne!" Jonas knelt down and turned the box back right side up and dumped the slices of pizza back in it. "That was my fault."

How the hell it was Jonas's fault, she couldn't imagine, but at least someone was apologizing. "It's okay. Accidents happen." As do bitchy spoiled women going postal from lack of calories in their diet.

Suzanne suddenly wanted to cry. And she never cried. Ever. Only very, very rarely when she was extremely pissed did she find herself getting a little misty-eyed from pure frustration.

But they never left her eyeballs and she damn well wasn't going to let them do it now.

She widened her eyes, horrified at herself. This was not tear-worthy.

So Nikki was a Bridezilla and she and Ryder were still married.

There were worse things.

Like a full frontal lobotomy.

But she would get it together by sheer will and grit.

"Alright, Nikki, why don't you come on over to my computer with me?" Suzanne said. "We can look at some venues. I'm guessing you'll want to have the reception in a hotel, then? It would be the closest to what Elvis did shy of going to Vegas. I have a few ideas for great hotel ballrooms we could use."

That way Nikki would be a solid eight feet away from the pizza aroma. "And do you want a popsicle from my freezer? They're only fifteen calories a pop. It isn't pizza, but it's better than licking the air."

"Really?" Nikki's face lit up. "Can I have grape?"

"Sure." Suzanne headed to her kitchen and caught Ryder's eye.

Something she saw there made her very uneasy.

It was almost like admiration.

And while she could handle irritation, sexual desire, or bravado from him, she could not handle anything that smacked of genuine feelings.

"You're being about as useful as a trapdoor on a canoe," she told him. "Now will you stop staring at me and see if you can download some pictures of Elvis and Priscilla's wedding?"

Her intention was to make him angry, but Ryder just grinned at her. "Yes, ma'am."

Yeah, she was feeling all sorts of uneasy. Ryder wasn't supposed to agree that easily with her.

But she needed to plan a wedding and a divorce, so she really didn't have time to worry about it.

BY the time the last of the bridesmaids had taken their leave, and Nikki and Jonas were heading to the door, Ryder was feeling Suzanne's pain. He could honestly say that if he ever had a career-ending injury he was not going to go into the wedding consultation business.

Brides were nuts.

At least Nikki was, and Ryder was paying the price of bringing up Elvis as a joke. If he had to watch one more YouTube video of the King and Priscilla passing cake into each other's mouths, he was going to look up their divorce decree and plaster it all over Nikki's bridal magazines.

The girl didn't understand subtlety, that's for sure. He had mentioned the King's marriage for the very reason that it hadn't worked out, and yet that one had gone right over Nikki's head, and now Suzanne was pissed off at having to do this kind of wedding.

She wasn't even hiding it very well, and that worried Ryder. He didn't want her to lose a client before her business even got off the ground. The media attention from this wedding would bring in a lot of future brides for Suzanne and he knew she was counting on that.

"You ready to go?" Ty asked him, swiping the half-empty case of beer and tucking it under his arm.

"You all go ahead. I'm going to help Suzanne clean up."

"Uh-huh." Ty shot a look over at Suzanne, who was stomping around her dining room gathering up dirty paper napkins and tossing them in an empty pizza box. "Have fun with that."

"Hit the road, McCordle."

Elec was in the doorway. "How are you going to get your car?"

"Suz can drive me to it."

A snort came up from Suzanne, but Ryder gave the guys a reassuring smile. "See you later."

They left, and Ty pulled the door closed behind himself, murmuring, "Good luck, man. Call if you need help getting to the ER."

"Go away." Ryder sped up the process of closing the door, nearly taking off Ty's foot. He did not want Suzanne to hear Ty's ribbing.

"Let me get that stuff, babe," he told her. "I'm the one who ordered the pizza." The whole reason for the guys being at this meeting had been pointless, and he'd been hungry. It had seemed like a good idea at the time until Nikki had snarled at the poor pie.

"Yes, you did." Suzanne whipped a balled-up napkin down on the table and stood up. "Why are you even in this wedding, by the way?"

"Strickland asked me." Ryder went in the kitchen and pulled a clean trash bag out from under Suzanne's sink. He flicked it open and started shoving pizza boxes in it. "This will be a good thing for your business, you know. With all of us drivers in the wedding party, there will be media buzz. Which means people will see your name and your work. You'll have clients from here to the next decade."

She gave him the look, the one that made his nuts want to withdraw back into his body.

"Who exactly is going to want to hire me after they see this mascara-laden paper bell wedding from hell?"

There really wasn't any good answer to that.

"Well, but—"

Her hand shot up. "I don't want to hear it."

"It's not like—"

"Stop talking."

Ryder narrowed his eyes. Damn, he hated it when she talked to him like he was a naughty child. They were divorced. He was under no obligation to put up with that.

Wait a minute. They weren't divorced.

But still. That was just a technicality. Ryder crammed the rest of the trash in the bag and sealed it a little tighter and with more force than was necessary. "I didn't think Nikki would take me serious. I was just trying to help them brainstorm, get the juices flowing, you know."

"She has no juices!" Suzanne shoved all the bridal magazines together on the table in a stack, her movements jerky and agitated. "That girl is so dumb, if she threw herself on the ground she'd miss."

Ryder blinked, then he couldn't stop himself. He busted out laughing. "Well, that's probably accurate."

"What?" She glared at him, but her lips were twitching with the urge to smile. "Don't make me laugh. I'm determined to stay pissed off."

Ryder grinned, sauntering in closer to her, leaving the trash behind on the floor. "Come on, it's not that big of a deal. Truthfully, the more over the top the wedding, the more of a news bite you'll get."

"That might be true," she said with great reluctance. "But don't ruin my bitterness for me."

Ryder had moved really close to Suzanne and he could smell her perfume, could touch any part of her body with any part of his with just one little shift. He could feel her warmth radiating from her, see the dimples she was struggling to suppress. Ryder had always loved Suz's dimples.

He wanted to kiss her. Badly.

But he knew the reaction that would get, and despite the optimism his dick was displaying at the moment, he knew it would be less than happy when Suzanne's knee made contact with it.

"You're not bitter, babe," he said. "Just stubborn." Ryder did put a finger on her waist, drawing it back and forth over the bottom edge of the sweater. "Now give me the papers."

She didn't move, didn't knock his hand away. But she smiled, a slow, sassy upturn of her full lips. "Nice try, Jefferson."

"I haven't tried anything," he murmured, wanting more than anything to peel off that sweater and lick her from head to toe.

"Go under my sweater and you'll live to regret it. The

papers aren't even there anymore. I haven't been walking around for the last hour and a half with a manila envelope up my shirt."

"Who says I'd be looking for divorce papers under there?" He gave her a wicked grin.

"Yeah, but you have a follow-through problem, remember? And I'm not interested in anything else being left half done."

Ryder froze. Now that was below the belt. He had never, never, ever, not once in all their years together left her unsatisfied.

Or any other woman for that matter.

Ryder took a step back. "I may leave loose ends, but you have tunnel vision. Lose the attitude, Suz, or you're going to lose your wedding-planning business before you even start it."

Her head tilted. "Screw you," she said in a low, even voice that didn't fool him at all.

One more word from him and she'd probably blow. Which didn't stop him from opening his mouth. "I'd love to. You start it and I'll finish it."

Then Ryder turned and headed toward the door, figuring he could call Ty for a ride. Hell, he'd walk, but he needed to get out before Suzanne hit him. Too late. He jerked forward when a magazine hit him square in the back. He saw the smiling cover bride staring up at him as it smacked onto the hardwood floor of the foyer.

Ryder opened the door and turned and gave her a smirk, his ego smarting more than any bodily damage she could do with a bridal magazine, regardless of how hefty their advertising was. "This was fun. We should find out we're still married more often."

"Why, so every day can be a special new plunge into hell?"

Ouch. But he refused to let her see she'd nicked him. "Nobody I'd rather burn with than you, babe."

With that, he left, plunging his hands into the front pockets of his jeans as he stomped down her front walk.

CHAPTER
THREE

SUZANNE groaned out loud after Ryder left. God, that had been such a ridiculous and overdramatic thing to say to him. Plunging into hell. Geez. She hated losing control like that. She prided herself on her control and she'd had literally none since her doorbell had rang for the first time three hours earlier.

Glaring at the grease stain on her carpet, Suzanne wrapped her arms around her middle and fought the urge to kick the full garbage bag Ryder had left sitting there.

Her cell phone rang and she pulled it out of her purse on the table, praying it wasn't Ryder or Nikki. She needed a breather and possibly a cocktail before she dealt with either of them. Fortunately, it was Imogen, her friend and Ty's fiancée.

"Please tell me you want to meet for a drink in the next half an hour," Suzanne said by way of greeting.

"I'm sorry, I can't tonight," Imogen said, her crisp voice apologetic. "I have exams to grade."

Make them wait, was Suzanne's feeling on it. She certainly remembered professors taking nine million years to grade her exams in college. "You're really going to leave me to drink alone? Do you know how pathetic that is?"

"You don't need a drink," Imogen said. "You just need to vent. Ty told me you and Ryder had a bit of an altercation."

"I guess you could call it that if you want to be polite. I like to think of it more as a rip-roaring fight." Where she'd thrown a bridal magazine at his back, which she had to admit had been totally childish. But Ryder just pushed all her buttons, always had.

"What happened?"

Suzanne kicked off her shoes and padded into the kitchen, retrieving the envelope with the letter from the lawyer from the pantry where she had shoved it when Ryder wasn't looking.

What happened?

Life as she knew it had just been knocked on its ass.

"Ryder gave me a letter from our lawyer. It says we're still married." Even saying the words created a lump in her throat.

"Excuse me? Are you saying you're still legally married to Ryder?"

"Yep." Suzanne rubbed her forehead. Tears were threatening to make an appearance again and she was going to halt those suckers in their tracks.

"Well, that's something of a shock."

And that was something of an understatement. "No shit."

"But I assume this can be easily resolved. Is it just a matter of filing the correct papers again?"

"I don't know. I need to call the lawyer tomorrow. Ryder said he would, but I seriously doubt he will. If he did what he said he was going to, then we would have been divorced all along like we were supposed to be." Suzanne leaned over and dug around in her refrigerator. She was sure she had a tub of cookie dough in there somewhere and she was damn well going to eat it.

Ryder had always had a problem with finishing what he had started. Not in the bedroom—that had been a dig just to piss him off. It had been more that he always said with the best of intentions that he would cut the grass or plan her birthday party or get his license renewed, but then he never did and she was stuck dealing with it.

Annoying, yes, but not the only reason they had wound up divorced. That had just been the day in, day out reality, and it had worn her down. When she heaped that on top of the fact that Ryder had never intended to marry her in the first place, she'd felt like his assistant with sexual benefits, not the woman he loved. Add in that he had been content to remain childless while she had craved a family, and that their fighting had escalated to nonstop, and the split had been the inevitable outcome.

"But Ty said you and Ryder looked extremely tense. This doesn't really sound like it warrants ruining your friendship with him."

Almost knocking over the jar of pickles on the top shelf of the fridge, she rolled her eyes. Did she really have a quality friendship with her ex? That was questionable. It wasn't like they went on nature hikes together and talked about their feelings. They didn't talk about anything at all that mattered. Mostly they engaged in superficial sparring and made fun of each other's dates.

"I realize it's unnerving and probably has dredged up memories, both pleasant and unpleasant, but honestly Suzanne, this is merely a technicality. You have been emotionally divorced for two years, and that doesn't alter that."

Screw the cookie dough. She went into the freezer for the vodka. Emotionally divorced? That sounded about as torturous as Nikki's lettuce diet. "Do I seem like a woman who knows how to emotionally divorce myself from anything? Imogen, I'm the queen of stuffing shit down so deep I need laparoscopic surgery to pull it back out."

"Then perhaps instead of arguing with Ryder, you should just call the lawyer together."

That was crazy talk.

Suzanne put the cold vodka bottle on her forehead. Or was it? "Why would I do that?" she asked Imogen suspiciously. Imogen was so logical sometimes Suzanne had trouble following her.

"Instead of him trying to prove to you that he can handle this process, and you doubting his ability to handle it, you should just handle it together. A simple conference call with both of you and the lawyer should take care of all of your questions and concerns and won't result in an argument over who did what."

Huh. It did sound kind of simple when Imogen put it like that. "You really think so?"

"Absolutely. Call Ryder and suggest you set up a time with the lawyer."

"I guess I could do that." Suzanne continued to hold

the vodka but didn't take off the cap. She suddenly felt guilty about the fact that Ryder had walked out of her house with no ride. "Did Ty pick up Ryder?" she asked.

"No. He said that you were giving him a ride home. Isn't that what you did?"

"Not exactly." Shit. He must be still walking. "Look, I'll call you tomorrow. Have fun grading papers. Show no mercy."

Imogen laughed. "I'm brutal."

Please. What Imogen was was frighteningly fair. Maybe Suzanne should take a cue from that.

With a sigh, she redeposited the vodka in the freezer, said good-bye to Imogen, and dialed Ryder's number.

RYDER was freezing his ass off. It was damn near Thanksgiving and he was hoofing it three miles to the stupid bar to pick up his car in a town that didn't believe in allowing people to walk anywhere. If you weren't driving, then good luck. He had trudged his way along the yellow line, perilously close to speeding cars who weren't used to pedestrians. After a suburban housewife nearly took him out with her Hummer, he moved off the blacktop into the damp and soggy grass. If he was going to die in a car collision, it was going to be on the track, not walking through Mooresville like a loser.

Race car driver run over by a soccer mom. Now that would be humiliating.

Even more humiliating than the fact that he was still so easily rattled by his ex-wife.

His phone rang in his pocket and he pulled it out, afraid

it was one of his friends. He didn't want to explain to anyone why he was walking.

Even worse, it was Suzanne.

He thought about ignoring her call, but in the end, he couldn't stop himself from answering it. "Hello?"

"Where are you?" she asked.

Straight to the point, as usual. "I'm walking down the road. I should be back to my car in about twenty minutes if I don't get sideswiped by this MINI Cooper crawling up my ass. If that happens I'll be there in twenty-five minutes with a leg injury or two."

"I'll come and pick you up. I'm walking out the door now."

It wasn't an apology, but he was still touched. Which meant there was something really wrong with him if he felt like a begrudging concession to rescue him from the cold after she'd thrown him out in it was a sweet gesture.

"It's not a big deal. I'm almost there." His fingers were all numb and his nuts had probably dropped off a mile back because he couldn't feel them, but he wasn't about to admit that.

"Don't be stubborn. I'm in the car."

"Oh, *I'm* stubborn?" Ryder lost his footing and almost fell into a ditch full of kudzu. Was she freaking serious? "Honey, if I'm stubborn then we need a new word for what you are, because you've got me beat in that department."

"I'm trying to be nice here and now you're starting shit."

Oh, Christ. Ryder didn't say a word. What was there to say, really? Most of the time it felt like they were speaking two different languages anyway.

He heard Suzanne huff. "What road are you on?"

For a split second, Ryder debated telling her to just forget it, but he couldn't. Ever since the first day he'd met her, he'd had a soft spot for Suzanne. They may be toxic as a couple, but he could really never tell her no, not even now. Especially since she was being so nice and all.

Ryder looked around and gave her his approximate location. "I'm going to stop in this gas station and just wait for you then."

"I'm close enough that I can see it."

The damn shame about that was he had been walking for what felt like half his adult life, and she'd eaten up the same distance in the time it had taken to argue about whether or not she should pick him up. No wonder he loved his career. He got to fly around the track every weekend at ridiculously fast speeds, which was seriously more fun than walking.

Suzanne pulled in a second later, driving the black mini-SUV he'd bought her a few years back. A punch of melancholy hit him and Ryder mentally shook his head. Clearly, watching an unlikely couple like Strickland and Nikki throwing themselves into marriage had him feeling nostalgic.

He opened the passenger door and climbed in. Before he even had the door shut, Suzanne blurted out, "Sorry."

"What?" He was so startled by that word coming from her mouth that he turned and stared at her blankly. She wasn't looking at him, her eyes forward, hands gripping the steering wheel.

"I shouldn't have made you walk."

Now he really was touched. Saying the S word was comparable to running a marathon for Suzanne. "It's okay.

I think being sideswiped by those papers with all those people around did a number on both of us. I'm sorry for egging you on."

She finally looked at him, a smile tugging at her lips. "Holy shit. Are we actually maturing or something?"

Ryder grinned back. It was an interesting theory. "Maybe. Or maybe we've just beaten each other down so much we're too tired to fight anymore."

She made a face. "Six years of beating you down? Is that how you see our relationship?"

He hadn't meant it like that. He had just meant that instead of talking, they fought out their differences, and it hadn't gotten them anywhere. "No, that's not how I see our relationship." Maybe it had just been too long of a day, with too many weird twists and turns, but as Ryder studied Suzanne's profile, her narrow, straight nose, her plump lips, her smooth skin still holding a touch of color from the summer sun, her dark blond hair tumbling down onto her shoulders, he felt the rush of former emotions, ones he no longer had but remembered clearly.

"I was happy with you," he said simply, because it was the truth. He had loved this woman when she'd been his wife.

Of course she was *still* his wife.

Suzanne gave a sharp laugh, breaking the mood. "Now you're smoking crack. You were not happy with me."

He had been, once upon a time, before he'd fallen into a pit of relationship quicksand he hadn't been able to haul himself out of. "Ten bucks says I was."

She pulled up to the road, looking left for traffic. "Please. How are you going to prove it one way or the other? I'm not taking that bet. Where is your car?"

"At Slim and Chubby's bar. Next intersection."

"What an awful name for a bar," she said absently as she whipped her SUV out into traffic.

He didn't give a shit about the offensive bar name. What he cared about was getting Suzanne to understand, to acknowledge that, at times, their marriage had been good. He wasn't sure why it mattered right then and there, but it did.

"Come in and have a drink with me."

She raised her eyebrows, but she said easily enough, "Okay. One drink. I thought maybe we could call the lawyer and leave him a message that we want to have a conference call to discuss what we need to do. Are you cool with that? That way we're both hearing what he says, so we both feel in control."

"Sure." He didn't have the same need she did to be in charge of the situation, but he wanted her to see that he could do what was needed. That he wasn't always a total screwup who forgot everything.

"Great." Suzanne parked her car next to his truck in the bar's parking lot and pulled out her cell phone. "When can you take a conference call? How does tomorrow at noon sound?"

Ryder scanned his mental calendar for conflicts and didn't come up with any. The next few weeks were the lightest of the whole year for him since the season was over and they wouldn't start intensive training for Daytona until December. "That works."

"Great." Suzanne dialed a number and left a message asking for the lawyer to call her at noon the next day. She hung up and gave a huge exhalation of air. "That's done. Hit me with a big old martini."

"My pleasure. It's been a long day for you, you deserve it." Ryder got out of the car and waited for her.

Suzanne followed suit and beeped her SUV locked. "Lord, tell me about it. The next five weeks are going to be hell working with Nikki. It's a lot to pull together in a short amount of time even with an intelligent bride."

Ryder grinned, holding the door to the bar open for her. "And no one is ever going to accuse Nikki of intelligence."

"Nope."

They went into the typical bar, with its dark wood and stale air. The bartender looked bored, and there were only a few patrons in the place, most staring sullenly at the big TVs mounted over the liquor bottles. Suzanne sank onto a bar stool and sighed.

"An appletini, please," she told the bartender. "And if you put sugar on the rim, I will love you forever."

The man, just an average-looking guy in his late twenties, smiled at her, his lip ring flashing in the overhead light. "You got it, sweetie."

Ryder felt a rush of jealousy, which was so stupid he didn't even want to acknowledge that's what it was. But when his ex-wife, excuse me, wife, laughed and smiled back, there was no denying those ugly feelings.

"I'll have a whiskey," he told the bartender. "And leave *our* tab open."

Suzanne gave him a funny look, but the idiot behind the counter got the message. "No problem," he said, running his eyes over Ryder like he found him lacking.

"You better be paying," Suzanne said to him.

"Don't insult me, Suz." She had changed her clothes,

exchanging the skirt for a pair of jeans and some short black boots. Ryder liked the softness of the jeans, the casual way her knees fell slightly open. "When have I ever been a cheapskate?"

She nudged his leg with hers. "You got me there. You were always generous, still are. Except for the granite countertops in the motor home. Do you remember how much shit you gave me over that?"

"They were expensive! It seemed stupid for just our RV. I know I'm in it every weekend, but those countertops cost as much as a used car."

"We didn't need a used car. We needed granite countertops. And I bet they still look fabulous."

The bartender placed his whiskey down in front of him and Ryder took a sip before giving her a smile. "They do. But I open my beer bottles on them. Does that piss you off?"

She laughed. "Of course you do, and of course it pisses me off." But she didn't sound remotely angry as she picked up her martini and drained half of it, then sighed.

"Damn, you thirsty? I'm going to end up driving you back home if you down them like that."

"I guess I could think of worse things."

They sat in companionable silence for a few seconds, and Ryder felt his muscles relaxing. It was nice just to hang out with her, to feel comfortable. Maybe he shouldn't go there, wreck the few moments of peace between them, but there was something he'd been curious about for a long time. "Hey, Suz, I always wanted to ask you, why didn't you change your name back to your maiden name?"

She shrugged. "Too much paperwork."

He'd figured it had to be something as simple as that, and not anything to do with nostalgia. That really wasn't Suz, but it still deflated him a little. "Well, I can understand that. You know how I am with paperwork."

She laughed. "Oh, trust me, I know how you are with paperwork. Besides, it was a good name to have doing my work for the foundation . . . Everyone associated with racing in any way knows who you are, of course." Then she shot him a grin. "And you know what my maiden name was. Did you honestly think I was dying to return to being Suzanne Hickey?"

Ryder was so used to thinking of her with his name, sometimes he forgot what her maiden name had been. He laughed. "When you put it like that . . . I guess I never thought about the fact that it's not that enviable of a name."

Suzanne slapped her glass back down on the bar, causing it to splash, and gave him an incredulous look. "Are you kidding me? You teased me about it mercilessly the very first night we met! You're lucky I thought you were hot or I would have clocked you."

"You thought I was hot?" he asked, liking the sound of that.

She rolled her eyes. "Duh. You knew that."

"All I remember knowing is that you were the prettiest woman at that wedding and I would have used any stupid line or excuse to talk to you. I guess I wasn't very smooth if I made fun of your name." He honestly didn't remember a damn word he'd said to her. What he remembered was turning around at his cousin Brian's wedding and seeing Suzanne talking to the bride at the back of the church.

She had been wearing a soft floral dress, her hair loosely pulled up, a smile on her beautiful face, her tan legs a million miles long. Ryder hadn't realized she'd been the wedding planner; he had thought she was a friend or a relative of the bride. She could have been the queen of England, for all he cared, his only thoughts were how to find out if she was married and if not, finding an opportunity to talk to her.

"Yeah, I thought you were hot," she said softly, staring down into her martini glass.

"I thought you were beautiful. I still do." Knowing she would probably protest if he delved too deeply into the present, he kept talking. "I must have asked about ten people who you were and if you were married. I think they were starting to whisper I was some kind of stalker."

"I'm glad you did," she said simply, glancing over at him, her brown eyes wide and open, her expression tender instead of sarcastic or closed.

Ryder felt emotion revving in him like his car engine pre-race. He was pushing his luck, he knew it. One more second and she would probably turn on him, but he couldn't stop himself. "So you don't regret meeting me?"

"Of course not, you idiot."

Ryder grinned as she made a face and turned to the bartender. "This is a little sweet, can I have another splash of vodka, please?"

"I don't regret it, either," Ryder told her. "Not one minute of it."

Okay, maybe he could do without some of their knock-down, drag-out fights, but hell, he had been happy married to her. "What did you do with your wedding ring?" he asked, taking a sip of his whiskey. "I kept mine, you know. I couldn't part with it."

"You're really asking for it tonight, aren't you?" she asked, moving restlessly on her stool. "This is what I get for being nice and picking your ass up?"

"You get what—compliments? That's not such a bad deal, is it?" Ryder moved closer to her, letting his leg rest against hers, his arms leaning on the bar in front of her, so that he was only a few inches from her face. "You really are an amazing woman."

"How long have you been drinking today?" she asked, wetting her lips nervously.

"I'm sober." He was. That subzero wind had iced any beer buzz in his veins he had been feeling and he'd only had about three small sips of his whiskey. "I guess that letter from the lawyer has me thinking, that's all."

"The past is the past."

He didn't say anything, just stared at her, thinking that he would give just about anything to feel his lips on hers, to taste her sweet, moist tongue, and wrap her in his arms again.

Her breath had quickened, like she realized the direction his thoughts were taking. "I kept it, too," she blurted. "My ring. It's in my jewelry box, which is stupid, given what it's worth. I should have it in a safe-deposit box or sell it, but I . . . can't."

That's all he needed to hear. Ryder closed the distance between them and covered her mouth with his.

The very first touch had his body jolting and his soul sighing.

He was the stupidest man alive for ever letting this woman go.

So he deepened that kiss and waited for the slap.

But instead, Suzanne just opened her lips and slipped her tongue into his mouth.

No victory had ever been sweeter.

CHAPTER
FOUR

RYDER had lost his ever-lovin' mind.

Actually, *she* had lost her ever-lovin' mind because while he had kissed her first, she was kissing right back.

She hadn't meant to. She had thought to herself, when she'd recognized that look in his eye, that she should put her hand out, stop him, before he even got close enough to kiss her. But not only hadn't she stopped him, the press of his lips on hers had felt so good she had opened her own mouth and was giving him back as good as she got.

Granted, it had been a long, less than stellar day, but that didn't explain doing a tongue tango with her ex.

Or why it felt so damn good.

Suzanne felt her eyes drifting closed, her body shifting into his, her desire stirring to life from the center out. She'd been lying about him leaving her unsatisfied. In bed, he had always satisfied her. If he had satisfied her any more, he'd have likely killed her, and her girl bits clearly remembered him, because she was suddenly and achingly wet.

Her fingers had mysteriously worked their way into the back of his short hair, and she kept thinking that this was a bad idea, but kept doing the opposite of stopping.

It had been a long, long time since they had kissed, and it was amazing to feel that not a millimeter of their spark had disappeared. That same intense, hot, consuming passion still burned between them.

When Suzanne found herself reaching down between his legs to stroke his erection beneath his jeans, she suddenly remembered where exactly they were, and that she no longer had any right to touch wherever and whenever she wanted.

Jerking back, she stared at Ryder, who looked as stunned as she felt. He was breathing audibly, and he was gripping the edge of the bar like he'd float away without it anchoring him.

"Will you go home with me?" he asked without preamble. "I want you really bad, Suz."

Not trusting her voice not to squeak, Suzanne just nodded. Her whole body felt like it had been dipped in melted wax, tight and hot and startled, and she was aware of every single nerve ending from scalp to toenail.

She'd barely finished her up and down nonverbal confirmation when he barked to the bartender, "Close our tab, please."

Suzanne put her hand on her belly and concentrated on taking deep breaths as Ryder overpaid the bill and declined the offer to wait for change.

What the hell had just happened? She hadn't even given one second's thought to deliberating the pros or cons of having sex with her ex-husband. A few kisses, and she was ready to sheet dive.

Which scared the shit out of her.

So even as she stared at Ryder, thinking it was possible she would curl up into a ball and die if she didn't get to feel his penis inside her in the next ten minutes, she was also thinking that the very second her body had been satisfied and he pulled out, regret was going to come crashing in on her like a flaming meteor.

It had been a while since she'd had sex, that was true. Her body would be very, very happy if she threw caution to the wind and let a man at her who knew all the right ways to please her.

But . . .

Ryder stood up. "Let's go."

Suzanne followed suit, grabbing her purse off the bar and slinging it on her shoulder. Damn, she was so outrageously aroused, even walking did funny things to her hoohah.

But . . .

"You can either ride with me or follow in your car," Ryder said. "I'd love the company of having you in the truck with me, but truthfully, you probably shouldn't leave your car here overnight. You should probably follow me."

Overnight. Gak. Suzanne wasn't sure what time it was, but it was still pre-primetime. And Ryder was already concluding she was spending the night. She gripped her purse tighter as they stopped in the parking lot in front of his truck.

"Suz?" Ryder studied her face and then sighed. "Hell, you're not going to do either one, are you?"

"No." She mentally slapped herself, hating what she had just done. "Shit, I'm sorry. It just seems like a really bad idea, but you know what I think of a dick tease, and I wasn't trying to tease, honestly. I really meant yes when I said yes."

"But now you mean no?"

Her inner thighs gave a whimper of protest, especially when she couldn't stop herself from glancing down and seeing his erection straining against his jeans, but she nodded. "Yes, I mean no. I just think it's a bad idea, especially when it's so impulsive."

"What if we plan it?" he asked, looking slightly hopeful.

Suzanne gave a soft laugh. "Nice try, Jefferson." Feeling a lump crawling up her throat like a scurrying crab, she reached out and touched his hair, running her fingers through the short dark strands. "I'll talk to you tomorrow, okay?"

A cool mask had slid back into place on his face. "Sure, babe. But if you get lonely before then, you know how to reach me."

For the second time that day he turned his back on her.

And both times she had pretty much given him no choice.

RYDER stared at his computer screen blankly. He couldn't even process the words in front of him, he was so distracted by thoughts of Suzanne.

That kiss.

It had lit a fire in him that was still smoldering and

he was really damn annoyed by that fact. He only had a few weeks off before the new season started up and he didn't want to spend it with his hand.

Next season promised to be brutal and challenging, given that he had finished a heartbreaking second place in the race for the cup this season. He would be damned if he didn't win next year, and he wasn't about to let Suzanne distract him from the time he needed to relax and regroup before the hard work commenced.

But he couldn't help it.

His thoughts were stuck on her and the way she had opened her mouth and pressed inside him with passion and enthusiasm. When they had been together, that's the way it had always been, but it had been two years since he'd kissed Suzanne. To be honest, he had expected her to stop him. Smack him. Act indignant and huffy. Tell him to take his tongue to the nearest bimbo, or something similar.

Not to kiss him back.

He had been so shocked, he had actually paused for a split second before recovering and kissing her back with everything in him.

Man, he wanted to make love to her again. Just one last time.

He could remember the last time they'd had sex, and it had been a stilted, angry affair, not the way he would have wished their last time to be. But he hadn't known that was it. He had still been fooling himself that they could work things out.

He wanted to do it right, to hold Suzanne in his arms with all the good memories intact and the bad tossed. To lay her down and give her pleasure. To bury himself inside her, and feel that connection again, just one more time.

But he wasn't going to beg, and she had changed her mind, leaving him feeling like a jackass.

Ryder abruptly turned off his computer without even shutting down the browser. He just flicked the off switch, annoyed with himself. What had he expected? It had been something of a mystery why Suz had even kissed him. She wasn't going to have sex with him.

Frankly, she didn't even like him all that much most days, and she probably had men crawling all over her. Why the hell would she need him to get her off?

Just thinking about giving her an orgasm had Ryder groaning out loud. His erection throbbed like he was four-teen and had stumbled across a *Playboy*. He stomped away from his desk and toward his bedroom. He was going to sleep, and he was not going to do a damn thing about his prize boner, no matter how much it was demanding attention.

Sullen masturbation was not his style.

Laying in bed staring at the ceiling and feeling sorry for himself was much more his style.

Feeling like a total dumb ass, Ryder stripped down to his briefs and slid underneath his sheets, feeling so surly he consciously skipped brushing his teeth, something he never, ever did. Bad breath would teach her.

He should have kissed Suzanne again in the parking lot. At least tried to get her to come home with him. But as soon as she had changed her mind, he'd cut and run, like a big giant weenie.

Not that he wanted to think about that particular word.

Flipping onto his side, he punched his pillow.

He could have tried to coax her all he wanted. If she had changed her mind, she'd changed her mind. Suzanne was never coaxed into anything.

So it had been stupid to kiss her in the first place.

Yet he didn't regret it.

He regretted that she wasn't naked on top of him at the moment, but he didn't regret the kiss.

Which made him one hell of a glutton for punishment.

SUZANNE lay in bed, completely unable to sleep, condemning herself as the biggest damn fool ever to reside in the state of North Carolina.

She could be playing cowgirl over at Ryder's instead of wearing fuzzy pajama pants and wishing her sheets were a little more aggressive in caressing her. Why the hell had she suddenly gotten some kind of conscience and sent him home alone?

So it would make their relationship complicated the morning after.

When wasn't their relationship complicated?

Hell, they were still married, and that was pretty damn complicated in its own right. What difference did having sex make?

Which even to her own ears was pretty shitty rationalization, but she was willing to go with it when she was feeling this desperate.

She was edgy, unable to sleep, aching with want, wet with desire. Still. Two hours later and she was still damp, which was pathetic.

Damn if she would be pathetic.

Suzanne threw back her covers and sat up.

Ryder wanted to have sex.

She wanted to have sex.

Why shouldn't they have sex?

He had told her she knew where to find him if she changed her mind. That was a clear invitation to seek him out if she wanted to pick up where they'd left off with that seriously kick-ass kiss. Plus for the last two years she'd been fending off sexual innuendoes from him. She didn't doubt for a minute he would be on board with her changing her mind yet again.

Ryder would probably give her shit about it, but only after the fact. She could live with that if she could get multiple orgasms out of the deal. And she would make it clear this was just a onetime event.

As Suzanne pulled on a pair of jeans, she tried to ignore the voice in her head telling her this was a flat-out dumb idea. She figured if she didn't go over to Ryder's she'd never get any sleep, and with Nikki as a client, she was going to need all the sleep and patience she could muster for the next month.

And if she felt a little bit stupid, she wasn't going to admit it. She was a woman who went after what she wanted, and she wanted Ryder tonight. Plain and simple.

She got halfway there before she regained control of her senses and realized this was setting herself up for disastrous consequences. Showing up in the middle of the night to have sex with her ex who really wasn't her ex was opening up a Texas-sized can of worms.

Smacking her hands on the steering wheel and letting out a groan of frustration, Suzanne glanced right to see if she could pull into the shopping complex and turn again. The man in the car next to her was staring at her like her boobs were on her back instead of her front.

"What?" she asked him out loud, even though he obviously couldn't hear her.

Nothing, he mouthed, shaking his head rapidly.

The man acted like he'd never seen a sexually frustrated woman in his whole life, and judging from his slack jaw and vacant stare, Suzanne was guessing he'd seen plenty of them.

The light changed and she waited until he had pulled forward, then she changed lanes, whipped into the shopping center parking lot, and redirected her car to head back home.

Her big lonely bed was waiting for her.

Yay her.

Suzanne hit the steering wheel again and cursed Ryder from here to Talladega for kissing her.

Then she cursed herself for kissing him back.

RYDER knew he was risking Suzanne being royally pissed at him, but then again, he pretty much risked that on a regular basis just by breathing.

He pulled into the parking lot of her condo complex at a quarter to twelve, noting her car was in its assigned spot. There was no doubt in his mind that she had intended them to have this conference call at separate locations, but after last night, after that kiss, after her rejection, he wanted to see her.

He knew why she'd changed her mind, and hell, she had probably been smart to do it, but he couldn't help but think they had some seriously unfinished business. Maybe the long night spent tossing and turning in his empty bed had affected his brain cells, because normally he avoided poking the bear, but today, he wanted to look Suzanne in the eye and discuss the fact that he had kissed her and she had kissed him back.

When he rang her doorbell, she answered right away, and her face was pinched but resigned. "I meant for us to do this call at our own houses."

"You never said that," he pointed out, which was the truth.

"You knew what I meant."

"Maybe. Maybe not. I'm not all that bright." He gave her a smile.

She shifted, one hand still on the door like she might slam it shut in his face. She was wearing jeans again and a black sweater. A shiny belt buckle drew attention to her flat stomach and Ryder marveled again how much he was attracted to her still. It seemed like at some point he should have stopped thinking of her as the hottest woman to grace the planet, but he hadn't.

"Well, that's true," she said, but she tempered the words with a smile of her own. "You certainly don't have any sense of self-preservation."

"I'm a race car driver. I like to take risks."

"What you're risking is becoming a serious pain in the butt." But she moved out of the way. "Since you're here, come in, and let's get this taken care of."

"Such warmth, such enthusiasm." Ryder followed her into the house. Her dining room table was still covered with bridal magazines and her computer was open to a picture of something that was either a wedding gown or a tablecloth, he wasn't sure which. Seeing the grease stain from the pizza still glaring up at him on the carpet, Ryder felt guilty.

"Sorry about the pizza incident. I had no idea Nikki would go nuts like that. You want me to call the carpet cleaners?" He knew she'd say no, but he had to offer.

"No, that's okay, I can do it. It's not your fault she lives on iceberg lettuce, with a little romaine tossed in when she's feeling downright wild." Suzanne flopped onto a chair and dug through a pile to get out the manila envelope from the lawyer. "Damn, I'm tired. I must be getting old."

He figured this was the best opening she was ever going to grant him, so Ryder sat in the chair next to her and went for broke. "I'm tired, too. I didn't get much sleep last night because I kept thinking about you."

She shot him a nervous look but didn't say anything.

"Suz, are we going to discuss the fact that we kissed last night?"

"No, we're not going to discuss it. It was a long day, and we were feeling nostalgic, fueled by alcohol and this." She held up the packet and shook it. "It doesn't change anything."

"No?" he asked mildly. He knew when to retreat with Suzanne. And when to push. "Alright, then. Guess that means I can kiss you again and it won't matter either."

Her eyes went wide and she shoved her chair back, away from him. "No!"

Ryder suppressed the urge to grin. "Why not? It doesn't change anything, you said it yourself."

She recovered and stuck out her finger. "Don't get smart with me. Kissing you was a mistake."

"So you admit you kissed me back?"

Her eyes narrowed. "I never said I didn't. Now drop it. It was a bad idea."

"That's just your opinion." Ryder settled back into his chair, getting more comfortable. "I happen to think it was a damn good idea."

"But you also admitted you're not very bright."

That drew out a short laugh from him. "Throwing my own words back in my face. I love it."

I love you, was on the tip of his tongue before he caught himself.

Unnerved by how easily that thought had popped into his head, he sat straight up.

Did he still love Suzanne?

He wasn't sure.

There were feelings there, definitely, a sense of caring and a physical attraction, a soft spot for her, and a desire to see that she was financially secure and well taken care of. Was that love, though, or just strong feelings for a woman he'd been married to?

Ryder cleared his throat when Suzanne picked up her phone and dialed the lawyer's office.

"You know, we never even got confirmation from him that this time was good for him," she said. "You might have driven over here for no reason."

Again, he'd have to disagree with her. He'd had every reason to want to see her after that kiss. Now he was glad he had. It seemed he had some serious shit to consider when it came to his ex-wife.

Wife. Still wife.

"I wasn't busy," he told her, which was a lie. There

were a million things he could be doing on any given day, as his PR person would gladly remind him.

But it turned out that the lawyer, Jackson Reed, a guy Ryder had known from high school, was perfectly willing to talk to them.

"It's crazy that you're still married, isn't it?" Jackson said, a chuckle in his voice.

Suzanne had put her phone on speaker and set it on the table. "Yeah, it's just hilarious," she said, rolling her eyes. "So what do we do to fix it? And do I have to file an amendment to my taxes?"

"Yeah, we're going to have to file a correction. You've been claiming alimony as income, when technically that's not income, just an allowance from your husband. So this will actually work in your favor."

"Don't we have to file jointly?"

"No. Given that you don't have any mortgage interest, this is simpler and quicker to just do it this way. I'll talk to the accountant and we'll get it straightened out."

Suzanne gave a sigh of relief. "Alright, that sounds good. Because I don't want some massive tax bill biting me in the ass."

Ryder didn't want that either, because then he would pay it, and Suzanne would be even more pissed at him.

"It's all good, we'll get it straightened out." Jackson didn't sound worried about anything whatsoever. Then again Jackson was the one who had never followed up on the paperwork in the first place. "And it's Ryder who is being audited, not you, Suzanne."

Suzanne shot him a funny look, like she realized how tacky that was of Jackson to say with him sitting right there. "Well, I don't think anyone wants to get audited but hopefully between you and the accountant we can have this straightened out by the first of the year. The taxes as well as the divorce."

Ryder figured it was time he piped in and actually proved to Suzanne that he was contributing. "What do we actually need to do to make the divorce legal?"

"There will be a court date. I'll get you one as soon as possible. We'll go into court, they'll ask some basic questions, and bam, we're done. I think I can get you a date in the next month or so."

"Good, because come January my schedule is jampacked." And he didn't want to screw this up again, because Suz would skin him.

"Now, just to make sure, before we go to all this trouble, is this really what you all want?"

"What do you mean?"

"Do you really want a divorce?"

Ryder wasn't sure, to be honest. He had strange feelings swirling around in him, ones that made him very uncomfortable.

Suzanne, on the other hand, seemed to have no reservations.

"Are you smoking crack?" Suzanne asked, staring down at her phone like Jackson could see her incredulous expression. "We've been separated for two years! I don't think we're going to reconcile at this point, Jackson."

Nothing like telling it like it was.

Glad to hear he was totally delusional for even thinking for one second that Suzanne had put some genuine emotion behind that kiss the night before.

"Ryder?" Jackson asked. "That your answer, too?"

Suzanne's head swung toward him, her eyes snapping, and if he wasn't mistaken, a little bit scared.

"Sure," he said calmly. "Nothing there to save, Jackson. Is there, Suz?"

CHAPTER FIVE

MAYBE Suzanne had spoken a little too vehemently. She knew immediately she'd hurt Ryder, which hadn't been her intention. But when he got that cool, detached look on his face, she always knew she'd pushed him too far, and he was retreating into nonchalance.

Funny thing is, for the first time she saw with total clarity it was a pattern they'd had for years. She panicked, used sarcasm to hide her emotions, and Ryder retreated behind a shield of bravado and mockery.

It was a stunning revelation, one she wasn't at all sure what to do with, and one she definitely didn't like.

"Just get us our court date," she told Jackson, watching Ryder uneasily. "And please call me as soon as you know. Is there anything else you need from us right now?"

Ryder was sitting back in his chair, looking very relaxed, which made Suzanne nervous. It was a deceptive stance. She could tell by the set of his jaw that he was downright furious.

"No, I'm good. You all have a good day, and don't worry. I'm on this. You'll be divorced before you can say Daytona."

That got a reaction from Ryder. His hand jumped a little on the table.

Suzanne cleared her throat and rushed Jackson off the phone. After she hung up, she clasped her phone and turned to look at Ryder. "Well, um . . ."

The corner of his mouth turned up. "Are you actually speechless? Never thought I'd live to see that day."

That made her feel defensive and she reacted. "Well, hell, Ryder, this is weird! What am I supposed to say?"

His fist slammed down on the black-painted table.

Suzanne jumped a little, startled at his sudden explosion of anger. She knew he was ticked off, but she wasn't entirely sure why. The situation was crazy and unexpected, but what exactly was he pissed off about?

"You're supposed to say that while we may have had our fair share of problems, our marriage didn't totally suck ass! You're not supposed to act like being married to me was the worst goddamn thing that ever happened to you."

Good Lord, never in a million years could she have predicted he would say that. Suzanne just gaped at him. "What the hell are you talking about?"

"I'm talking about the fact that you act like being my wife was akin to hell on earth."

The man was smoking crack right along with their lawyer. "Are you nuts? When did I ever say anything like that?"

"You've said it a thousand times out loud and in a million ways without words."

Now he was just being overdramatic. If he threw out his hand and started spouting words from a dead guy, she was out of there. And it was her damn house.

"I have never said that. And you sound like a girl so just calm yourself on down." So maybe that was a childish and rude dig, but he was freaking her out, and God knew Suzanne had never handled emotion well. He should know that about her by now.

Ryder threw his hand up in the air and gave an exasperated groan. "That explains everything then. No wonder you hated being married to me . . . I'm a girl."

"I did not hate being married to you! And I didn't say you're a girl, I said you sound like a girl."

He stood up. "I'm a goddamn idiot. I keep doing this. Just setting myself up to get knocked down. Over and fucking over. You think I would have learned by now, but no, I keep doing the same damn thing hoping that one day you'll actually validate my feelings and our marriage, and that makes me a moron. You never wanted to marry me in the first place, you only did because I talked you into it, and you're happy as a clam without me. I get it. I finally fucking get it."

Suzanne leaped out of her chair, too, shocked at the words coming from Ryder's mouth. "You get nothing! I did not marry you because you talked me into it. I was dying to marry you, but I didn't want you to think I was trying to trap you. I was a poor girl who got knocked up on our first date and you were an up-and-coming race car driver . . ."

She almost blurted out that she hadn't been good enough

for him, but she stopped herself just shy of that. He didn't need to know her deepest insecurities at this point.

Ryder's anger deflated, and his shoulders slumped. "I never thought of you as a poor girl who got knocked up. I thought of you as the woman I loved, and it was . . . bad when you lost the baby."

Tears were suddenly in her eyes, and fuck, she didn't want to go there. That had been the worst day of her life, when she had realized she was bleeding out the baby she and Ryder had conceived. This was something they had never really talked about, and she sure in the hell didn't want to now, when it no longer mattered.

"It was bad. Very bad. But there was good between us, too. I wanted to marry you. Can we just leave it at that?"

His hands opened and closed in fists at his side, and his jaw shifted, but he just nodded. "Yeah. We can leave it at that."

The doorbell rang.

"Fuck me," Suzanne said, in exasperation. This conversation didn't feel even remotely finished, yet she didn't know what else to say. "That's Nikki. We're going to look at hotel ballrooms this afternoon."

"I'm leaving anyway." Ryder headed to the door and Suzanne followed him.

She wanted to say something to defuse his anger, to finally, after two years, reach a real level of friendship with him, but she didn't know how to do that. She never had, and while she cared a hell of a lot about Ryder, the truth was, they didn't seem to know how to be in each other's lives.

Nikki was smiling when she pulled open the door. "Hi, Suzanne. Hi, Ryder. What are you doing here?"

Ryder pulled his keys out of pocket. "Suzanne and I just had some business to take care of, but I'm heading out now."

"You know, for being divorced you guys spend a lot of time together. It's kind of weird." Nikki stepped into the house, her nose wrinkled. Then her eyes got bigger. "Ooooh, I get it. You have sex with each other!"

Suzanne wished.

Or did she?

There was that whole complicated issue, as was evidenced by the circular argument about nothing they'd just had. "We don't have sex," she told Nikki.

"No, because I'm a girl," Ryder said, shooting her a look as he skirted around Nikki and stepped out onto her front stoop.

Suzanne rolled her eyes. He was never going to let that one go. "Well, you're certainly pouting like one right now."

"That's a joke, right?" Nikki clutched her giant handbag that probably cost the same as a small house on half an acre and twittered nervously. She looked downright scared at the thought that maybe Ryder was a very masculine and hairy woman.

"Yes, it's a joke." Suzanne had no patience to explain humor to Nikki. Or to get her to understand that there was clearly tension between herself and Ryder and that maybe she should excuse herself for a minute.

That kind of subtlety was beyond this one.

Ryder was leaving, just heading on down the walkway without a word. "Well, good-bye!" she called. "Have a wonderful day."

His response was to lift his hand in a backward wave, but he didn't look back at her.

Jerk.

Suzanne tried not to be hurt, because really, what was different about this than any other day she encountered Ryder?

But she was, in a way that irritated her. Two years, and she was still hurting. Two years, and they still couldn't manage to have a conversation without misunderstanding each other.

And yet, the night before she had seriously considered having sex with him.

Which made her a complete masochist. Or an idiot. Or both.

"If he was really a girl, you'd know, right?" Nikki asked.

Suzanne felt reassured that she wasn't such an idiot after all. Nikki had the market on stupid cornered.

"I would know," she reassured her, reminding herself that she had to stop at the bank to deposit that check from Jonas. "Now are you ready to go? I really think you're going to like the Hilton. It has everything you're looking for and it will be easy to give it that faux middle eastern feel the Aladdin had."

"But it is classy?"

Classier than the bride. But Suzanne gave her a bright smile. Honestly, it wasn't Nikki's fault she had breasts ten times the size of her brain. "Of course."

Nor was it Nikki's fault that Ryder Jefferson still managed to get under Suzanne's skin, festering like a splinter she couldn't extract.

She should have a little more sympathy and compassion and patience for Nikki, and she vowed to do just that.

* * *

EIGHT hours later, she was only thinking it was a good thing Nikki's neck was so scrawny because it would be much easier to wrap her hands around it and choke the life out of her.

"None of these appealed to you at all?" she asked Nikki again, just to confirm that out of six very elegant ballrooms, Nikki hadn't found one that she liked. They had crisscrossed town, shaken hands with six different fawning catering managers, and Suzanne had been forced to use two public restrooms. Her feet hurt, her head hurt, her nerves were shot, and her thoughts had never so frequently strayed to homicide. Not even when she was with Ryder.

"No. They're just . . . wrong. That one was too big, the other too small, the one had those gross pillars, and one had blue carpet. I mean, eew." Nikki shuddered, like blue carpet was a personal affront to her.

The wind was cutting through Suzanne's peacoat as they stood in the waning darkness of the hotel parking lot. This was unreal. Every one of those rooms had been perfectly acceptable. "Virtually anything in a ballroom can be obscured or altered with the right decorations," she told Nikki, praying for patience, something she'd never had a hell of a lot of.

"You can't change blue carpet." Nikki pulled a hair off that had gotten stuck to the lip gloss on her plump lip.

"You want to bet? I can change anything," Suzanne said, feeling a rise of defiance. She wasn't going to lose this wedding, and she wasn't going to be forced to jump through any more hoops. They were going to pick a venue today if it killed her, or hopefully, if it killed

Nikki. "I can lay down a series of rugs that match the theme in a pattern, and stitch them together. Or put a circular rug under each table. I can do whatever you want, but we can cover the carpet." She really wasn't sure she could, but once she'd spoken the words, she knew she'd find a way or die trying.

"I can change anything," she repeated, wishing that were the case in her personal life. If she could just cover her shitty feelings with a carpet, she could sell that secret for more than a dollar.

Nikki tilted her head, clearly contemplating this. "Okay. Let's go with the blue carpet place then. I liked the entrance. Can we go back there tonight? I'll call Jonas and he can meet us there."

"Sure." The sooner she had Nikki and Jonas sign on the dotted line with the hotel, the better.

Because then she could take a swan dive into her bed and not reemerge for a good twenty-four hours. She felt beyond whooped.

Checking her own phone while Nikki called Jonas, Suzanne saw she had a voice mail. It was Jackson, the lawyer.

"Got a court date. December twenty-third. Merry Christmas, here's your divorce." He gave a chuckle then said, "Call me if you have any questions for me."

She did, like how had her life become such a joke?

Chances were he wouldn't have a clue, any more than she did.

A sour taste was in her mouth, like she'd eaten too much chip dip and it had curdled. Suzanne fished in her purse for a stick of gum and contemplated a divorce decree under her Christmas tree. That was festive.

Nikki's wedding was December twenty-second, after which she would undoubtedly be exhausted and cranky. Then came the divorce, and finally, to cap off the week just right, she would have a Christmas to spend all by her lonesome while everyone else in America opened presents together.

Where was a goddamn violin when she needed one?

And she didn't even have any freaking gum left.

Suzanne closed her eyes briefly and wondered if this day would have gone differently if she'd had an orgasm at Ryder's hands the night before.

Probably not.

But it would have been good while it was going down. While he was going down.

Suzanne sighed.

Her phone vibrated in her hand and she glared at it for scaring her.

It was a text from Ryder.

I'm sorry, was all it said.

So was she.

For all the things she'd said, and all the things she'd never said.

Me, too, she wrote.

Ryder sent her a smiley face back. It was so unexpected, Suzanne laughed. He'd never texted her a smiley before.

Girl, she wrote, adding a smiley of her own.

Punk, was his answer.

"What's so funny?" Nikki asked her.

"Just a private joke." Suzanne held her phone tightly in her hand and decided that the day didn't suck so bad after all.

CHAPTER
SIX

"*THIS* is the way it should be," Ty said as he settled back into a folding chair, the flames from the fire pit dancing in front of him. "Just us guys, relaxing in nature, no women, no complications."

There were murmurs of approval from the other guys around the fire, a sort of forced joviality. Ryder gave a similar lackluster response. He wanted to enjoy himself, wanted to sit there in the woods around Lake Norman without a care in the world, drinking beers with his buddies, but he was having a hard time getting into the spirit of this guys' weekend.

It had been five days since he had seen or talked to Suzanne. It had seemed like they'd ended on a positive note with their teasing texts, but then nothing. Not a word. And it bothered him, he could admit it.

"Maybe another time we could bring the women with us," Jonas said casually, his eyes on his beer can.

They had decided to start including Jonas in their outings since he had invited them into his wedding, but those kinds of comments weren't going to win him friends, not when Ty and Evan were determined to pretend they were having fun without female companionship. Elec had stayed home with his wife Tammy and her kids, pleading bonding time with his stepchildren. Nobody had dared argue with that, and Ryder had to admit he envied the guy at the moment. Not that he wanted to be at home, because in his case, he'd be all alone, but he envied Elec his family.

"What would be the point in bringing the women?" Ty said, but he spoke a little too quickly, a little too sharply. "This is about us, the men. Doing men stuff."

"Like what?" Evan asked. "Freezing our asses off together?" He stomped his feet on the ground and shoved his hands deeper in his pockets.

"Like fishing and hiking." Ty threw a peanut violently into the fire and watched it burn. "Look, I love Imogen to pieces, and I want to spend a hell of a lot of time with her. But I want to spend time with my friends, too. Excuse me."

Ryder laughed, despite his own determination to feel gloomy. "Hey, I for one appreciate you planning this, McCordle. Otherwise, I'd be home watching the Food Network and denying it."

"Truth is, I'm just jealous I don't have a woman to bring," Evan said. "My sleeping bag is a little lonely these days. You know what I'm saying, Jefferson."

Yeah, he knew, and thanks for the reminder. Ryder wasn't normally hurting for female companionship, not because he was such a good-looking stud or anything, but because he was a race car driver. Women were always willing to go out with him. But lately, he hadn't been giving chase, and had been ignoring some obvious invitations from various acquaintances, and he wasn't sure why.

Hell, yes, he did. He was too worked up over Suzanne and dating anyone else wasn't appealing. For months, ever since Suzanne had started dragging Ryder into her matchmaking efforts for her friends, Ryder had been preoccupied with Suzanne and hadn't slept with another woman in longer than he cared to consider.

Which made for a damn cold sleeping bag. "Glad I can be in the lonely hearts club with you, Evan." He crushed his empty beer can in his hand with a satisfying squeeze.

"Hey, I'm not looking for love." Evan held up his hand. "Or marriage. But I'd like some reliable booty, if you know what I mean."

"Is that your pick-up line?" Ty asked him with a grin. "'Hey, sweetheart, wanna be my reliable booty call?' No wonder you're sitting here with us then."

"No, I don't say that," Evan said in clear annoyance that his lothario skills would be questioned. "But I do make it clear I'm not looking for marriage."

"What do you have against marriage?" Ty asked, looking ready to defend the institution like any recently engaged man would. "Your brother is mighty happy with his wife."

"That's Elec. It works for him. But dining in the same restaurant every night doesn't do it for me. I know myself too well and that's not realistic."

Ryder leaned toward the cooler containing the beer and thought about that phrasing . . . dining in the same restaurant every night. That had never even entered his head when he had married Suzanne. He had been thinking that he was the luckiest man alive to get her locked in and signed on the dotted line as his.

"Wait until you meet the right woman," Jonas said, glancing up from his lap. "Then you'll change your mind."

Whatever Ryder thought of Jonas's choice of a wife, he had to admit, the guy seemed happy. In fact, if he wasn't mistaken, Jonas had his cell phone in his lap. "Are you texting Nikki?"

Jonas gave a sheepish smile. "Yeah. I can't help it. It's so hard to be away from her."

"That is a guys' weekend violation," Ty declared. "Hand over the phone." He switched his beer to his left hand and held out his right.

"No." Jonas clutched his phone tighter. "Nikki's feelings will be hurt if I don't answer."

Ty had no doubt that Nikki with hurt feelings wouldn't be pretty. He pictured the pizza box hitting the carpet. "Let him text his girl. It's not a big deal."

Jonas looked wistful and pleading.

Evan looked like he wanted no part of the argument.

Ty looked disgusted, then resigned. "Fine. But if you can text Nikki, I can text Imogen."

Ryder almost rolled his eyes, but restrained himself. "Text whoever you want. There aren't rules here, you know. We're just supposed to be having fun, hanging out. That doesn't mean you can't check in on your fiancée. My feelings won't be hurt if you send her a dirty message."

He might wish he could send his own dirty text to a certain someone, but he could lament that at home just as easily, and at home he wouldn't have his friends to talk to. And if he did send that dirty text either here or at home, he'd be shot down like a goose in hunting season.

"Alright, just one," Ty said, holding up his finger.

Jonas was already typing furiously on his phone's keyboard.

"So do you have any plans for the next month?" Ryder asked Evan. "The season's right around the corner."

"I'm heading to Mexico for a week for some chill time, but that's it. We've got the wedding, but mostly I need to get back to work, because I'm not finishing twenty-goddamn-fifth again next season."

"No, you're going to finish fortieth," Ty said, ribbing him.

"Shut up and send your damn text."

Ryder glanced over at Jonas, wishing his toes weren't going numb. He should have put on a second pair of wool socks. Jonas was staring at his phone, his expression stricken.

"What's up, Strickland? Trouble with Nikki?"

Jonas was a big guy for a driver, with a slow, ambling speech, and he always reminded Ryder of a soft teddy bear. Right now he looked like a teddy bear who'd just had the stuffing yanked out of him.

"Um . . ." Jonas shifted on his nylon chair. "It turns out Nikki and her girlfriend are on their way up here. Just to drop by for a few drinks."

Right then Ryder felt his own phone vibrate with a text message.

"What?" Ty yelled. "Tell her no."

Ryder pulled out his phone and read the message. Uh-oh. This was bound to get interesting.

SUZANNE had just put on her pajama pants when Nikki called her. She seriously considered not answering it, then figured it was better to just get it over with and deal with whatever it was Nikki wanted. "Hello?"

"Hey!" Nikki's voice was loud and there was a lot of giggling in the background. "Can you like come and pick me up?"

"What? Why?" Suzanne ran her free hand through her hair. If Nikki needed to be bailed out of jail, she hoped it wasn't because she'd killed Jonas. That wouldn't be the kind of publicity she would like for Weddings by Suzanne.

"Me and my friend are going up to the lake to crash in on Jonas's boys' weekend and we totally need you to drive because we're drunk."

Now what was the proper response for that? "No," Suzanne said. Was the girl nuts? She wasn't hauling her drunk skinny ass out to the lake. Jonas probably wouldn't mind but the other guys would kill her for dumping Nikki in their laps.

And Ryder was there. No way was she driving out to the lake with Ryder there.

She hadn't heard a word from him in five days and she was weirded out by that. While they certainly didn't talk every day, this seemed like a glaringly long gap in communication. Then again, maybe she was just hypersensitive since they'd shared that kiss. Hell, she was, she knew she was. In the past two years, there had been times when she'd gone weeks without talking to Ryder and hadn't thought anything of it. They were divorced after all.

Sort of.

But that had been before he'd planted his lips on her.

"You have to!" Nikki wailed. "If you don't, I'll get arrested for DUI and then I won't be able to get married!"

The girl had a point. And if she didn't get married, Suzanne didn't get paid.

Damn it.

"Alright, are you at home? I'll be there in ten minutes." But she was picking up Imogen first, because there was no way in hell she could be in a car with Dumb and Dumber all by her lonesome.

Imogen resisted the idea, but caved after Suzanne threatened her with getting Ty drunk and having Imogen's face tattooed on his backside.

"Ty is going to be upset that I'm crashing his guys' weekend," Imogen said, pushing up her glasses after closing the car door and fastening her seat belt.

Probably, but Suzanne would be damned if she'd admit it. "No, he's not. I bet he's been texting you all night, hasn't he?"

As she pulled down the street and headed toward Nikki's apartment, she glanced over at Imogen. Her silence spoke volumes. "I'm right, aren't I?"

"Yes, he has been texting me, that's true. But that doesn't mean he actually physically wants me present."

"Are you kidding? Once Nikki and her friend blow in, Ty's going to want to jump onto your lap and be held." The very image was about the only thing amusing Suzanne lately. "He might even call you mommy."

"That's disgusting," Imogen replied. But she did smile. "Maybe you're right. It's a bit awkward for him with Nikki sometimes, since they used to date."

"Yeah, I don't get how that really works. I mean, you

think Jonas would feel some kind of guilt, or jealousy, or something, but he seems to think it's totally normal that Nikki cheated on Ty with him. And now wants him in his wedding party? It's kind of weird."

"I think it would be significantly more awkward if Nikki or Ty had genuine feelings for each other. But theirs was merely a mutually satisfying temporary arrangement."

Booty call. Suzanne got that. "Well, it's a good thing my life isn't complicated like that," she said with a healthy does of sarcasm. "I mean, I'm just still married to my ex-husband. That pales in comparison."

Imogen laughed, then her amusement was cut short as they pulled up in front of Nikki's apartment building. Nikki and one of her bridesmaids whose name Suzanne couldn't remember, were doing stripper dances on the telephone poles adjacent to the parking lot. "Oh, my goodness."

"Good Lord." Suzanne shook her head. "I was young and stupid once, too, but I like to think I saved my gyrating for men, not inanimate objects. Somehow that just seems a notch classier."

"Are they even old enough to drink?"

"Nikki is twenty-two. All grown up." Suzanne got out of the car and yelled to Nikki, "Come on, let's go. Time's a wastin' when there's wine to be tastin'."

"There's wine?" Nikki asked. "Hooray!" She threw her arms up and stumbled over to Suzanne in her fuzzy boots and fuzzy coat. "You're the bestest, greatest, most awesomest ever."

Suzanne accepted the hug, patting Nikki on the back. When she wasn't tossing pizzas onto the floor or screaming at her fiancé, Nikki was a sweet girl.

The other girl said, "I'd better get laid once we get

there. That's the only reason to go into the woods at night."

Charming. Though the girl kind of had a point.

Nikki burped loudly. "Evan Monroe is there."

"Ooohhh. That will work." Her eyes widened and she hiked up her skinny jeans, a smile on her face.

Suzanne got in the car and shot Imogen a look. Imogen looked as nervous as she felt. Pulling out her phone, she texted Ryder.

Incoming blondes. Retreat if possible.

She did still care about the man. It was only fair to warn him.

RYDER heard Nikki and her friend before he saw them. They were singing a song at the top of their lungs, though it was so garbled he couldn't have said what song it was. He had appreciated the warning from Suzanne, but he couldn't abandon Ty and Evan.

Besides, he'd ridden up with Ty, and he knew McCordle wasn't going to surrender their camping trip without a protest.

Jonas actually smiled as he heard his fiancée's wobbly voice. "Hey, that was fast. They're here already."

"Yippee," was Ty's opinion.

His own thoughts matched Ty's, but Evan was the one who gave voice to the basic problem in front of them.

"Great. Now I have to be cold *and* annoyed."

Nikki saw Jonas as they came up the path and she ran to him, tripping and nearly landing in the fire pit. Jonas grabbed her arm and prevented a barbequed Nikki. "Whoa, babe. You alright?"

"I'm drunk," she told him with a giggle.

"What did you drink?" he asked. "You never drink."

"Skinny bitches," she said, her words slurring a little as she collapsed onto his lap, her fur coat lifting up to surround her cheeks. "Vodka and Diet Coke with a lime. The other drinks have too many calories." She smacked her own bottom. "Can't get fat."

Ryder was about to ask how many skinny bitches the skinny, uh, Nikki had consumed when he realized Imogen and Suzanne had walked into the campsite, too. He sat up straighter and pulled off his knit cap. Damn it, now his hair was fucked up, and Suzanne looked smoking hot in jeans and a puffy white vest with a tight black turtleneck under it. He crammed the stupid hat back on his head, figuring that was better than jacked-up hair. Though he wondered exactly why he cared, as Ty jumped up out of his chair.

"Imogen! Darlin', what are you doing here?" A smile split Ty's face, and for a guy who'd been holding tight to the ban on women, he looked pretty damn giddy to see his fiancée.

"I'm here for moral support," Imogen said, giving Ty a kiss on the cheek as she moved around the campfire. "Suzanne needed some help delivering her client."

That was obvious. Nikki was trying to climb up Jonas's lap, but kept sliding down his legs. Finally Jonas put a big hand on her tiny butt and hauled her up onto him, holding her firmly in place.

Ryder stood up. "Hey, Suz, have a seat."

She gave him a weak smile. "No, thanks. Now that Jonas has Nikki, I'm going to head home."

"You just got here. You don't really want to turn right

around and head back do you?" Meaning he didn't really want her to turn around and head back. Ryder was drinking in the sight of her, her legs long and naturally muscular, her ass high and perky in those close-fitting jeans. Not that he had anything other than stupid small talk to say to her, but he still wanted her to hang around awhile.

The other girl who had stumbled up behind Nikki had plopped herself on Evan's lap. He looked equal parts horrified and turned on. Ty was kissing Imogen on the neck and she was laughing and trying to push him away. Nikki and Jonas were making out, aggressive little sounds of pleasure coming from the bride-to-be.

Yeah, there were half a dozen reasons he didn't want Suzanne to head out, not the least of which was that he didn't want to be left lone man out in what was quickly turning into a love fest around the fire.

"No, trust me, I really do want to leave."

He gave her his most charming smile. "If you leave me here alone with all of them, I will cry, Suzanne."

"You've never cried once in your entire life."

Actually, he'd cried twice in his lifetime. The first time was the day Suz had miscarried their baby. The other was the day she walked out of their house and didn't come back. But she didn't know that, so he just said, "I'm going to start."

"Whatever," she said, but she did plop down into his empty chair. "I'll tell you what, Ryder, I don't mean to complain, but this is a hard way to make a living. I'm a wedding planner not a designated driver."

"You did the right thing. Jonas can handle her."

He turned and looked at Jonas, who was managing to contain a wobbly and giggling Nikki.

"How many drinks did you have, honey?" Jonas asked her.

"Three. But I haven't eaten since yesterday. I think they went straight to my head."

"Nikki, you have to eat," he told her in a gentle voice. "It's not good for you, and you look amazing the way you are. You'd look amazing at any weight, you know." He looked around her at the crowd. "Did we bring any food that isn't junk food?"

"I sent a vegetable tray with Ty," Imogen said. "Where is it, Ty?"

"In the cooler. I'll get it." He fished around in the second cooler and emerged with a plate full of carrots, cauliflower, and broccoli. "Here you go, Strickland."

While Jonas coaxed Nikki to eat a carrot, Ryder studied Suzanne. She looked exhausted. Even in the dark night, with only the light from the lanterns and the fire, Ryder could see the dark circles under her eyes. He squatted down next to her. "Has all week been like this?"

Suzanne started to wave her hand, but then she just gave a nod. "Pretty much. This girl is running me ragged."

"At least we got our court date ironed out," he said, then immediately regretting bringing that up.

Her eyes narrowed and her voice was suspicious. "Yeah, at least there's that."

They sat in what Ryder was pretty sure was an uncomfortable silence. A glance over showed Evan was trying to back up in a chair that wouldn't allow him to go anywhere, while Nikki's friend groped his jock. He kept moving her hand away from his jeans, but she always managed to find her way right back. The girl had awesome reflexes if she could pass in that tight of a space.

Nikki held a half-eaten carrot in her hand as she kissed Jonas enthusiastically. Imogen and Ty were snuggling in his chair, talking quietly.

"Well, this is somewhat awkward," he told Suzanne.

"If you think this is awkward, you should have been in the car when Nikki was describing Jonas's penis to us in great detail."

Ryder felt his skin crawl. "Damn, am I glad I missed that."

"Yeah, well, I don't think we heard an ounce of truth, because if you listened to that girl, Strickland is as thick as a jar of pasta sauce and as long as a garden hose, both of which I'm pretty sure are physically impossible. If he was packing the way she claims, he couldn't climb in the car to drive."

Ryder was momentarily stuck on the image of a penis as thick as a jar of pasta sauce, but then he said, "Well, I guess it's sweet she's bragging about him, in a weird, creepy sort of way."

"I can't figure those two out," Suzanne said, hands reaching up to adjust the loose bun she'd put her hair in. "I mean, what do they see in each other? What do they talk about? How do they ever make decisions? But I guess we all have to admit they do seem happy together."

"So, did you ever brag about me?" Ryder asked before he could stop himself. Not that he was insecure or anything, but it would be nice to hear confirmation that he was no slouch.

But given the look on Suzanne's face, he was seeking reassurance from the wrong source.

CHAPTER
SEVEN

SUZANNE gave her ex-husband an incredulous look. He was really asking if she had run around bragging on his dick size. Men were unbelievable. "Of course. I even took out a newspaper ad, then posted it all over the Internet."

"Ha, ha," he said petulantly.

He was hunkered down on the ground next to her, and Suzanne studied him. Ryder didn't look like he was in much of a better mood than she was. He was still damn cute though, despite the goofy striped knit hat he was wearing to combat the cold. Hands in the pockets of her vest, Suzanne sighed.

"Are you really asking me if you were up to snuff?"

"No, of course not. I was joking."

Sure he was. "You have nothing to worry about. Your penis is very pretty and more than enough to make any woman happy."

How many women it had made happy in the last two

years she didn't even want to contemplate. Not that she'd been celibate, but just thinking about him making love to another woman got her back up. Drivers had bimbos throwing themselves at them all the time, and she was sure Ryder had partaken a time or two, or twelve. Thinking that he might have enjoyed sex with some chick ten years her junior more than he'd enjoyed it with her stuck in her craw.

"Pretty?" he said in horror. "Wow, thanks, Suz, that's what every man wants to hear. You make it sound like I should slap a bow on my dick and take pictures of it."

"I'd pay money to see that. Not that I have any money. But I'd dig in the couch cushions for change for a glimpse of a pink bow around you."

"It's not going to happen. My pretty little penis is staying naked in my pants."

"I never said it was little."

"Just pretty." Ryder picked up a stick and hurled it into the fire, where it collided with a log and sent sparks popping and flying.

Lord save her from men and their fragile egos. "What should I have said? It was daunting?"

"Never mind. I'm sorry I brought it up."

"Me, too, because I feel like you're trying to ask me something, only I don't know what the question is."

"There's no question." Ryder had his hands dangling over his knees and she wondered how he could keep his balance like that. The man was definitely in better shape than she was.

"No?"

"No. I know the answer. Sex between you and me was explosive. It was hot and wet and exciting, every single time. My body belonged inside your body and we drove each other wild."

Suzanne could honestly say she hadn't expected him to say that. Holy sexy . . . Sucking in her breath she stared at Ryder, his expression smoldering and intense and determined. Her nipples had hardened beneath her vest, and her inner thighs were tingling. The man spoke the truth. They had driven each other wild, and just thinking about it now was doing interesting things to her insides.

She didn't know how to respond, her thoughts were jumbled and confused, the only thing coming through with any clarity was the fact that her body was one hundred percent aroused by Ryder's words. Her girl bits were saying they knew exactly how to talk to Ryder.

"If we were alone, I'd kiss you again," he said.

That wouldn't be a bad thing.

"I would make you so hot, so desperate for me, you wouldn't be able to walk away this time."

Oh, really? He'd had her at the description of their love life. She'd even been leaning toward the kiss. But then he ruined it with that last part.

Suzanne tamped a lid on her libido and stood up. "Well, this is me walking away. There is no kiss and I'm out of here."

Arrogant son of a bitch. Telling her that she wouldn't be able to walk away. Please.

"What?" Ryder leaped to his feet. "Why? Where the hell are you going?"

"I'm going home." Suzanne fished in her pocket for her car keys. "I'm tired and this is pointless. I brought Nikki here safe and sound and now she's Jonas's problem." A glance over showed Jonas didn't look like he minded the burden in his lap, given the way his hand was making in-roads on Nikki's inner thigh. "As for me and you, it's pointless to even talk about our sex life. That's over and done."

"You're not really driving all the way home are you? If you're tired, just stay here."

Ryder reached for her arm but she dodged it. "Imogen, I'm heading home. Are you staying or riding with me?"

Imogen looked to Ty. "Am I staying or going home?"

"Hello. Staying." Ty made a face like it wasn't even worth a question, his arm snugly around her shoulders. "Thanks for driving on up here, Suz. Are you sure you don't want to stay?"

Nikki and Jonas were still making out, and at some point Evan and Nikki's friend had disappeared, presumably into his tent. "At Camp Get-It-On? Sweet of you to offer, but no thanks."

"I'll ride home with Suzanne," Ryder said, heading toward one of the tents. "Just let me grab my duffel bag."

And who exactly had he asked if that would be okay? "No, you're not."

Ryder stopped in midstride. "You're not driving back alone."

"I'm a big girl. I can manage."

"You're tired. I'm going with you." Ryder gave her a stern look, one that irritated the shit out of her. "Give me two seconds to get my bag."

As if. The minute he entered the tent, Suzanne waved to Imogen and Ty and whirled around to head to the driveway.

"Suzanne . . ." Imogen was pushing herself out of the lawn chair. "I'll go with you."

"I'm fine. Stay with Ty." She gave her a friend a look that said to drop it. Imogen knew her, and knew when she said it was fine, it was. If there was one thing Suzanne could say with certainty it was that she always spoke her mind with her friends.

Imogen nodded and sank back down. "Alright. Text me when you get home so I know you're safe."

"Of course. Have fun." She was just starting down the path when Ryder reemerged, bag in hand.

"Damn it, Suzanne, wait for me."

You know what? She just didn't feel like it. It was childish and petty, but she was exhausted and fed the fuck up with her week, her bank account, and her life.

So she walked faster.

Beeping her car unlocked, she jumped in and started the engine.

Ryder tried to get in the passenger door but it was locked. Suzanne put the car in reverse and took her foot off the brake so that it started to roll. Ryder pounded on the window. "Let me in."

"No!"

"Suzanne, I swear to God, I'll jump on the hood of your car if you don't stop."

He wouldn't do that. "I'm not stopping." Suzanne glanced behind her and gave the gas pedal a slight push to emphasize her point.

The pounding impact had her whipping her head around and slamming on the brakes. He'd done it. Holy shit, he'd actually done it. Ryder was on the hood of her car, struggling to hold on to her wiper blades. "What the hell are you doing! Are you crazy?"

His face was only a foot in front of hers, even though

a sheet of glass separated him. "Unlock the goddamn door."

The expression on his face was so scary, Suzanne didn't even hesitate. She hit the button, not wanting to be responsible for him falling off the hood of her car and being run over when she starting driving, which she was going to do. Damn, he pissed her off. Of all the nerve, leaping on her car to prove a point, which was a stupid point to begin with.

"You have sixty seconds to get your butt in this car or I'm hitting the gas, and I don't give a shit what I run over on you. Your pretty dick is going to lose its place in the penis pageant after it's had an SUV roll over it."

She held the brake, seething, and fairly certain she and Ryder had reached a new low in their relationship as he hopped into the car and glared at her. Stomping on the gas, she flew backward, braked, then went into drive and peeled out down the gravel road, all while his door was still in the process of closing.

"You wouldn't run me over."

"Don't test me, buddy."

"Why are you so pissed? I just didn't want you driving home alone. Can't I even express concern for you?"

"Concern is nice. Meddling is not welcome. I don't need you telling me what to do."

"I wasn't telling you what to do!"

Suzanne's wheels spun a little on the gravel and she slowed down. Just a little. It was a thirty-minute drive home and that was about twenty-nine minutes too long. Whatever patience she'd had for the day was used up on Nikki and she did not want to do this with him. "Whatever."

The road was dark and she was shaking, she was so annoyed.

"That's it? *Whatever*. Oh, that's classic Suzanne. And you say I don't finish what I start. You never share your emotions. Ever."

That was it. She couldn't fight with him and drive at the same time. She slammed on the brakes and threw the car into park. "You want emotion? I'll give you emotion. My life sucks, okay? Aside from the money for Nikki's wedding, which I can't use until after the thing is over and done with, I have exactly two hundred and twelve dollars to my name and the gas and electric bill are due next week. I realize I'm lucky that I have a condo and a car, but neither one of them were paid for by me. You gave them to me. I'm thirty-three years old, I'm single with no money, I have no children, and I've done nothing, not one thing, that I can consider a success. Aside from my charity work, there is nothing I am proud of in my life, and I can't even do that anymore because I can't afford to. I'm a big, fat failure. How's that for emotion? You like that?"

She pounded the steering wheel in frustration. "Does it make you feel good to finally get me to break down?"

He didn't say a word and she was afraid to look at him, knowing she would see pity on his face. But she was so spitting mad, she couldn't bring herself to regret her outburst. She would tomorrow, for certain, but for right now, she still had a thing or two to say. "So as for your concern, you can keep it. I don't need your emotional or financial charity. I've been taking care of myself since I was eighteen years old, and I'll figure this out, too. I'll survive Nikki and I'll make something out of this god-damn wedding-planning business if it kills me."

Then she sat and waited for him to tell her he was sorry, that he felt bad, the sympathy dripping from his voice, making shame ooze out of her pores.

But he didn't. Instead he just said, "I have no doubt that you will make something out of it. You are a strong woman, one that I've always admired. Generous, determined, a survivor."

Suzanne glanced over at him, wary. He didn't sound like he was feeling sorry for her.

"And you're also the sexiest, hottest goddamn woman I've ever met in my life."

Nope. No pity there. That was razor-sharp lust. Suzanne could practically smell the testosterone rolling off him, and steam might as well have escaped his nostrils, he sounded so raw and aroused.

Oh, boy. She had a sudden feeling she was about to get that kiss he'd been threatening her with earlier.

She opened her mouth to say something, anything, she wasn't sure what, but she was right about that kiss. There was no time to spit out a single word before Ryder was on her like stink on pigs. In one rapid motion, he had just eliminated any and all space between them and he was kissing the bejeezus out of her.

Suzanne did manage a startled squeak, but that was it. Then his mouth was covering hers, his tongue making teasing little inroads inside hers, his hands in her hair, gripping her tightly. It was the kind of kiss that didn't start out slow and burn steadily. It exploded with the first touch, a hot, wet, anxious kiss that collided her frustration and passion with his, and when he started pawing at her vest to get it off, she was neither surprised nor opposed to the idea.

Goose bumps had popped up on her flesh, a shiver of desire rushing down her spine, and every inch of her body jumped on the happy bandwagon. The kiss just went on and on, their breath jagged and eager, her hands reaching out to grip his sweatshirt, to drag his sexy self closer to her.

If she had wanted him earlier in the week, she had to have him now, and there was no thought, no brakes, no reality other than him on her and how goddamn good that felt. Suzanne moaned when he kissed her neck, the tip of his tongue trailing across her bare flesh, hands sweeping down over her breasts and tweaking at her nipples. Leaning forward in her seat to get closer to him, she slipped her hand onto the front of his jeans, finding his erection with the ease of familiarity, regardless of how much time had passed since she had touched him there.

The sharp catch of breath he gave as she stroked emboldened and satisfied her. Ryder had the right of it. Sex between them had always been amazing, and she was going to get herself some of that right now.

"Thank you. Now make me hotter."

Ryder didn't even bother to stifle his groan at both Suzanne's words and the way she could go up and down on him with just the right amount of pressure, driving him wild even through his jeans. A quick study of her eyes, glassy with desire, her posture, open and abandoned, her voice, sassy and laced with arousal, assured him she wasn't going to change her mind this time.

He wanted her in the backseat, where they could have more room to maneuver, but he was so hot for her, it seemed like a ridiculous waste of time. Popping the snap on his jeans, he took down his zipper, and let his erection bound free. If she were going to call a halt to this, now would be the time.

But he knew immediately she wasn't going to do anything of the kind because her eyes lit up in a way that had him gritting his teeth. When she bent over him, Ryder gripped the door handle on the car and considered himself very, very fortunate that Nikki couldn't hold her liquor.

That first touch of her soft, warm lips over his erection had him moaning. "Suz . . . God."

"I don't care what you say," she murmured, her breath dancing across his flesh. "I still think it's awfully pretty."

"Call it whatever you want," he said, and he meant that most sincerely.

"Mmm," was her only answer before she flicked her tongue over the tip of his shaft, then slid her mouth fully over the length of it.

The hot, wet slide had him closing his eyes and white-knuckling the door handle. She gave one slow pull back, then she picked up the pace, up and down, her hand gripping the bottom of his cock, her saliva creating a slick surface for her mouth and her fingers. Ryder thought it might be the closest he'd ever come to dying from pleasure, it was such an unexpected jolt of ecstasy. It was only a minute or two before he simultaneously couldn't take it, yet wanted more.

Her. He wanted her. Gripping her cheeks, he stopped her. "Take your pants off, babe."

Even in the dark, he could see her smile over his cock. "Good idea."

Suzanne sat up, and while she unzipped and wiggled out of her jeans, Ryder shoved his own down to his knees, both of their movements impatient and desperate. After several precious seconds were lost to her battling the denim off over her ankles, he said, "Forget it, just come here." Her panties, turtleneck, and puffy vest were still in place, but he didn't care.

To prove his point, he ran his hand over her thigh, slipped under her panties and drove his finger straight inside her.

She froze in the process of fussing with her pants at her feet and let out a groan. "Damn, Ryder, give a girl some warning."

The slick reception his finger was receiving left no question Suzanne was as ready as he was. "Okay. I'm warning you that I'm going to pull you over here and onto me."

Her hips started to move, rocking her into his finger, and he let her, for about three heartbeats, then pulled out of her. She gave a groan of frustration, but Ryder just grabbed her by the hips and yanked her toward him.

Suzanne gave a yelp of surprise, but once she realized his intent, she grabbed the back of his seat and helped him maneuver her body toward his. It was awkward, it was frustrating, but lust prevailed. After clearing the gearshift, Suzanne fell onto Ryder with a soft oomph, her warm thighs delicious on his own bare legs. They were both fully dressed from the waist up, her nylon vest making a soft scratching sound as it rubbed against his sweatshirt.

He debated wrestling her out of the ridiculous piece of clothing but decided it was a waste of energy. He wanted to focus on kissing her instead. Which he did, with more urgency, more passion, more desperation than he thought he'd ever felt in his whole life. As their lips melded together, their hips rocked in unison, his cock pressing against the front of her panties with each soft collision.

Suzanne was trying to both kiss him and push her panties down. Ryder helped her out, shoving the silky fabric down, his hands skimming the warm flesh of her tight, firm ass. She had to lean forward onto him, straightening her legs, so the panties could make clearance past her hips and knees, and her hair fell out of its bun with their jerky movements. The scent of her hair, the perfume she'd worn for years, the tang of her arousal, all flooded his senses, and Ryder closed his eyes for a brief second to take it in.

This was what he had missed, and damn, she felt so good. Even better clasped around his cock.

So he picked up her hips and guided her down onto his erection with one smooth motion. When her soft, slick heat enclosed him, Ryder moaned, all thoughts gone from his head, nothing but him and her, and the need to take, to own, to drive it hard and finish their mutual pleasure.

"Suzanne," he said through his clenched teeth.

Her response was to lift her hips, pulling herself slightly back, then driving down onto him, their bodies as close together, him as deep inside her as was possible. Ryder swore, using her hips to brace himself as he took over the rhythm, thrusting up into her, their urgent breathing filling the front seat.

Ryder watched her, her hair tumbling loose, her eyes glazed before they drifted closed, her cheeks blooming pink from exertion. Frantic bursts of air came out of her mouth, punctuating each push of him up inside her.

Then she stilled, her eyes flying open, her fingers squeezing into his shoulders. Suzanne's breathing paused, her inner muscles contracting over him, and Ryder felt his own arousal spike in response. She was so amazing, so sensual, so damn hot, that he heard his own voice get louder as hers disappeared. He was thrusting and moaning and she was absolutely silent as her orgasm burst, her head snapping back, thighs clenching, fingers pinching. Her mouth was open, but Ryder knew her throat was closed off. Suzanne held off her breath when she came hard, and she was doing that right now.

That sent him over the edge, knowing he had made her come so soon and so hard, and Ryder let go of his own control and joined her. Her eyes had opened and he stared into them, the amber depths darker than normal, a rawness of passion in them that he was sure was reflected in his own as he pulsed inside her.

At the first feel of his orgasm, she let her breath go in a huge exhalation, and the warm burst of air over his face pleased him, made him want to swallow her whole, be back with this woman in body, mind, soul.

God, he loved her, but as his orgasm burst before tapering out, he clamped his lips shut so he wouldn't blurt that sentiment to her. He knew Suzanne. Dusting off the L word now would just send her scrabbling away from him, both literally and figuratively.

As their bodies quieted down, she collapsed against him, kissing the side of his jaw in a way he found ridiculously sweet before she dropped her head onto his shoulder. "Good Lord. We just went at it like a couple of high school kids," she murmured into his sweatshirt, but she didn't sound remorseful.

Ryder loosened his grip on her hips. He wasn't sure what to say, not when over-the-top flowery emotions were at risk for leaping off his tongue at any given second. So he just said gruffly, "Sex happens."

Suzanne laughed and pulled back to look at him.

"It does. But at least we know what we're doing, unlike teenagers."

There was a compliment buried in there, and he was going to take it. Knowing it might send them into dangerous territory, he still said, "It works between us. It always did."

She didn't agree, but she didn't get defensive either, which he took as a positive step.

Pushing her hair off her forehead, she wiggled a little, still on him, their bodies warm and moist. "I'm hotter than two rabbits screwing in a wool sock. This vest has to go."

Ryder laughed. He loved the way Suzanne used metaphors. He loved her. God, it was so obvious, so right there still in his heart, so like the past two years were a bad dream and they could be together again, as they were meant to be.

"You are the hottest thing I've ever met," he told her, nuzzling into her neck. "Let me go home with you tonight and we can do this again, in a soft bed with cool sheets."

"No gearshift in my thigh? No vest around my ears?" Suzanne clenched her inner muscles onto his cock, making him start to swell again. "That sounds like a plan, my friend."

Friend was not the label he was going for.

Ryder wanted to be Suzanne's husband again, not just on paper because he was a bonehead and forgot to sign something, but because she wanted to be with him, in his house and in his heart.

It was crazy. It was dangerous, foolhardy, arrogant, and blind.

They hadn't worked for a reason. Probably for more than one reason.

But Ryder was starting to think that maybe their paperwork not being filed properly wasn't just happenstance, that maybe it was fate. Maybe it was saying that yes, they'd had problems, but they were still meant to be.

They were still legally married and he wanted another shot at making that legit.

Tonight was as good a night as any to start persuading Suzanne that maybe they should hit pause before they headed to court and signed a damn thing.

CHAPTER
EIGHT

SUZANNE was sweating in places sweat should never be, her hair was stuck to her lip, her thighs were burning from the awkward position, and her panties had cut off circulation to her ankles, but she wasn't complaining.

She had needed that orgasm desperately. Tension had been building up in her for weeks, and the last five minutes had gone a long way toward relieving that.

It had probably been stupid as hell to have sex with her ex, but at the moment, she didn't care in the slightest. She'd done it, it had been hot and frantic and satisfying, and she was about to do it again.

"I guess we should move," Ryder murmured lazily into her neck.

Suzanne knew he was right, but it was relaxing lying against him, the familiar smell of his cologne enveloping her, his touch light on her bare hips. It was odd that it didn't feel more wrong, that she wasn't freaking out and worrying about the ramifications. It just felt . . . pleasant. Not completely comfortable, but satisfying.

Maybe it was like putting on the jeans you'd worn at your thinnest. They weren't a great fit anymore, but it made you feel good to try them on and get them over your hips. A turning back of the clock.

Suzanne peeled herself off of Ryder and smiled at him. "You owe me oral sex." With that, she separated their bodies and flopped half on her seat, half on his, trying to figure out how to right her twisted panties and get them back into place.

"I'll give you all the oral sex you want," he said, tucking his semi-erection back into his jeans and zipping up. "I'll oral sex you to death."

Leg muscles protesting, Suzanne paused in her panty pursuit and laughed. "Is that a threat or a promise?"

"I'm saying I'll go until you can't take it anymore."

That sounded promising. But she wasn't about to let him know about the shiver of anticipation that danced across her flesh. "But until I'm dead?"

"If that's what happens, so be it."

Suzanne laughed. Very few men could amuse her, but Ryder had always been able to catch her off guard and make her laugh with his nonchalant wit. "Yeah, but if you kill me, you'll have to finish planning Nikki and Jonas's wedding."

His lip curled. "Shit, I'd better be careful then. I don't want to get stuck with that hot mess."

"But you are the best man, after all. How's that going for you?" Suzanne managed to get her underwear up to approximately where they should be. The puffy vest was still driving her nuts, so she stripped it off and flung it in the backseat. That made getting ahold of her jeans at her ankles a bit easier.

"Well, it's not that bad, really. It mostly just involves listening to Jonas do Elvis imitations."

Suzanne suddenly realized the reason she was so over-heated had only partially to do with Ryder. As she shifted to haul the denim over her butt, a blast of scorching air hit her in the arm. "Shit, I left the car running this whole time. No wonder I'm burning up. And what a waste of gas."

But Ryder raised his hands, tilted his head, and curled his lip. Jesus, he was about to do an Elvis imitation, she could feel it coming on. Like a cold sore.

"Stop right there." Holding her hand out, she said, "I'm begging you. I can't have any more faux Elvis in my life. I'm up to my eyeballs in kitsch and memorabilia trying to put together a reception that makes Nikki happy. If you imitate the King, we may wind up with you back on my windshield."

Not that she meant it. And he knew that.

Ryder laughed and leaned over and gave her a big, smacking kiss. "Whatever you say, gorgeous. Tonight is all about you. And by the way, we should switch seats so I can drive. You've had a long week and you should just relax."

"Okay," she said readily enough. She was tired. She was relaxed and lazy and postorgasmic blissful. She was giggly and enjoying herself more than she had in weeks. It was nice to have someone at her back, wanting to help her out.

Dangerous, too, but she'd worry about that later. For now, she was just going to enjoy the moment with Ryder.

They got out of the car and moved around the hood to change seats, and Ryder stopped her by blocking her path, like she knew he would. Like she wanted him to. He moved up nice and close, his chest against hers, his hands encircling her waist and sliding under her sweater to the small of her back. That confident smile was one she was familiar with, one that had been turning her on since the first night they'd met at that wedding over six years ago.

"You want something?" she asked him, licking her bottom lip slowly.

"I want a kiss." His fingers had moved below her waist and were skimming the top of her backside inside her jeans, and his mouth was mere inches from hers, but he hovered, waited for permission.

Why make it easy for him? "Say please."

Ryder gave a soft laugh. "Please."

Then without waiting for her answer, he took her mouth with his and owned the kiss. Suzanne could only hang on to his arms and spread her lips for him, letting him work his magic. God, the jerk could kiss, all the right pressure, the right rhythm, the right angle, to make her hot and wet and incoherent all over again. Just when she was beginning to maneuver her body closer to his, seeking his erection, and contemplating sex on the hood of her car, it was over.

As fast as he was on her, he pulled away. "Thanks," he said mildly and moved on past her to the driver's side of her car.

Suzanne took a deep breath and shivered in the cool night air. "You'd better watch it, Jefferson, or you'll get yours."

"I'm not afraid of you." Ryder closed the door behind him to prove the point.

Left standing there horny, Suzanne had no choice but to get into the passenger side, contemplating smacking him upside the head with her puffy vest. But it was too far to reach it in the backseat, so she settled for considering ways to sexually torture him all night.

"Oh, and feel free to give me a blow job while I'm driving," he said, grinning as he threw the car into reverse.

Subtle. "Why are we going backward?" she asked, well aware he wasn't serious about the oral sex request. Which would be the perfect way to get back at him. Once he started driving, she was so going down on him. The man drove nearly two hundred miles an hour on a looping track with forty plus other cars in close contact with him. He could handle driving her SUV at forty miles an hour with her mouth on his cock.

"Getting my duffle bag. I dropped it somewhere back there."

"Sorry about that," she said, grinning.

"No, you're not."

He knew her so well. "No. I'm not."

Ryder stopped the car, hopped out, retrieved his bag, and tossed it in the backseat. Suzanne let him get settled and let him start down the road in companionable silence for a few minutes before she shifted in her seat.

When she bent over his lap and undid his zipper Ryder gave an audible groan and the car lurched a little. "Careful," she told him, reaching in to stroke his warm flesh.

"You're not really going to . . ."

She popped him free from his jeans and closed her mouth over him.

"Shit, yes, you are."

Pulling back, she glanced up at him. "You told me feel free."

"But you never do anything I suggest."

Suzanne laughed. "True that. But then again, I never thought I'd be having sex with you again either."

"Which makes it a good night all around." The car came to a halt when she flicked her tongue up and down the length of him.

"Keep driving. It's more fun that way."

"I'm going to hit a tree."

"You are not. You're a professional driver." Then Suzanne was done with talking. She closed her mouth over his cock and slid up and down, enjoying the feel of him hardening under her touch. He swelled fully erect in a matter of seconds and she felt her own arousal increase as he filled her.

It was delicious, to drive him wild while he was driving her car, to take him deep into her mouth over and over, her fingers cupping his testicles through his jeans. There was something so freeing and powerful about it, her rhythm steady and controlled. The sounds he made pleased her, his low steady moans a testament to how he was enjoying her touch, and how he was fighting to maintain control.

"We're coming up on the main road," he told her.

"So?" Suzanne paused and tried to look up at him, but she could only see his chest.

"So, I'm going to pause before I pull out onto the road, and come in your mouth."

Oooh, she liked the way he thought. Ryder braked, threw the car into park and buried his hands in her hair, helping her pick up the pace of her strokes.

Suzanne briefly worried about his ability to get it up again later, but then figured it didn't matter. She was just going to lie back and receive oral sex until death as he'd already indicated. So Suzanne added her hand to the slide of her mouth, squeezing a little at the base of his cock, his skin slick from her tongue.

His fingers paused in her hair, then he exploded, filling her with his salty, hot taste. He was the only man she ever let do this, the only man that she actually took a certain amount of satisfaction in having him finish while still in her mouth. It struck her suddenly that even after two years apart, during which time she'd never let another man even come close to this, that she hadn't even hesitated with Ryder.

Pulling back, she wiped her lips and tried to slow her suddenly pounding heart. Those feelings, the ones she'd convinced herself were dead, were swelling in her chest, and she wasn't sure what to do with them. She just knew she wanted to grin like a fool, laugh like a hyena, and swear like a sailor.

She still loved the bastard.

Which was just so wrong. As was the fact that it took a blow job to get her to realize it.

But there it was. She still loved him.

Which meant that she needed to make sure he understood that this was it, just one night. Any more than that, she seriously couldn't handle because nothing that had been wrong before had changed.

But tonight, she wasn't going to worry about any of that; she intended to just enjoy herself.

"That was . . ." His words tapered off.

"What?" Suzanne sat up and adjusted her seat belt. She gave him a very sly smile. "Fast?"

He let out a crack of laughter as he rezipped. "Yes, you sexy bitch. I have no control when you're doing that."

That was a compliment she'd take.

And he'd used to call her sexy bitch all the time. It was a term of endearment some women might not like, but she loved it. It had told her that Ryder got her and her sense of humor, and he'd always said it with a grin, a satisfied smile, or an indulgent exasperation. Tonight it was a satisfied smile.

"Good." Suzanne stared at Ryder's profile in the dim light. She knew every inch of his face, his body. There had been so many times in the past two years where she had wanted to reach out and touch him, just a hand on the arm, her head on his shoulder, a quick kiss like she had always done, only to remember that she no longer had the right to do any of those things.

Leaving him and their marriage had not been an easy decision, and there had been a thousand little things that had all piled up like bricks day in, day out, until the wall between them was so high that the sense of comfort, ease, love had been gone, replaced by tension and accusations. While they could never go back, tonight it felt like they had taken a jigsaw and carved a little window in the wall.

So she reached out and ran her fingers through his dark hair as he pulled out onto the main road, loving the feel of the soft bristle-short strands, before wandering down to his neck and massaging him. If he was surprised, he didn't show it, he just gave a low grunt of approval.

"That feels awesome," he said. "But I think you're the one who deserves a neck rub after all the maneuvering around this car you've been doing."

"I'm not going to argue with that." Ryder had amazing hands that really dug into her muscles and worked them loose. "Should you text Ty and let him know you left with me?"

"I think he can figure it out, and by now he's probably getting busy in his tent with Imogen."

"So the guys' weekend turned into a sex-fest from the looks of it."

"Indeed. I think we actually all owe Nikki a giant thank-you." Ryder glanced over at her, but she couldn't see his eyes in the dark. "Hopefully you thought it was worth having to put up with Nikki on the drive."

"So far so good." No reason to swell the man's head. He still had all night to disappoint her.

Not that he would. She knew that. In the bedroom was never where she and Ryder had disappointed each other.

That was everywhere else in their lives, their marriage.

But damn if she was going to think or worry about that at the moment.

That reality belonged in the past and for tomorrow.

Right now she was going to live in the present. Naked.

AS they got closer to town, Ryder asked Suzanne, "Your place or mine?" He was thinking his place was closer, but then again, they had lived in his house together for four years. It had memories, good and bad. It had been the house they had picked out together, where he had carried her over the threshold, where they had planned out a nursery, and where Suzanne had packed a bag and walked out the front door the day she'd left him.

Ryder had offered the house to Suzanne, but she had

bought her condo instead, a fresh start he had imagined. He had thought about selling, but he hadn't ever gotten around to it. Two years had taken some of the emptiness out of the place, and he had gradually replaced blankets and dishes she had taken with his own choices, and he had taken over the master bathroom entirely.

Maybe he didn't want Suzanne in his place either now that he thought about it. Awkward.

"My place, if you don't mind. I need my pillow."

It could mean simply that Suzanne liked her pillow, or there could be a larger meaning behind what she'd said, and suddenly it felt like there was a giant elephant sitting on the gearshift between them.

"Sure, not a problem."

"Do you remember when we went to New York for the end-of-the-season awards ceremony that one time and they put us up in that really nice hotel and we got in a pillow fight? The people in the room next to us called and complained about us laughing and shrieking."

Ryder smiled. He did remember that weekend well. Suzanne had been bounding around the bed in her bra and panties taking swipes at him until he'd dropped her to the mattress and kissed her breathless. "We weren't shrieking. *You* were shrieking. Until you were moaning."

"I remember."

The tension Ryder had felt shifted, the energy in the car between them heated and sensual. Just like that, he was hard again. "It was a good weekend."

He pulled into the parking spot in front of her condo and turned to her.

"It was a fucking great weekend," Suzanne said, the vehemence in her voice catching him off guard. Her eyes ran over him, up and down the length of his body, the parking lot lights casting a glow over her pinkened cheeks.

Ryder felt a rush of blood down south under her scrutiny and from her words. "Get inside," he told her. "Or I'll take you in the car again."

She opened the car door but paused, glancing back at him over her shoulder. "Just so we're clear on it, this is just tonight, this doesn't mean—"

Ryder cut her off, not wanting to hear the speech of how they weren't together. He knew they weren't together. He lived it every day.

"I know. I understand. I don't expect anything." Ryder ended that thread of conversation by getting out of the car and slamming the door shut. He came around to the passenger side and hauled her door open the rest of the way. "Now get inside, Suz."

He took her hand and tugged her out of the car toward him.

"Well, aren't you bossy as hell," she said, but her voice was breathy, taking the sting out of the words. "But I can be bossier."

"As if I ever doubted it." He handed her the key ring. "Open your front door and get inside. Now."

"Fuck you," she said, yanking the keys out of his hand, her voice more turned on than angry.

"That's the plan." Ryder followed her up the walk, unable to resist reaching out and cupping her ass in her jeans as she paused at the front door to insert the key.

Without even looking at him, she said, "You're really playing with fire tonight, Jefferson."

Ryder picked up her hair and kissed the back of her

neck, taking in her scent, one hand still on her backside, caressing, gliding toward her inner thigh. "We've already both been burned. What's a few more flames?"

God, he wanted to be with her so bad, even more than he wanted to win a championship. He knew it was stupid to think that Suzanne would want him for more than tonight—she'd just flat-out told him that's all it was—so he needed to be careful, to guard himself. But for now, for tonight, he was going to take whatever she was willing to offer.

"Taking risks is dangerous." Suzanne shoved her door open.

"And when have you ever played it safe?"

She turned and shot him a look over her shoulder, one he couldn't decipher. "Oh, I think I've always played it safe. I just do it with attitude."

That puzzled him. He would have never called Suzanne cautious. But before he could question her further or turn it around in his head more than once, she peeled her sweater off and tossed it to the floor. There was a light on in her kitchen and the beam filtered down the hall, casting her head in shadow, putting her now bare back and legs in a soft glow. Suzanne unzipped her jeans and shoved them down, bending over and giving Ryder a hell of a view of her red panties.

Trying not to swallow his tongue, he said, "I'm about to have an attitude."

"Really, why?" Suzanne turned to face him, her body fully displayed for him in a cleavage-creating bra and those scrap-of-nothing panties, and he was certain for a second that he had actually inhaled his tongue because he couldn't speak.

As she walked toward him, Ryder enjoyed the view, his anticipation building with each step, until she skirted him, her arm barely brushing his, and walked right on past him. She slammed her front door shut and locked it.

"Chances are, you'll never have as much attitude as me."

"I think we've already established that." Suzanne was about to sidle on past him again, the little tease, but Ryder blocked her by turning his body. She retreated a step and wound up close to the wall. Perfect.

Ryder took her by the shoulders and pushed her the rest of the way until her back made contact.

"What are you doing?" she asked.

"I'm going to kiss you."

"That's all you better do. I want my oral sex and I don't want it against this wall."

"You'll take it wherever I give it to you," he told her, fingers stroking across the front of her panties, enjoying the heat coming from her. "And like it."

Suzanne's breathing was increasing, just from his light touch across her clitoris, but she gave a scoff. "Who says I'll like it, you arrogant ass?"

But there was more arousal than scolding in her voice and Ryder kissed the corner of her mouth, lingering over the taste of her. "You would if you weren't so stubborn. Just relax and let me kiss you."

Suzanne gave a short nod, and Ryder closed the gap between them, his legs on either side of hers, hands on her neck, his mouth falling onto her soft, sweet lips. But when he kissed her, she bit his bottom lip, just a quick nip to show him she wasn't about to be submissive.

"Oh, we're going to play it like that, are we?" Ryder used his foot to shove her legs farther apart.

"Like what?" she asked, eyes open in mock innocence. She leaned against the wall, her breathing quick, torso tilted up toward his body.

"This power play. We're going to fight for control."

"Let's not fight. It's such a waste of energy. Just give all the control to me."

Ryder took her mouth with a hard kiss, wanting her so bad he couldn't believe that it was possible to want that deep, that hard, that desperate. "I'll give it to you."

"I bet you will," she said, her hands sliding down and grabbing his ass. She squeezed and fondled him with a total lack of inhibition he found very hot.

Ryder ripped her bra straps down and yanked the cups so her breasts spilled out. He was losing it. They were crashing into what was about to be rough sex against the wall, right next to her framed picture of the Eiffel Tower. Bending over, he nipped the creamy swell of her breast, earning him a hard swat on the ass.

"What, you don't like that?"

"I want more," she said. "Suck me."

Since that was punctuated by another smack, Ryder had no problem obliging. It was on. All his blood was rushing south, his mouth was hot, his dick hard, his muscles tense. He tore at her bra until it was down by her belly button, and then he covered her nipple with his mouth and sucked. Suzanne gasped in pleasure and Ryder wedged his knee up farther between her legs, rubbing his thigh against the slippery satin of her panties.

Her nipple was hard and slick, a tight little bud that felt amazing in his mouth, so good that he had to bite it.

"Ah!"

The little gasp of shock and pleasure egged him on. He

bit a little harder, cupping the weight of her full breasts in his hands. Suzanne had deliciously round and perfect breasts, naturally large enough that Suz had always joked they were officially hooters. Ryder didn't care what they should be called, he was just grateful for their soft fullness and for the fact that they were one hundred percent real, giving Suzanne plenty of sensation in them.

She smacked at his head even as she arched her back, guiding her breasts back to him when he pulled away. "Too hard."

"No, it's not. You like it hard." Ryder flicked his tongue over the taut bud, giving it a third nip.

"Shit, you're right." Suzanne's fingers clamped onto his hair. "You make me nasty."

That was one of the nicest things she'd ever said to him.

Ryder dropped down to his knees and stripped her panties to her knees. Pulling apart her blond curls he studied her dewy, shiny pink sex, knowing the longer he waited, the more she would squirm. When her legs shifted restlessly and her fingers tugged relentlessly on his hair, he still paused, blowing a stream of warm air over her clitoris. Her hips bucked forward in a blatant invitation, but he resisted the urge to touch her with his tongue, his lips, his fingers, instead just breathing steadily, his thumbs holding her apart and open, his cock throbbing intensely in his jeans, as he watched the wetness of her arousal increasing. As it trailed down her thigh, he wanted to reach out and lap it off her warm flesh, but he resisted.

"Touch me," Suzanne demanded.

"No."

"Well, then I'm leaving," she said, voice shaking with

irritation and arousal, hands shoving his head, hips lifting off the wall so she could move past him.

Which was exactly when Ryder used his arm to push her back and his tongue came out and lapped at her, a long bold stroke. Her body jerked in reaction, but she still tried to escape. Ryder applied more pressure to her hips with his arm and sucked her clit.

"Shit, stop it, let me go."

He pulled back, but gave a random flick here and there, knowing this conversation wouldn't last long. "You don't want me to let you go."

"Yes, I do."

"Why?" Ryder plunged his tongue up inside her and she dug her nails into his shoulders.

"Because you're an asshole."

He pulled out completely. "So you've been telling me for years. Speaking of which . . ." Ryder slid a finger through her juicy inner thighs, then kept going down and around and slipped it inside her back door.

She gave a strangled gasp, her thighs trembling. When he ate at her, licking and sucking and stroking, his finger moving in tandem, he felt her entire body tensing around him. Fingers squeezed him, knees bucked against him, cries grew louder and louder, the scent of her sex swelling up around him.

When he knew she was going to come, he paused, finger inside her, tongue hovering over her clitoris. "Oh, wait, you want me to let you go, don't you?"

"If you let me go, I'll rip your dick off with my bare hands."

That's what he loved about this woman. Balls to the wall, and she still came out swinging.

"That won't be necessary," he told her and finished the job, reveling in the sensation of her coming over, on, and around him.

Suzanne screamed as her body exploded and contracted, and Ryder was really damn grateful that she liked getting nasty with him.

CHAPTER
NINE

IF Ryder's arm hadn't been holding her up, Suzanne would have dropped to the hardwood floor in a postorgasmic puddle. She hadn't come that hard since . . . she had been married to Ryder.

Trying to breathe, she leaned against the wall and looked down at him, expecting to find him grinning in triumph. He wasn't. His expression was all business as he ripped her panties down the rest of the way and lifted her foot out, one after the other. Then he stood, hands moving up her legs, her hips, her sides, as he rose, the denim of his jeans and the cotton of his T-shirt erotic brushes against her bare flesh.

While his fingers unhooked her twisted bra, which had drooped to her stomach, his mouth covered her breast, like he couldn't control himself. Suzanne understood the feeling. She wanted him inside her now, do not pass go, do not collect two hundred dollars. Just get her done.

But when he pulled back, she realized that wasn't his plan. He was gathering his control, damn it. After a deep breath and a hand through his hair, he pulled off his T-shirt and tossed it to the floor. Then he bent over, hands out, and Suzanne realized what he was about to do.

"Ryder, do not pick me up." She screamed when he did it, a hand sliding under her butt, another across her back. Still a little oxygen depleted from what he'd just done to her, the movement of having her legs yanked out from under her made her dizzy.

"Quiet," he told her.

If she'd had more strength, she would have fought him, hating how being lifted made her think about everything on her that jiggled and how broad her butt was. But she was too sapped to protest further, and actually, when she banished all those worries rolling through her head, it was sexy. The way he carried her effortlessly down the hall, the way her breast touched his bare chest, the way her still damp inner thighs were forced together.

By the time he deposited her down on her bed, it felt like every inch of her skin had been stroked and caressed. Even the comforter, cool against her warm bed, was tactile and arousing. Suzanne spread her legs for Ryder as he shucked his jeans at the foot of the bed.

"I'm on top," she told him, deciding she needed to re-assert herself.

Flicking on her lamp, casting the room in a soft glow, he raised an eyebrow. "Doesn't look like that's what you want to me at all. Given that your legs are open in such a gorgeous invitation."

"It is what I want." Suzanne shifted a little on the bed,

raising her arms above her head, brushing her fingertips over her nipples on the ascent.

"I think you just want it any way you can get it, isn't that right?"

It was so bizarre that those words outside of sex would have had her contemplating murder, but in the bedroom had her nipples tightening and a low burn firing low in her belly. "No," she said carefully, her mouth thick and hot with desire. "I want to be on top."

And she closed her legs, intending to sit up and switch positions.

But Ryder wasn't about to concede that easily. With quick reflexes from driving, he had her legs apart before she could make a further move, his body over her, erection pressing against her in a delicious teasing pressure. God, was there any moment of greater anticipation, any moment of more heightened senses than that split second before he entered her? When her whole body tensed and quivered and focused right on that small spot between her legs, and she hovered, breath held, waiting for that eye-rolling connection to happen.

"You'll take what I give you," he told her, his dark eyes stormy, the muscles in his forearms bulging as he held himself over her.

"It doesn't seem to me like you're giving me anything," she told him, smacking his ass, knowing it would have exactly the result she was looking for.

It did.

He pushed inside her with a hard thrust, sinking deep into her wet body, as her eyes snapped closed and her breath rushed out in ecstasy.

"Yes."

Ryder let out a low moan, his cock throbbing as he paused, buried in her, then pulled back, starting up a quick, pounding rhythm. Leaving her legs flat on the bed, open wide, Suzanne let him take her, reveling in the hot swirling intimacy, the intensity he could drag out of her, the feeling of being his, only his.

When she thought she might come, her muscles contracting, her back starting to arch, Ryder pulled all the way out.

"Now. On top." He flipped on his back, pulling her with him.

Chest on chest, Suzanne moved her legs to either side of him and kissed Ryder hard. Teasing him for being so damn bossy, she slid her clitoris over his erection, sending pleasant little shivers through her body. He moaned, and she smiled down at him, her hair falling onto his cheek.

Ryder tried to enter her, but she shimmied out of the way, going lower on his thighs.

"Don't start something you can't finish," he told her, hands digging into her arms as he tried to pull her back up onto his cock.

"I'll finish it." She flicked her tongue across his lip. "My way."

Sitting up, she pressed her hands on his abdomen, sliding her moistness down the length of him again. It was a delightful sensation, one that kept her arousal sharp, body ready. Then lifting up her hips in a move that her muscles would protest tomorrow, one hand stroking Ryder, lifting his erection, she joined them again.

Being on top was something she had always loved, the freedom, the control, the deep penetration, and she flung back her head, hands behind her on his legs, and rode him like a rodeo star.

"There you go," he told her, head on the pillow, fingers gripping her knees as he watched. "Damn, that feels good."

"It does, doesn't it?" she asked breathlessly. It had been a long time since she'd been this aroused, this abandoned with a man, and it was because she trusted Ryder, and because he'd always been able to do this to her. Drive her past desire to desperate.

"You don't even know," he said, eyes dark, jaw clenched. "Suz, I need to come soon."

"Well, that's good." Suzanne slid him in and out of her, her hips bucking, pace hard and determined. "Because I'm coming right fucking now."

"You go, you sexy bitch."

"You know it." Then Suzanne couldn't speak because a loud, wild wail came out of her mouth as her orgasm broke, sweeping in her, over her, around her.

Ryder swore and paused inside her, before she felt him coming, a hot rush of release into her open and pulsing body.

As the sensations claimed her, owned her, shook her to her core, and left her flopping weak onto his chest, she had to admit they were good at this.

His skin was dewy, his breathing ragged, and he stroked her backside softly. "Jesus. You're amazing."

Her eyes were already drifting closed, so with great reluctance she disengaged them and slid down his side to the mattress. Hand on his chest, leg draped over his, she murmured, "I told you I would finish it."

"That you did. But Suz," he said in her ear, his lips

brushing up and down her jaw, "I don't think any of this is finished. It never was."

For the first time in a long, long time, Suzanne actually agreed with Ryder.

SUZANNE'S first thought when she opened her eyes and saw Ryder lying naked next to her, softly snoring, the sheet just barely reaching his waist, was that she had just had an awesome night of amazing sex.

Her second thought was now what the hell did she do with him?

The room was lit with the morning sun streaming in and she was curled up snugly under the sheet and comforter on her bed. Rolling onto her side, she studied him. Damn, he was just as cute as he'd ever been, perfect lips, perfect nose, perfect eyebrows that were not too small and not too big and bushy. Cute, cute, cute, the bastard.

When it was good, it was good, and last night had been just that.

Why couldn't they make it work?

Suzanne wasn't even sure anymore, and that was dangerous. There had been reasons, solid, legitimate reasons. She had not walked away lightly, in fact, she'd agonized over it, yet here she was telling herself that maybe there was a chance . . .

She sat up in bed, tossing the covers aside and shivering when the chill of the room hit her. Time for a dose of cold November air on her ridiculous thoughts. Which was good timing, because as she padded across the room toward her bathroom, stepping over the pile of Ryder's clothes, his phone went off on the nightstand.

Ryder groaned and silenced his phone before asking in a groggy voice, "Where are you going?"

"Bathroom."

"Can I come with you?"

"You want to watch me pee?" Suzanne shot a glance at him over her shoulder, wondering why on earth she suddenly felt self-conscious being naked in front of him. It wasn't like he hadn't seen her ten thousand times before. But she was feeling oddly vulnerable, and Lord knew, she couldn't stomach that. "I don't think so."

"Hurry back. I have plans for you."

Just to prove to herself she could, Suzanne stopped in the bathroom doorway and turned, putting one arm up on the door frame and posing, giving him a full frontal view. Not that it was meant to seem posed, but she wanted him to look at her and see all her stuff. And get that lusty look in his eye that he was already getting. It made her feel more in control.

"Suzanne . . . damn, you're gorgeous." He tossed the sheet aside so she could see his erection. His hand enclosed it and he stroked lightly up and down. "Come on, babe, come back to bed."

"I have an appointment with Nikki to try on wedding gowns at ten." A glance at her bedside clock revealed the ugly truth. "It's nine already. I'll be lucky if I can shower the smell of sex off me and still get there on time."

His hand fell off his penis. "Well, that totally sucks." Then he gave her a wheedling smile. "Just five minutes? What are the odds Nikki isn't totally hungover anyway. And maybe Strickland didn't realize she was supposed to meet you and she's still up at the lake with him."

"No, I can't. She texted me that she'll be there." Which

was a total lie, and Ryder was probably right, she would find herself at the bridal shop solo as Nikki slept off her skinny bitches, but she had to leave. She was feeling all sorts of tied up in knots, and suddenly like she might cry again, an annoying emotion that seemed to raise its sissy head only when Ryder was involved.

She expected an argument but he just nodded. "Okay. I understand."

Dropping her arm, she cocked her head at him. "That's it? You're not going to try and talk me into it?"

"Do you want me to talk you into it?"

"Yes and no. I wouldn't mind going for a pony ride, but I really can't be late for this appointment with Nikki."

"And I get that, so I'm saying I won't push it."

She stared at him, not sure what to say. "Why do I feel like we're supposed to fight here, but there's nothing to fight about?"

Ryder grinned. "Old habits die hard." He got out of bed and padded over to her, stretching his arms over his head as he yawned. When he reached her, he kissed her forehead. "But I was thinking that maybe it would be nice if for once we walked away content with each other instead of pissed off. What do you think?"

Suzanne ran her fingers lightly over his back, dumbstruck and touched all at once. "I think sometimes you have kick-ass ideas, Ryder."

"Why thank you." This time his lips brushed hers before he backed up. "I'll use the other bathroom so we don't put you behind schedule. I can be ready in ten minutes."

Ryder bent over and scooped up his clothes and ambled toward the door to the hallway.

"There's towels under the sink," she told him, just standing there, watching him walk away. She should be hurrying, yet she felt no urgency. Quite the opposite, in fact. Ryder had eradicated her fears with his reassurance that he wanted no drama either, and watching him, she just felt . . . happy.

That sad little sack in her chest was all puffed up and telling her that things were good with a capital G. Whatever they had been, whatever they would be in the future, Ryder was and always would be in her heart, and at the moment she wasn't minding that one bit.

Until she opened her bathroom drawer in pursuit of her hairbrush and saw her birth control pills sitting there. Well shit fire and save the matches. She had forgotten to take one the night before. One didn't matter though. Did it? Of course not. The timing was all wrong anyway. Popping it into her mouth, she told herself that the odds of getting pregnant were slimmer than Nikki's forearms, and promptly put it out of her head. No sense in adding more pointless worry to the heaping pile she had already going.

Twenty minutes later she and Ryder were out the door and she drove him home, hitting the drive-thru for some coffee for her and muffins for him. A glance over showed he was destroying the giant blueberry concoction, balancing his black coffee between his knees.

"You'd better not be getting crumbs in my car."

"I'll lick them up if I do." He wiggled his tongue at her and moved his eyebrows up and down. "I'm good at licking."

Oh, Lord. Men never changed. "Uh-huh," she told him,

choosing not to give him a hard time, because she was feeling rather pleased with him.

Ryder laughed and leaned over and gave her a crumbly kiss on the cheek.

When she pulled into his driveway, she had a weird nostalgia fall over her like a blanket. They had done this before, pulled into this driveway together, many times when they'd been married. This had been their house, not his.

Shaking off the melancholy, Suzanne smiled at him. "Thanks for making sure I wasn't the only woman around the campfire last night who didn't get some action."

"Likewise." Ryder shot her a grin then opened the car door. Reaching in the back, he grabbed his duffel bag. "Have fun dodging Bridezilla's tail today. I'll talk to you later."

"Thanks. Have a good day."

As she pulled away, Suzanne wondered if that was it. She guessed it was.

"THESE are the ugliest suits I've ever seen in my life," Evan said as he checked himself out in the dressing room mirror. "I feel like a Ken doll."

"You look like one, too," Ryder told him, adjusting his own tie in the mirror next to the other guys. "And I think technically these are tuxedos."

"I don't give a damn if it's a suit or a tux or a leotard, I feel ridiculous wearing it."

Ryder wasn't feeling the look either. "I hear you. I feel like I'm in an emo band with these skinny pants and skinny ties."

Ty put on his jacket, then took it back off. "These are just weird. I feel very uncomfortable with all of us standing around in this room together trying on androgynous formal wear."

"It was the style back in the sixties," Elec said. Then he added in a low voice with a nod at one of the closed dressing room doors, "And just be grateful none of us are wearing paisley like Strickland."

Ryder would raise a glass to that. Nothing about paisley on his body appealed to him. But if there was ever a day to cram him into something stupid, today was it, because he was feeling the afterglow, no doubt about it. Suzanne had been smoking hot last night, and while his eyes felt like he needed toothpicks to prop them open from lack of sleep, he was high on endorphins.

They'd left it, well, okay, too, which was good. Nobody had stormed off. Objects hadn't been thrown.

That was the definition of progress.

They hadn't talked about anything of importance or how they would handle seeing each other again, but that didn't matter. One thing at a time.

"We're supposed to be fishing today out at the lake, not stuck in this store trying on these dumb suits." Ty unbuttoned the neck on his shirt. "Feel like I'm choking."

"Yeah, well, as soon as everyone had a woman with them, guys' weekend went out the window," Evan said. "And with Jonas having to bring Nikki back for her appointment, Suzanne figured we should get this taken care of, so here we are. You all are lucky I got lucky last night or I'd be really pissed."

"You didn't want to be out at the lake anyway," Ryder told him. "So what are you complaining about?"

"Oh, I can always find something to complain about," Evan said.

Ryder let out a crack of laughter. "True that."

"Guys, I don't know about this . . ." Jonas came out of his dressing room trussed up in black satin paisley.

Not a good look for a big guy. He looked like a marshmallow crammed into a wet suit.

"Uh . . ." was Evan's response.

"Holy shit," was Ty's.

"It looks better than I thought," was Elec's opinion.

Ryder was thinking they needed Nikki and Suzanne's green light before they went ahead and paid for this mess. "You know, Strickland, let's take a pic with your phone and send it to Nikki so she can see it. Maybe she'll want you to go with the regular suit instead of the paisley."

"You think so?" Jonas wiped his forehead. "I think only certain guys can pull this off and I'm not one of them."

Truer words were never spoken. Ryder held out his hand. "Give me your phone. Let's consult the women."

SUZANNE took another sip of her lukewarm coffee and tried to keep her eyes open. She had been at three bridal salons with Nikki over eight hours and was ready to crawl under the velvet bench she was slumped on and fall asleep. It was a cruel irony that after not eating for two days and getting loaded on vodka, Nikki had absolutely no sign of a hangover today, trying on dress after dress with boundless energy. Suzanne hadn't had a drop of liquor and she wanted to collapse into bed and sleep for the next twelve days.

"I'm getting old," she told Tammy, who was sitting on the bench next to her, a crumpled-up rejected bridesmaid dress in her lap. "I need more sleep than I used to."

"Eww," was Nikki's opinion as a new gown option was held up in front of her by the increasingly hostile saleslady. Not a single dress was pleasing Nikki, and Nikki wasn't pleasing the salon staff with her obnoxious attitude.

The other bridesmaids had left when Nikki hadn't been able to focus on finding dresses for them, preoccupied with her own gown. Tammy had been out shopping and had popped in to say hi to Suzanne after they'd texted and realized they were in the same shopping complex.

"Are you staying up too late? I can't do that anymore either."

Time to fess up. "Yeah, I stayed up late last night. Having sex with Ryder."

"*What?*" Tammy sat up straight on the bench next to her and turned to face her. "Did you just say what I think you said?"

"Yep. I did the nasty with my ex-husband. Only he's not really my ex-husband, he's still technically my husband, which should make it okay, but makes it even weirder." Suzanne shoved her shaggy bangs off her forehead, knowing she'd probably just made them stick straight up but not caring. "But I can't say I regret it."

"Oh. Okay, then. I take it it was . . . good?" Tammy studied her carefully.

"Of course it was good. Ryder's a sure thing, if you know what I mean."

"No. I really don't."

Sometimes Tammy's naivete scared the shit out of Suzanne. She'd had more street smarts at six than Tammy had now, but that was part of her friend's charm. "A sure thing. I know he can always get me off, no questions asked. Multiple orgasms."

Tammy blinked, her cheeks a little pink. "Oh, well, that is good then. But how do you feel about it now? Are you seeing each other?"

Could hope and sheer terror coexist? Because Suzanne was sure she was suddenly feeling both. She tamped the feelings down. "No, absolutely not. It was just a fun one-night stand. I think we both needed a little closure."

Uh-oh. Tammy's head had tilted. Suzanne smelled a lecture coming on.

"Closure by sex has really never worked, that I'm aware of. Most of the time it just reopens old wounds and feelings."

"Well, it didn't." So there.

"Suzanne!"

Nikki's high-pitched voice nearly made her spill the remnants of her coffee on her lap. "Yes?"

"None of these dresses work! None of them look like Priscilla's!" Nikki was standing on the dress platform in an empire waist chiffon dress. She looked like a flower girl on steroids. "The sleeves are all wrong!"

"Remember what I said, we just need the basic outline to be right, then we'll do alterations. We don't have time to start a dress from scratch. Your wedding is four weeks away, so there's no way we can find a seamstress to do it in that time frame."

"I don't see why not." Out came the pout.

Trying not to sigh, Suzanne stood up and set her coffee down on the bench. She inspected the dress Nikki was wearing. "This will definitely work." It wouldn't look good, but it would work. "We just need the sleeves and some lace added to the bodice. Maybe an underskirt to fill it out a little."

Nikki's cell phone was suddenly blasting "Rock You Like a Hurricane" from her purse in the corner.

"Can you get that? It's Jonas."

"Sure." Suzanne dug out the phone and handed it to Nikki.

Nikki punched buttons and then let out a wail so loud the saleslady started and fell back onto her bottom from where she'd been pinning the hem on the dress.

"Jesus, what's the matter?" Chances were, it wasn't important, but given Nikki's trembling lip and watery eyes, this was a crisis Suzanne wanted to avert before it got worse.

"Look at Jonas in Elvis's tux!"

Nikki held her phone out and Suzanne eyed the picture of Nikki's fiancé looking a little . . . stuffed into a very shiny tux. "Hmm."

"It looks awful on him! He doesn't look like the King, he looks like a human Ding Dong!"

For perhaps the first time ever, Nikki had said something that Suzanne could find a measure of truth in. Trying not to giggle, she bit her lip hard. "Maybe it's just the angle."

"It's not the angle! It looks terrible. And I don't like this dress, and I was thinking if I have to dye my hair black it will take *years* to get it back to the perfect shade of blond again."

Alarmed at the hysterical tenor in Nikki's voice, Suzanne took her hand and squeezed. "It's okay, hon. We'll work it all out so you're happy. Maybe dying your hair and having Jonas in paisley is too over the top. Let's scale back and just go for a retro look, how does that sound? Just a pretty, simple dress, and a nice black suit."

"I don't want simple." Nikki yanked her hand away. She balled up her fists and screwed up her eyes and let out another fantastic shriek, that was punctuated by her hurling her cell phone across the room, where it hit one of the many mirrors dominating the room. The glass shattered and the cell phone dropped with a thwack to the carpet amid a rainstorm of mirror shards.

Holy . . . Suzanne stared at the mess in shock. "Nikki!"

"That's it," the saleslady said, her face a deep russet color. "Get the hell out of my shop. After you pay for that mirror."

"I'm really sorry," Suzanne said, already reaching for her credit card and mentally deducting broken glass from her check from Jonas. "Of course we'll pay for it."

The saleslady was unzipping the back of the dress Nikki was wearing. "What the hell are you doing?" Nikki asked. "I'm wearing this!"

"Not anymore."

"What if I want to buy this?" Nikki asked, her hands reaching back to shoo at the saleslady.

"It's no longer available."

The dress dropped to a puddle on the floor, leaving Nikki in her bra and panties. "Hey! I'm naked, you fat cow."

Oh, my God. Suzanne frantically turned, trying to remember which room Nikki had left her jeans and sweater in. Tammy was pointing. "That one."

"You have sixty seconds to get out of here before I call security," was the saleslady's response.

Tammy was already gathering up their coats and purses as Suzanne emerged with Nikki's clothes. She gave them to her with a stern look she hoped would get the girl to hurry. "What about the mirror?" Suzanne asked the sales-lady. "I can pay for it."

"Just get out," the plump middle-aged woman said, her lips pinched and fists clenched.

In another minute, they were outside on the sidewalk, Nikki blustering and threatening to sue, Tammy's expression appalled. Suzanne pulled on her peacoat and tried not to feel sorry for herself.

"Thanks for stopping by," she told her friend.

Tammy's eyebrows shot up. "Are you okay?"

She waved her hand, feeling oddly prosaic. "Sure. Fine. Whatever. Just a day in the life of me." If she stressed every time Nikki threw a tantrum, she'd be begging for a heart attack.

"Alright. Call me later. And I'll see you Thursday."

"What's Thursday?" Suzanne was drawing a blank.

"Thanksgiving! You'd better be at my house or I will hunt you down and drag you over."

Thanksgiving. Right. Another holiday to remind her everyone else on the planet had a family and she was the lone woman out.

"I'll be there. With a pie."

"Awesome. Everyone loves your pie."

Ryder had been loving her pie the night before. Suzanne felt her cheeks and her hoohah start to burn.

It suddenly occurred to her she hadn't heard from Ryder since they'd parted ways that morning.

And that suddenly sucked.

C H A P T E R
TEN

RYDER refused to be nervous about seeing Suzanne as he rang the doorbell to the Monroe's house on Thanksgiving. So they hadn't talked since he'd gotten out of her car after they'd made love all night. It didn't mean anything. Everything would be normal, fine, good.

Which didn't explain why he kept flattening the top of his hair and wishing he'd given his pits one more swipe with the deodorant. He was sweating.

It just now hit him that Suzanne might not even be at the Monroe's. He had assumed she would be, which was mostly why he'd said yes to the invitation. His own parents were in Hawaii for the holiday, and he was an only child, so it was either go to his cousin's house, go to the Monroe's, or fly solo. Seeing his godson Pete and Suzanne were what had tipped the scales to come here.

If Suzanne weren't there, he'd have to be content with

the company of good friends and Tammy's kids, which was a hell of a lot to be thankful for, he had to say.

Pete opened the door. "Hey, what's up?"

"Happy Thanksgiving, jerk," Ryder told him with a grin and a hand out to ruffle his godson's hair. Pete had shot up over the summer and Ryder felt himself on the verge of giving one of those stupid comments about growing that he'd always hated from adults when he was a kid, when he restrained himself.

He didn't get to see Pete as much now that Tammy and Elec were married. In some ways, Elec had replaced Ryder in Pete's life as a surrogate father. After Tammy's husband and Ryder's buddy Pete had died, Ryder had stepped into Pete Junior's life as the token guy. He'd enjoyed that, and felt a pang as he followed Pete into the house that he was no longer needed in quite the same way.

It made him wish all over again for a child of his own.

"I'm getting a tarantula for Christmas," Pete told him as he skidded down the front hallway in his socks, his khaki pants and button-up shirt already looking more than a little wrinkled.

"Oh, really? And your mom agreed to that?" That seemed a little too eight-legged and hairy for Tammy's taste.

"Elec said he'll talk her into it."

Ryder felt a smirk coming on and he cleared his throat. "I guess we'll see how persuasive your step-dad is, huh?"

They rounded the corner into the family room, which was bursting with people and the smell of cinnamon. He scanned the room, smiling and greeting everyone, wondering where in the hell Suzanne was, when she came in through the other doorway via the kitchen, a platter of cheese and crackers in her hands. She was wearing a black skirt with some kind of white pattern on it, a short-sleeve red turtleneck sweater, and boots that came to her knees and made him want to throw them up over his head.

Damn, she was gorgeous. He just couldn't say it enough.

Ryder knew he was staring at her, but he wanted her to look at him, to acknowledge his presence, to meet his gaze and have the secret running between them that he had spent half of the other night inside her.

He was well aware she had said more than once that one night was just one night and that there wouldn't be any more, and he respected that. He did. But that didn't mean he wanted her to pretend nothing had happened between them.

Tammy's parents, in visiting from Seattle, Elec's parents, his brother Evan, and his sister Eve, had all greeted Ryder. Tammy's daughter Hunter, a few years younger than Pete, was already climbing onto the tops of his feet with her patent leather shoes, her hot little hands gripped in his.

But Suzanne was ignoring him.

So he tamped down his disappointment and focused on the little girl in front of him, who was wearing a dress, shocking the hell out of Ryder. Hunter was the quintessential tomboy, with a burning love of stock car racing. "You're mighty fancy today, squirt. You look beautiful."

But Hunter made a face at his compliment. "Mom made me wear it." She turned a little to the side. "But she let me add this." There was an Elec Monroe button on the puffy sleeve of her velvet dress.

"Cool. That really makes the outfit." It had probably made Tammy wince, too, but Ryder had to admire a compromise.

Hunter gave one final tug on his hands then darted off, flapping her arms in some interpretive dance move Ryder didn't understand. Amused by her, he took a seat in an armchair next to Eve, who in addition to being their sibling, was Elec and Evan's PR rep. "Hey Eve, what's up?"

"Not much, how are you doing? Congrats on finishing second."

"Don't remind me," he told her with a smile. "Thanks, but second is like being one number off from the winning lottery number."

"Guess you'll have to be number one next season." Eve did a hair-flip thing, her head tilted, smile coy.

She was flirting with him. It had happened before and Ryder had flirted back, considering it harmless. He seriously doubted Eve actually wanted to date him, any more than he wanted to date her. She was attractive, a real shark in PR, and high energy, but he would have never considered getting involved with someone so closely tied to his team members, even if he hadn't just crossed the border into Suzanne Land.

But part of him wanted to flirt right now, to poke Suzanne. It was childish, petty, stupid, and potentially dangerous, but he couldn't help it. Suzanne hadn't even bothered to say hello to him and how childish was that?

"I guess I will," he said. "But shouldn't you be rooting for your brothers instead?"

She shrugged and waved her hand. "They'll be fine. As long as they finish above fifteen, we're not at risk for losing sponsorship. And Evan can't do much worse than last year; he needs a miracle more than my cheer-leading."

Evan was close enough to hear their conversation and he rolled his eyes as he leaned forward to grab some cheese off the platter Suzanne had set on the coffee table. "Heartwarming as always, Eve. And don't forget who funds your paycheck."

"Elec, that's who. The rookie made more than you did, little brother." Eve smirked.

So much for flirtation. She had totally forgotten about Ryder. Instead Evan was insulting Eve's intelligence and they were facing off for a sibling smack down.

"I swear I didn't raise them to be this competitive," their mother said, shaking her head from the couch. She turned to Suzanne. "Do you fight with your brothers and sisters like this? It's embarrassing."

"I don't have any brothers and sisters." For the first time since he'd entered the room Suzanne looked directly at Ryder. "Neither does Ryder."

That had been something they had both understood about each other, what it was like to grow up solo. But even that had been disparate. Suzanne had grown up dirt poor with her grandparents after her mother ran off when Suzanne was a toddler. Ryder had grown up middle class with parents who were pretty sure he could do no wrong. Occasionally, it might have been nice to have someone offering him a little discipline and guidance, but it hadn't harmed him beyond repair.

He didn't think. Maybe Suzanne had a different opinion on that.

"Well, you're both lucky," Evan said, with what Ryder had to assume was exaggerated envy.

"Actually, it was lonely." Suzanne shrugged. "I would have given anything to have a brother or sister to hang out with."

Ryder studied Suz's face. She looked upset but was covering it up. He wasn't sure what it meant, other than that her childhood had been hard and lonely, just like she'd said. He had always pictured her as a scrappy little blonde facing down cruel peers who were making fun of her clothes, or her lack of parents, or her tiny house, with defiance and wit.

Had he ever really acknowledged that to her? Probably not.

"You can have both of mine," Eve told her hopefully.

Thoughtful, Ryder lost the thread of the comments sallying back and forth and sank back into his chair. He wondered just how many times he had failed to ask Suzanne about her emotions, just waiting for her to speak them.

If he knew anything, he knew she wasn't the kind of woman who just offered up her feelings on a regular basis. He should have asked more. Like now.

When Tammy came to the doorway and yelled, "Dinner's ready! Into the dining room," Ryder made sure he aligned himself next to Suzanne for the migration.

"Hey," he told her. "You look nice."

Her eyebrows shot up but she said, "Thanks."

"How are you? How are things going with Nikki?"

"Well, she changed her mind about the Elvis and Priscilla theme after seeing Jonas in that suit and she got us kicked out of a bridal shop by breaking the mirror. Other than that, we're good."

"Wow, that's intense, I'm sorry. Though I have to agree

with her on Strickland. It wasn't a good look for him. But I'm really sorry she's putting you through so much extra work."

Hunter appeared out of nowhere and tugged his hand. "Sit by me!"

With an apologetic smile, Ryder leaned in and murmured to Suzanne, "Sit by me."

The urge to kiss her was strong, but since they weren't alone, he resisted, settling for briefly touching the small of her back before letting Hunter drag him off to the other side of the crowded table.

SUZANNE stared at Ryder's retreating back as he let Hunter pull him along and tried to figure out what the hell was going on. He was freaking her out with his soul-searching looks and empathy for the Nikki situation. Not that Ryder was normally a total jerk, but he didn't usually express so much outward concern, and it was unnerving.

But the looks were really making her squirm. He looked thoughtful, like he was seeing her for the first time.

Running her sweaty palms down the front of her skirt, Suzanne assessed the table, wondering where to sit. She supposed she could sit next to Ryder if there were no other empty chairs, but to just go right to him and sit there, well, people would think it was weird. Wouldn't they? Maybe no one else thought twice about it, but to her it seemed obvious, like it would scream that she and Ryder had crossed the line exes normally don't venture across.

Then again, she was probably drawing even more attention to them by not speaking to him when he had come into the living room. That had been stupid, not to mention rude, but her heart had sped up when she'd seen him and she had been unable to meet his eyes, not sure what to say. So she had ignored him and that made her a bitch.

Shit.

Tammy was still bustling around the table laying down dishes, as was Mrs. Monroe and Tammy's mother, but everyone else had taken a seat around the massive oak table. The only available chairs were next to Elec and Mr. Monroe, which had clearly been left open for their respective wives, and the one next to Ryder.

Trying to move neither quickly nor slowly, just some kind of normal, Suzanne went to the chair next to Ryder and sat down, yanking her chair in closer to the table and fussing with her napkin so she didn't have to look at him. That resolve disintegrated when she felt his hand on her knee. Swinging her head to the left, she gave him a questioning look. Ryder just smiled and squeezed her knee.

With a frown, Suzanne focused on her dinner plate. It had a turkey design on it, a plump elegant gobbler, which freaked Suzanne out. It seemed downright bizarre to be eating turkey off of a turkey. Not that it was going to stop her. She was starving and the food aromas were assaulting her from every direction, and she was going to do some eating, and nothing was going to distract her from that.

Ryder's hand moved an inch higher, leaving the safe territory of her knee and venturing into the danger zone of the thigh. What the hell was he doing? They hadn't spoken in days and he was going to choose a family dinner with small children around to get frisky?

She shifted her leg so his hand dropped off.

Elec was carving the turkey, and a bottle of wine was

being passed around. Hunter, who had a voice that could overpower a race car engine, held up her hand and yelled, "Wait! Before we eat we should go around the table and say what we're thankful for. I'll start."

"That's a wonderful idea, baby girl," Elec told her.

Hunter listed all of her family, her godfather Ty, who was with Imogen and his parents for Thanksgiving, sunshine, and stock car racing as things she was thankful for, and tacked on Suzanne and Ryder at the end as if she'd realized they were sitting right by her. Even if she was just an add-on, Suzanne was touched. When Elec mentioned his family and his wife, the look he gave Tammy was so loving, Suzanne felt a lump forming in her throat. She was so happy for her friend that she'd found a second chance at love.

Mrs. Monroe gave a touching speech about family and the joy of having step-grandchildren, and even Evan managed to give a genuine statement of thanks for his family and friends, though he ended it with, "And I'm thankful for the opportunity to have a career I love, that pays well, and allows me to spend more time with my family. Wait, I guess that's what you call a mixed blessing."

He grinned and turned to Pete. "Your turn, buddy."

Pete, being a ten-year-old boy, said, "I'm thankful for turkey and sweet potatoes, if I ever get to eat them."

Suzanne was hungry herself and feeling an uncomfortable anxiety creeping over her. While she wanted to be thankful, she wasn't sure she was. There was a certain melancholy in listening to a large family appreciate each other. It was just her, still, and that kind of hurt.

So for her turn, she did what was typical for her when she was feeling bad—she gave a lighthearted pat answer and hoped like hell they'd just keep on moving down the line. "I'm thankful for my health, Black Friday sales at Macy's, and my friends."

Hunter, who had cross-examined everyone on their blessings, asked, "What about your family? Aren't you thankful for them?"

You know, she loved the kid, but really? Maybe Hunter would like to poke Suzanne in the eye, too.

"Hunter! That's enough," Tammy said, her look to Suzanne sympathetic.

Oh, well, whatever. There was the truth and Suzanne had lived with it long enough. "I don't have any family, honey. My granny and granddad raised me and they passed away. I don't have any brothers or sisters or aunts or uncles."

"Oh." Hunter's little face crumpled. "That's sad. But we'll be your family, right, Mom?" She looked to her mother for confirmation.

"Of course. We love Suzanne."

Oh, shit, now she had tears in her eyes. She was going to humiliate herself right here in Tammy's country chic dining room with this dumb turkey plate in front of her. "Thanks, honey," she managed to force out. She reached around Ryder, careful not to look at him, and rubbed Hunter's back. "I love y'all, too."

"Isn't Ryder your family?" Hunter asked. "You were married and everything."

"And everything" pretty much summed it up. Suzanne fought the urge to sigh. Somebody better have poured her wineglass straight to the top after all of this.

"Alright, it's time to eat," Elec said. "Food's gonna get

cold. Ryder, you have anything to be thankful for? You're
the only one left to answer."

What Ryder said just about scared the skirt off of Suzanne. He looked at Hunter and said, "Yes, I am Suzanne's
family. And I'm thankful for every day that I've been in
her life."

Then he leaned over and kissed Suzanne on the temple.

Making her actually blush for the first time in over
twenty years.

RYDER watched Suzanne running across Tammy and
Elec's backyard, football tucked under her arm, dodging
Pete's attempts to tag her. There was something very sexy
about a woman willing to put on a borrowed pair of sweatpants and a sweatshirt and get out in the yard on Thanksgiving Day for a pickup game of touch football. Suzanne
had always been like that though, willing to dive in, ready
to try anything.

He supposed he ought to help Pete out since they were
on the same team. Evan was also on their team, but he had
paused to take a sip of his beer. Hunter was blocking Pete,
and it looked like their sibling rivalry was alive and strong
as they shoved each other a little harder than was necessary. Ryder jogged over and scooped Hunter off the
ground and put her under his arm like Suz had with the
football.

"Pete, you're clear, tag Suzanne."

"Hey!" Hunter protested, wiggling in his arms. "Put
me down!"

"Nope." He bounced her a few times and she laughed.

Pete started charging toward Suzanne, who squawked and took off running again.

Hunter got too heavy so Ryder put her down and they both took off after Pete and Suz. Hunter collided with her brother and Ryder grabbed for Suzanne. She gave him a challenging smile as she slipped out of his grip. Her cheeks were pink from the cold and she was breathing hard from the exertion.

"You'll have to tackle me to get this ball."

"It's touch football."

"Scared you can't do it?"

"Oh, I can take you down." Ryder grinned and did a small circle around her. She spun around, wary. "You sure you want me to do this?"

"Give it your best shot."

Ryder shoved her into a giant pile of leaves. She stumbled and went down on her butt, laughing even as she fell. "You still don't have the ball."

He dropped down and hovered over her, wanting to suck her juicy bottom lip, stained the color of raspberries from the cold. "It's too bad we didn't play this game shirts and skins. This would be even more of a fun position than it is."

Her eyes were shiny and leaves were sticking to her hair. "You're a dirty man. There are children present."

Those children were also landing on his back. Someone hit him hard with a monkey move, all arms and legs all over him, and suddenly there were four of them in the pile, laughing and tossing the fiery dried leaves in the air and at each other.

Watching Suzanne laugh and smile, his own grin splitting his face, Ryder had a hell of a lot to be thankful for.

* * *

ELEC sat next to the fire pit, keeping one eye on the logs he had burning there and another on his step-kids playing in the yard. His wife was on the chaise lounge with him, nestled between his legs, her back on his chest, and he kissed her shoulder, perfectly content.

"So what do you think is going on out there?" he asked Tamara.

"Hmm? What you mean?"

"Ryder and Suzanne. There's a . . . vibe between them."

Tamara glanced up at him, biting her lip. "They slept together the other night."

Well, that explained a lot. "Really? I thought that was over and done a long time ago."

"Yeah, me, too. And I'm worried about Suz. She said it was no big deal, but you know her . . . she says everything isn't a big deal. But I don't think she's ever really gotten over Ryder, and if he's just playing around, well, I'm worried she's really going to be hurt."

Elec studied the pair rolling around in the leaves with Hunter and Pete. They both looked to be having fun, and at dinner Ryder's words about Suzanne had sounded sincere. Elec didn't think he was just fooling around to fool around. "I thought Suz was the one who wanted a divorce."

"Technically, but it was complicated. She didn't leave him because she didn't love him. It was other . . . stuff."

"Huh. Well it looks like that other stuff isn't mattering so much right now. They seem to be getting along just fine."

"Maybe."

Elec laughed and nudged Tamara with his knee. "Don't be cynical."

"I'm not! I just care about my friend. I want her to be happy, happy like me."

"Oh, are you happy?" Elec teased her, stroking the back of her auburn hair. "I wasn't sure."

"I'm very happy. The only thing that could make me happier would be if you kissed me."

"I can do that." Elec kissed his wife and forgot all about Ryder and Suzanne.

CHAPTER

ELEVEN

SUZANNE stared at Nikki across the sampling table at the bakery on Saturday and wondered if it were possible for her head to float off of her shoulders and out the front door, and if it did, if that would really be such a bad thing. She was so exhausted her head felt like a helium balloon, and she was fighting random waves of dizziness.

While everyone else in America had spent the day after Thanksgiving cashing in on all the Black Friday sales, Suzanne had been building storyboards of various wedding themes for Nikki. Using pictures of cakes and gowns, along with fabric samples of color palettes to display options, Suzanne had created eight very different, but all very elegant weddings for Nikki to choose from, knowing they were so tight on time at this point that a decision had to be made today or they might as well just book city hall and call it good.

Between working on the storyboards, worry that Nikki would throw another tantrum, and distracting thoughts about Ryder, Suzanne had gotten zero sleep and had the headache to prove it.

But Nikki, bless her little heart, was actually very seriously and quietly studying each one of the storyboards, sometimes making little sounds of pleasure, and occasionally reaching out to touch a fabric. Suzanne would actually feel somewhat proud and pleased if she had been able to focus her eyes. As it was, all she could think was maybe she'd given Nikki too many choices and would overwhelm her.

Fortunately, Nikki shifted to another board and her eyes lit up. She smiled, a sweet almost innocent smile. "Oh, Suzanne, this is beautiful. This is it."

Suzanne perked up and managed to sit up straight, relieving her hand of its duty attempting to prop her suddenly abnormally heavy head up. "Which one?"

Sighing with pleasure, Nikki said, "Cinderella. It's perfect. I'm beautiful like Cinderella . . . Jonas is totally Prince Charming. Our love is magic, and so our wedding should be, too."

"Um-hmm," Suzanne said, hoping that would pass for agreement. She was just so relieved that Nikki was pleased and had made a decision that she would listen to Nikki waxing poetic about her relationship for hours. Wait. She already had. And gotten a rundown on Jonas's penile appearance. Yet she couldn't ever quite manage to give their relationship the enthusiastic endorsement Nikki clearly wanted. All she could do was applaud her decisions that would move this wedding planning forward. Finally.

"That's an awesome choice, Nikki. I'm sure you'll be

really happy with the way it turns out. And we can keep the same ballroom for the reception, we'll just change the décor."

"Great." Nikki was still fondling the fabric for the gown, her face the picture of contentment. "The carriage you have on here is perfect. I should definitely arrive in a carriage."

"And since it will be chilly, we'll have a cape and muff made for you in white to match your gown."

Nikki's sigh was beatific, and when her fiancé walked in a moment later, she smiled at him. "I love you."

It should have made Suzanne happy. Nikki wasn't screaming or throwing things and she had made a decision she seemed thrilled with. Yet some small part of her was suddenly and quite appallingly jealous of Nikki's look of love and devotion. Maybe, just maybe, Nikki and Jonas did actually give a shit about each other. Maybe—and Suzanne couldn't believe she was even thinking it, but she was—maybe their marriage would work out.

Which meant Suzanne might as well just hang it up, because if those two knew more than she did she was in serious trouble.

Time to accept she was going to be alone forever.

The doorbell tinkled and Ryder walked in.

Christ.

She was too foggy to deal with him at the moment. Thanksgiving had ended with Ryder simply getting into his car and leaving, no mention of seeing her again or calling or anything. Not that she would have agreed to see him, but it just seemed like he should have *tried*. Maybe that was dumb, since she'd told him more than once during their night together that it wasn't going to happen again, but still. The man should look a little more cut up about being denied future sex with her.

Instead, he had a very calm expression on his face as he said, "Hey, Suz, what's up?"

What was up was her hackles. She was exhausted, Ryder was blowing her off, and Nikki had found the secret to happiness. It was not a combination designed to make her feel good about herself and life, and she was starting to wonder if she hadn't chosen someone who sucked as a husband maybe she would actually still be married.

Not that that was remotely fair or true, but in her current mood it felt wonderful and liberating to blame everything on Ryder.

"What are you doing here?" she said, trying to ignore the fact that Nikki and Jonas were rubbing noses.

"Nice to see you, too. I came to help Jonas taste cakes. Nikki doesn't want to actually eat any of the cake and she wanted a second opinion."

"I could have given you another opinion," Suzanne told Nikki, who was gazing blissfully at the images of a Cinderella wedding in front of her.

"Oh, you shouldn't be eating cake," Nikki told her. "Especially at your age. Not even Pilates will help."

She would not say what she was really thinking . . . Suzanne dug her nails into the denim of her jeans and kept her lips clamped shut.

"Suzanne can eat all the cake she wants, she's smoking hot," Ryder said.

That was kind of sweet. Suzanne felt sort of bad for irrationally blaming the horrific state of her life on him.

Nikki didn't respond to that. She just said, "So can this bakery do this cake?" She held up the image Suzanne had found of a four-tier cake in pink fondant, a glass slipper on top, and crystal wheels on either side of the cake, creating an elegant illusion of a carriage.

"Yes, I'm sure they can do something similar. Let me tell the baking consultant that we're ready for our appointment." And she might just tell the baker that the bride was a bitch. So much for Nikki's earlier brief moment of sweet complacency.

Ryder hovered along beside her. "Don't listen to Nikki," he murmured. "She's anorexic. You look amazing."

"My self-esteem is fine, but thanks, I do appreciate your concern." She also appreciated his penis. A little loopy from lack of sleep, Suzanne added, "But I'll give you five bucks if you wave a piece of cake in her face."

"Are you crazy? I'll end up with it crammed up my nostrils." Ryder stopped at the counter with her, his fingers automatically reaching out for a display of cupcakes before he stopped himself.

Amused by his transparent sweet tooth, Suzanne glanced around for a bell to ring for the consultant and said, "I did offer five bucks, and trust me, that's hard to come by these days."

"Is this stuff cash and carry?" he asked, scanning the glass case in earnest now.

"Probably. But you'd better not. You'll get fat before Nikki's wedding."

He snorted. Then he leaned close in to her and whispered, "OMG, get that cake out of my face, I'll be faaattt!" His voice was a ridiculous masculine mockery of Nikki's shrill tone.

She refused to laugh. "One of her is annoying enough. I don't need a second bride."

"You don't think I make a good diva?"

"No. You're too hairy." Feeling devilish, she pointed to a pair of candy apples, sitting next to each other on their paper doilies, and said, "Those are nice and smooth, shiny."

"What's that supposed to mean? I am not hairy," he protested. "Especially not down there."

"Where?" she asked with mock innocence. "Down where? I was talking about candy apples."

"Come on, you have to admit I keep my manscape tidy. No moss growing under my—"

Suzanne smacked his arm to shut him up when she realized the bakery consultant had stepped up in front of him. "Hi!" she said to her brightly. "I'm Suzanne Jefferson, we have an appointment."

"Oh, right." The woman frowned in disapproval. "I'm Joyce. Is this the groom?"

"Best man," Ryder told her with a charming smile, sticking his hand out. "Nice to meet you."

Joyce ignored his hand and came out from behind the counter. "Do you have an idea of what you'd like for a cake? How many guests?"

Ryder made a face at Suzanne as Joyce gave them their back. "Wow. A battle-ax baker. She's as scary as Nikki in a whole new way."

Suzanne rolled her eyes at him. "Maybe it's because you were talking about your mossy balls in front of her edible art."

"They are not mossy. They're"—Ryder held his hands up like he was cupping his own testicles—"nice."

Oh, God, she was going to laugh. She just couldn't help it. He was such an idiot, in such a cute, sexy, adorable way. "Friendly, too."

"Damn straight."

A little laugh did escape, but Suzanne covered it up with a cough. "Now use your lips for cake tasting instead of talking," she told him in a stern voice.

"Is that all?" he asked, his eyebrows going up and down.

"For now."

Her answer clearly shocked him because his look instantly shifted from teasing to lustful. "Later?"

She shouldn't, she really shouldn't go there again with him, but she was afraid she knew herself all too well and it wouldn't take a whole lot to convince her to sheet dive again, especially after the last few days of nonstop stress. There was something really appealing about just rolling around naked and laughing with Ryder.

Suzanne couldn't help but smile, even as she evaded the question. "Shut up and eat your cake."

NORMALLY sitting around a bakery while other people rambled on and on about the construction of a Cinderella wedding cake would have put Ryder to sleep in under sixty seconds, but he wasn't bored. Not watching Suzanne work. He had tuned out what they were saying a while ago, but just staring at Suzanne as she took charge and directed the conversation with class and efficiency was sexy as hell.

Content to just sit back and wait for his cake, Ryder wondered if Suz had been serious when she'd hinted about them hooking up later. She'd never been a tease. Usually if she threw something on the table, she followed through with it. Then again, she had bailed on him in the bar after they had kissed, so maybe she'd retreat on this one, too.

While he was perfectly willing and eager for another night with her, if that wasn't her intention, he would live. He was cool with just hanging with her, getting the opportunity to spend time with her and make her laugh. He had never stopped loving her, not even when he had tried to tell himself he had, and it was a happy relief to be able to let that out a little, to indulge himself in his feelings and in spending time with Suz.

Now there was even actual cake involved. He'd lost track of the flavors they had been discussing because they were nothing Ryder had ever heard of, but there was now a whole tray of little cake pieces in front of him and he was being urged to eat them. No one needed to ask him twice.

"That's lemon Maurice," Suzanne told him, pointing to the first piece. "A chiffon cake with a lemon mousse filling. What do you both think?"

He thought Suzanne had originally intended to sample the flavors herself, but now wasn't as a result of Nikki's stupid comment. Annoyed by that, and the whole ridiculous unearned pretentiousness Nikki was displaying, studying the baker's sketches and dimensions, he shoved a huge bite in his mouth. It was good. Not rocking his world, but tasty cake.

Jonas shrugged. "It's good." He swiped a crumb off his lip with the paper napkin he'd been handed by the saleslady.

"I think it's a little bourgeois," Ryder said, not sure what possessed him to assume the role of arrogant food critic, but quite confident the cake was just good, not great. "The flavor explodes too quickly, with no secondary undercurrent of flavor. You might want to tell Maurice that, whoever the hell he is."

Suzanne stared at him, Joyce the baker glared at him, and Nikki looked up from her papers. "Oh," she said. "That's bad, isn't it?"

"Just try the second one," Suzanne said, shoving the next sample in his direction from her seat next to him. "White with a raspberry filling and a buttercream icing."

Hmm. Ryder chewed thoughtfully. "Well, I appreciate the excitement the raspberry brings to the white cake but it's missing a certain mass appeal."

Joyce frowned. Nikki frowned. Suzanne frowned. There seemed to have been a tent sale on sour expressions, because they'd all picked one up.

"This is a peach champagne filling in a traditional white cake."

That didn't even sound good. Ryder put it in his mouth. Blech. It didn't taste good either. Dropping the role of verbose food critic, he just said straight out, "This is like eating bubble bath."

Jonas was shuddering, too, and looking like he wanted to spit the remnants in his mouth back into his napkin, but resisted. Swallowing hard, he thumped his chest and coughed. "Can I have a glass of water?"

"Shush," Nikki told him, but she did pull a water bottle out of her giant handbag and hand it to him.

"This is chocolate hazelnut meringue," Suzanne said, her voice getting a little clipped. She shoved the fourth piece at him.

The chocolate melted in his mouth, and Ryder longed

for a glass of milk. Now this was cake. "Two thumbs up. This is rich and moist, and the hazelnut hint keeps it from being pedestrian."

Suzanne's eyebrows shot up. "You've been watching the Food Network, haven't you?"

He was busted. "Maybe. Just a little. On Mondays."

There was a long pause where she just stared at him, then she started laughing. It burst out with a loud crack, and Ryder couldn't help but laugh, too. She might have been laughing at him, but it was still funny to see her cackling so hard tears were in her eyes and she was doubled over and wheezing.

"What's so funny?" Nikki asked.

"I'm sorry," Suzanne managed, trying to rein it in, using her finger to swipe under her eyes. "But the thought of Ryder watching foodie shows just really cracks me up. I mean, he has never cooked that I'm aware of."

Joyce, who was glancing at her watch, said, "I didn't realize you knew your clients so well."

"Oh, they have sex with each other," Nikki explained, sticking her finger in Jonas's piece of chocolate cake and lifting it to her mouth before catching herself and wiping it on his napkin with a little growl.

"We . . ." Ryder started, not sure what to say. They did have sex with each other, at least they had until two years ago, then again the week earlier, but he was pretty damn sure Suzanne didn't want everyone to know, especially not her bakery contact. "We're married."

The remnants of Suzanne's laughter cut out. She gave him an incredulous look and amended, "*Were* married. We're divorced."

Not so much. "Actually, not according to the lawyer—"

The rest of his sentence got stopped in its tracks by a piece of cake being shoved straight into his mouth by his ex-wife, current wife, whatever wife she was. Icing scraped over his teeth and his tongue recoiled from the weight of the cake unexpectedly colliding with it.

"Ahh," he managed before being forced to swallow. It was the shitty champagne cake, and while he didn't want it in his stomach, he definitely didn't want it lingering in his mouth either.

Wishing a beer would miraculously appear in front of him, he looked over at Suzanne as he reached for a napkin. "What the hell did you do that for?"

"To shut you up," she told him, her eyes sparkling with humor. "Nobody here wants to listen to our business."

"I do," Nikki said.

Ryder ignored the bride and licked more icing off his teeth. "You're not careful, Suz, you'll wind up taste testing yourself."

"You wouldn't dare."

"Don't test that theory." He turned to Jonas. "I'd go with the chocolate hazelnut if I were you, man. That cake rocks."

The diversionary tactic worked. When he whirled with a piece of lemon cake in his hand, Suzanne was totally unprepared. She didn't even have time to get a hand up to block before he had squashed the icing into her lips. He didn't actually want to put it in her mouth because he didn't want her to choke and have to be Heimliched, but he did want to make a point.

What that point was, he wasn't exactly sure, but the look on her face when he pulled back the slice of cake, leaving her with a half-inch layer of icing on her lips, was hilarious. Ryder laughed, reaching out and swiping his finger through the white cloud of frosting. "So what do you think of that?" He sucked his finger clean.

Her tongue came out and did a slow slide through the mess. It was meant to clean off her lip, but Ryder couldn't help but look at the tongue and have erotic thoughts that had nothing to do with cake and everything to do with dessert.

"I think"—she said, reaching for a napkin, the corner of her mouth trying to swing up into a smile she was desperately fighting—"that the lemon makes the cut. We should do the chocolate hazelnut and the lemon. Nikki and Jonas, is that agreeable with you?"

"Sure, if that's what you think," Nikki said, making it the easiest she had probably ever capitulated to anything in her life. "Jonas?"

"Whatever you want, baby. The chocolate was pretty damn good."

"Excellent." While Suzanne slipped back into professional mode, she nudged his leg with hers under the table.

He gave her a questioning look, wishing that Nikki and Jonas and Mrs. Fondant would just disappear, leaving the two of them alone with sugary icing that Ryder could smear on Suzanne's nipples and suck off, slowly and thoroughly.

Suzanne put her finger between her lips and licked it deliberately, her eyes darkening. When she dropped it back down, she mouthed to him, *Later.*

That was the second time she'd said that since he'd walked in the door, which meant it had to mean she was serious. Ryder could only hope she had managed to read his mind and later would start oh, say, now, and involved lots of licking and sucking on both their parts. She gave him a sly smile, like she knew the direction his thoughts were taking and she approved.

Now somebody needed to just sign off on this damn Cinderella cake so they could get the hell out of there.

"IS later now?" Ryder murmured to Suzanne after another thirty minutes. Joyce had run to answer the phone and Nikki and Jonas were making out on the other side of the table, so they were alone.

"No." Damn it. "In fact, you and Jonas can leave if you want after he gets done cramming his tongue down Nikki's throat. We're just about done here now that we've ironed out having twelve mini-cakes of Nikki in a Cinderella gown for each table, but then the bride and I are on to the florist." Where she arguably might pass out from lack of sleep, but maybe she'd land on a bed of roses. No one could say she didn't think positively.

"No private cake tasting?" Ryder looked crushed, which made her happy.

"Not unless you want it at about two A.M., because that's probably when I can break away. I'm sorry, I was thinking with my girl bits instead of my brain."

"You should do that more often," Ryder told her.

Suzanne laughed. "I'm sure you would like that, but my bank account wouldn't."

"Alright, I understand, but make sure you get some sleep at some point, okay? You're going to get sick if you don't slow down."

Her first instinct was to bristle and tell him she didn't

have a choice, but she decided to just take it the way Ryder meant it, as concern, not a criticism. "It should ease up after this weekend. Nikki is going to Champions Week with Jonas so we need to have all decisions made by Tuesday. Maybe next Saturday I'll even get to sleep in."

"No appointments next Saturday?"

"No."

Ryder's arm was on the back of the metal chair she was sitting on. He leaned closer, his aftershave scent drifting up her nostrils. "Hey, come to Vegas with me next weekend then."

"What?" Suzanne sat straighter, her palms instantly going damp with sweat. "For the awards ceremony? Are you crazy?"

"Why not?" He gave her a charming smile. "We'll have a great time. Lots of wine, food, shopping . . . sex. Sex again. And more sex. What could be better?"

"That sounds an awful lot like what married people do. What we did when we were married." She had to admit, it held a certain appeal, but it would more than muddy the waters, it would run them black.

"And we always had fun."

That he could sit there and look so endearingly confident that they wouldn't rip each other's throats out with mini-bar tools was damn cute. Enough that she actually entertained the idea for a split second before squashing it.

"Do you know what kind of attention we'd get if we showed up together? Tongues would be wagging for weeks."

Ryder wiggled his own tongue, making her laugh. "Let them wag. I don't give a shit what anyone thinks."

"You should, you dumb ass. You have an image to uphold." He wasn't going to sway her, he just wasn't. This was a big, bad, suck-ass idea.

Of course, she'd made a number of those lately, and she was actually kind of enjoying them.

"How does this damage my image? It's not like I'm walking in with a gaggle of hookers, you're my ex-wife."

"A *gaggle* of hookers? How many is that exactly? And if you walk in with your ex-wife, someone might start poking and figure out that the *ex* part is slightly exaggerated." Suzanne glanced over at Nikki and Jonas, but they weren't listening. They were whispering to each other, noses touching. What was their obsession with nose rubbing? It made Suzanne want to get really drunk so she'd pass out and not have to see that anymore.

Ryder just waved his hand. "No they won't."

"Hey, Suzy Sunshine, you're wrong. The media loves this kind of thing. Look, I appreciate the offer, and I'm tempted, really tempted to spend a weekend naked in Las Vegas with you, but it ain't going to happen, Jefferson."

CHAPTER
TWELVE

"*I* think you should go," Imogen told Suzanne, sucking down her margarita like it was water.

Suzanne eyeballed her friend. "Maybe you ought to slow down there, Shakespeare, because that tequila is clearly going to your head, given that you're talking crazy."

"I agree with her," Tammy said from across the table, relaxing back in her seat, her lips stained from the melon margarita she was sipping.

"You all have lost your minds," Suzanne said in disgust, pushing her own drink away from her. "Yuck, this tastes like shit. And why would it even remotely be a good idea for me to go to Vegas with Ryder for Champions Week?"

"Because clearly the two of you have unfinished business."

"I don't think a weekend at some swanky hotel is going

to finish it!" Were they nuts? Suzanne tugged at the neck of her gray sweater. She suddenly felt like she couldn't breathe. "It will just be all make-believe if I go. Like a rewind or something. It's not a good idea."

Because she was pretty sure she'd wind up with her heart kicked all over again, and she wasn't signing on for that shit voluntarily.

"Suz," Tammy said in a tone that was sympathetic, but firm. "You have never gotten over Ryder. Don't deny it, because the only people here are your best friends and the booze, and we all know the truth."

"It's not that I never got over him, it's just that I never really got closure." With that bit of nonsense, Suzanne lifted her own glass and sipped.

"I think that's somewhat of the same thing," Imogen told her, pushing her glasses up on her nose. "I wasn't around for your marriage to Ryder, but I think it's fairly evident that there are unresolved issues. This could be an opportunity for the two of you to really open up to each other and discuss the failure of your marriage."

Suzanne snorted. "Now that sounds like fun. You want me to go all the way to Vegas to talk to Ryder about why our marriage stank so bad it made a gut wagon smell good?"

"Your marriage was not that bad," Tammy told her, tucking her auburn hair behind her ear. "You loved each other."

"It wasn't that good either," Suzanne said. "And sure we loved each other, or at least, I loved him, but if we knew why we failed, I'm guessing we don't need to talk about it. It just is what it is."

Suzanne didn't want to talk to anyone about why her

marriage had failed. Not Ryder, not her friends, not her own self. There was nothing fun about remembering how Ryder had married her solely because she'd been pregnant in a quickie Vegas wedding to prevent any industry gossip. At the time, his sponsor had been a very well-known condom brand, and it would have been a huge PR nightmare if they had found out Ryder had knocked up his girlfriend of about ten minutes. And there was nothing worse in stock car racing than losing your sponsorship.

Ryder had said the right things to Suzanne and never even mentioned the irony of who his sponsor was, but despite being a poor country girl, she wasn't dumb. She figured it out on her own, and she'd known that if she weren't pregnant, there would have been no proposal. Their relationship probably would have burned out in six months instead of lingering for four years.

So what was there to talk about?

"If there's nothing to talk about, then there's no reason you can't spend the weekend with Ryder just enjoying yourself. You have nothing to fear from forty-eight hours."

Damn that Imogen and her logic. She had just turned Suzanne's words right on around.

"Yes, I do. I have his stupidity to fear." When cornered, come out clawing. It was a skill she'd perfected over a lifetime of poverty.

Except her friends weren't falling for it. Imogen's eyebrow went up, and Tammy just shook her head. "The only thing you think is stupid about that man is his inability to use a bottle opener. You can be real with us, you know."

Maybe she didn't want to be real. Suzanne crossed her arms across her chest and tried to hang on to her bitterness.

But as she looked around the crowded Mexican restaurant and bar that had become their favorite girl's hangout, she was having a hard time mustering up bitchy. Her friends meant well. They wanted her happy. Well, hell, she wanted herself happy, too, and maybe they weren't so crazy after all. If a weekend knocking boots with Ryder made her happy, why shouldn't she do it?

Because down that path lay heartbreak and a high standard for orgasms that ordinary men couldn't compete with.

"It's already complicated. I don't think tossing a romantic weekend away together into that is going to do anything but make it worse." Not to mention the last time they'd been in Vegas together they'd been getting hitched shotgun style.

"Since when is awards weekend romantic?" Tammy made a face. "It's a bunch of cameras in your face, speeches, and endless dinners. And you only have to show for the weekend. I'm stuck there for all of Champions Week."

"This is your first time doing this event with Elec. I can guarantee come Monday you'll have a different opinion on the whole thing."

Tammy shrugged. "I never really got into it, it's stressful."

"Then why the hell are you telling me to go?" she asked incredulously.

"Because you always had fun. That's your thing, socializing, and half the time you and Ryder were scrambling in at the last minute because you were having sex again."

That was true. Suzanne propped her chin on her hands and sighed at the memory of those trips.

"Sadly, my first husband and I were never late to anything. I'm not sure we ever even had sex on one of those trips."

"Pete was a good guy, but the two of you had about as much sexual chemistry as a couple of doorknobs." Unlike Suzanne and her first husband. Who was still her husband. And who wanted her to go to Las Vegas with him for a sex fest.

"I'm glad the two of you will be there," Imogen said. "I'm nervous myself, since this is my first big event since becoming engaged to Ty. Do you think we'll have time to see a show? I'm also having hair and gown anxiety. You're going to have to do my hair, Suzanne."

"I didn't say I was going," she pointed out. "So you'd better be booking a salon appointment."

"You're going," Imogen said. "You've already made up your mind, you just have to find an acceptable rationalization first before you can admit it to yourself."

Damn her. That girl was always so right in her annoying logic. Not quite ready to admit it yet, Suzanne complained. "Why did they move it to Vegas anyway? It's always been in New York. New York is tempting, but I can control myself in New York and get home quickly if I need to bail. I have serious doubts about my ability to be rational in Sin City. Ryder looks damn good in a tux, you know."

"Vegas is glitzy and glamorous and quite frankly, I'm guessing it's cheaper," Tammy said. "Not exactly kid friendly though. Petey and Hunter are disappointed they have to stay here with their grandparents."

"It will be like a second honeymoon for you," Imogen told her.

An image of her own honeymoon in Vegas rolled through Suzanne's head like a film. An adult film. They'd had a lot of sex and she'd worn a lot of sequins, both in bed and out.

What honest woman could resist the twin lure of bling and booty?

Not her.

RYDER was about to step on the plane for Vegas Monday morning, papers being shoved at him by his assistant, Carol, when his phone rang. A quick glance showed it was Suzanne, and he answered it, the tiny flicker of optimism he'd been trying to fan flaring up. Maybe she had changed her mind.

"Hello?"

Carol shot him a look of annoyance that he had answered the phone, but he ignored her, moving a few steps in front on the Jetway.

"Do you still want me to go to Vegas with you?" Suzanne asked without preamble.

His hope and other parts of him leapt up tall and proud. "Hell, yeah."

"You're going to have to lend me the money for the ticket and a dress."

"Don't insult me, Suz. I invited you. I'm paying."

"I'll accept the plane ticket, because at this late date, it's going to be about a grand, but I'll pay you back for the dress."

"Whatever, sweetheart. We'll figure it out." Later, in bed, when he had her mindless and incoherent, he would convince her to accept the trip as a gift.

"Are you sure you want to do this?" she asked, her voice skeptical.

Ryder paused at the door to the plane behind a little old lady with a walker who was being escorted on board. Suzanne had said questionable things before, but this was just dumb. "Yes. I want to do this. Hell, yes."

"It's going to be a media shit storm on the red carpet. Are you ready?"

"I don't care about any of that. I just care about you." The minute the words were out of his mouth, he realized they might scare Suzanne off, so he quickly amended, "Care about having fun with you. We're going to tear up Vegas, baby."

She sounded doubtful when she said, "Alright, I'll fly in on Thursday. At least I know I won't be on the same flight as Nikki."

"We're at the Wynn. Call me when you're leaving Thursday and let me know what time you get in. I'll have Carol call you and book your flight for you."

"See you Thursday and you'd better have some fucking bells on, Jefferson."

"Whatever you want, babe."

Ryder hung up the phone as he boarded the plane and turned to Carol, unable to prevent a grin from splitting his face. "You need to book a flight for Suzanne on Thursday morning to Vegas then e-mail her the details."

As he plopped his small carry-on down on his seat in first class, Carol frowned at him as she took the seat next to him. "Suzanne who?"

He looked at her in disbelief. "How many Suzannes do you think I know?"

Carol just shrugged, her navy blue blazer shifting on

her shoulder. Carol had been his assistant for years, and while sometimes he found her demeanor a little pinched and off-putting, she kept him organized. Back when he was a rookie, she had been instrumental in preventing him from making embarrassing media errors. Over the years her hair had gotten grayer and her lipstick had gotten bolder, but she was still essentially the same. Quiet, faintly disapproving, and so efficient the devil would never have a crack at her fast-moving hands.

"Suzanne *Jefferson*. She'll be flying in on Thursday and spending the weekend with me in my suite." Ryder sat down and hooked his seat belt. "When we get to Vegas can you make sure there's champagne and chocolate covered strawberries in the room for Thursday? And tickets to that magic show with that one guy, whatever his name is."

Suzanne had wanted to see that show when they'd been on their honeymoon, but they had been too late to buy tickets. Getting married on about three minutes' notice had made it sort of a cobbled together event. But this trip he would get magic show tickets if he had to pay a thousand bucks for them.

"You have events going all on week," Carol reminded him. "I seriously doubt there's time for a magic show."

"Well, pick whichever night has the least going on. Probably Thursday or Sunday night." He hadn't confirmed when Suzanne wanted to fly back, but Monday morning made the most sense. That's when he was going back. "And see if you can get Suz on the same flight back as me on Monday."

Carol didn't answer, just typed into her BlackBerry.

"What?" he asked her.

"I didn't say anything." She still wasn't looking at him, but her voice rang with disapproval.

"You think it's a bad idea to have my ex-wife with me for this trip, don't you?"

"It's none of my business," she said. She was a full foot shorter than him but somehow still intimidating. It was the twenty-five years she had on him, and the narrow glasses. It was like having a teacher send you to the office. "I'm just your assistant, not your PR person."

"You think I should tell Bill?"

"I think it would be wise," she said, still typing away, her black glasses sliding down her nose.

Yeah, but it would suck the fun right out of his day. Bill Coughlin saw potential disaster in everything. He didn't need to know that Suzanne was attending the awards ceremony with him. Nor did he need to know that technically Ryder and Suzanne were still married.

That was just between the two of them.

Just like the amazing sex they were going to share every spare minute of the upcoming weekend.

Pulling his sponsor's logo ball cap down low over his eyes, Ryder settled back to take a nap and anticipate a wild weekend in Vegas with the woman he still loved.

SUZANNE was in Vegas, for better or for worse. As the car Ryder had sent to the airport pulled up in front of the majestic glass hotel rising out of the desert, she took a deep breath. Six years since she'd been here, a happy and terrified bride. A lot had happened in that time. Hell, this hotel hadn't even been there then. Ryder had been a young up-and-coming driver, hoping to crack the top twenty. She had been pregnant.

Her stomach suddenly roiled and she swallowed repeatedly, keeping her mouth closed to fight the nausea. Her cheeks went hot and bile churned aggressively in her gut. Flinging a door open before the cab even came to a complete stop, she sucked in the crisp December air and felt her stomach settling down. Jesus. Maybe she wasn't used to traveling anymore, because waiting at the airport, the long plane ride, and the cab ride had kicked her butt.

Ryder must have been hovering in the doorway because he was suddenly beside her, his welcoming grin slipping off his face. "What's wrong? Are you okay?"

"Yeah, just a little carsick. It must be old age."

Or her gut telling her this was one of her dumbest ideas yet. She and Ryder hadn't spent more than a few hours in each other's company since their divorce. Alleged divorce. Presumed divorce. If you didn't count when they'd spent the night together two weeks earlier. Anyway, the point was, she wasn't sure they could really handle three days and four nights together.

But clearly there was something compelling her to try it on for size, because she'd packed a bag and put her ass on a jet and flown five hours west. Insanity was the only explanation. Or masochism.

Ryder reached for her hand and helped her out of the car. "You just need some air and a glass of water."

The gesture was thoughtful and appreciated, but Ryder didn't let her hand go as he paid the cabdriver and directed the bellman to take her bags. Suzanne felt truly stupid standing there holding hands like a couple of high school kids, or worse, honeymooners. She was thirty-three years old and pseudo-divorced. Holding hands was just dumb.

Ryder didn't seem to think so. He kept a tight grip on her as he led her to the front doors of the hotel. He even leaned over and kissed her forehead. "I'm glad you came. Thanks."

Now what exactly was she supposed to say to that? Suzanne hadn't felt this awkward since her granny had taken her to buy her first bra. "Let's just try to have fun," she said with a fair amount of resignation.

Laughing, Ryder swung their hands together as they entered the lobby. "Your enthusiasm is a little out of hand, you should take it down a notch, Suz."

She could say she was tired from the flight. That her stomach was making her cranky. That she hadn't slept well. All of which were true. But the greater truth was she didn't know what the hell they were doing and there was no sense in avoiding that. "Look, I'm sorry, this is weird, Ryder. Don't tell me it isn't. I don't know what the hell we're doing. A month ago we talked maybe every two weeks and thought we were divorced, now we're legally still married, we're doing the nasty, and we're in Vegas for Champions Week. It's weird and you know I don't do weird well."

Ryder pulled her to a stop in the middle of a very impressive and expansive lobby. Momentarily distracted, Suzanne glanced around her. The hotel was the bomb. Wow. Chic and modern and expensive.

"Suz." Ryder touched her chin, drawing her attention

back to him. "I know it's weird. I don't know what we're doing either. But I'm enjoying spending time with you and I just . . . I just want to make some good memories again, you know what I mean?"

"Yeah, I do." She wanted good memories again, too— badly. She wanted easy and relaxing and some small measure of security. Ryder was the familiar and maybe she just needed that right now.

But what she didn't need was the fool to kiss her in the lobby, sexy bedroom eyes or not, which was what he was about to do. "Alright, let's hit the pool, if there's an indoor one. There's a chaise lounge with my name on it." She managed to even extract her hand from his to clap her hands together in emphasis, a little chop-chop to get him moving. "What's our room number?"

"Ten sixty-nine."

Suzanne stopped walking toward the elevator and stared at him. "Are you kidding me? We have room sixty-nine? You're making that shit up."

"I'm not," he protested, hands up in the air. "And I didn't ask for it either, so don't go accusing me of being a pervert. It's a coincidence."

Somehow she didn't believe him. "Uh-huh."

"There's a ten in it, too. So really, you just need to get your mind out of the gutter." Ryder winked at her.

"I'll do that. I'll keep my mind on flowers and bunnies and the innocence of children, how does that sound? From the room next door to you."

"Liar. There's champagne, strawberries, and whipped cream waiting for us upstairs. Because I happen to like your mind in the gutter."

Suzanne's still slightly queasy stomach was overruled

by her suddenly alert girl bits at the thought of lounging in bed eating whipped cream off Ryder's . . . finger.

"Well, you know what my granddad used to always say."

"What?"

"That makes me happier than a dog with two peters."

Ryder laughed out loud. "I think I would have liked your granddad."

"I think he would have liked you, too." He would have. Her granddad and Ryder would have sat around shooting the shit and lamenting the state of the world together. Suzanne was sorry they'd never had a chance to meet.

Reaching down, he cupped her cheeks with both hands and kissed her deeply, boldly, affectionately.

And Suzanne let him.

CHAPTER
THIRTEEN

RYDER took Suzanne's suitcase and set it by the armoire as Suzanne strolled around the room gawking. "Good Lord, look at this room. Swanky, Jefferson. You've moved up in the world."

He shrugged. "I don't know. I think everyone got a room like this, it's a nice hotel. Let me take your coat, babe." He held out his hand and took her coat when she slipped out of it.

"Yeah, but this room is huge. And the view is killer." Suzanne whipped back the partially opened drapes the rest of the way and stared down at the Strip. "Who'd you have to do to get this room?"

"The only one I'm going to do is you," he told her, coming up behind her and lifting her hair so he could nuzzle the back of her neck. "But first I'm going to eat you."

She gave a sigh. "So are there really strawberries and

whipped cream or did you make that up to lure me to your room and have your wicked way with me?"

"There are strawberries and whipped cream. Chocolate, too, and champagne. You can eat them while I eat you."

"You keep mentioning eating me. You must be hungry," she teased.

"Starving." Ryder turned her around and kissed her, sliding his hands into her hair. "It's been too long since I tasted you."

"It's only been two weeks," she murmured between kisses, giving him token attitude even as she felt herself relaxing into the kiss. Ryder knew just how to kiss her. How was it possible that no other man could touch her with the same immediate reaction?

The few men she'd dated since she'd split from Ryder had all had pros and cons—one who was a killer kisser, another who had been particularly skilled at oral sex, a third who had excelled at straight-up stroking sex. Which were all great in different ways at different times, but ultimately never enough. She didn't want just the entrée, she wanted side dishes and dessert, too, for a balanced sex life. Which was why it was amazing to be standing in the arms of a man who could give her all three, a man who could just run a finger down her arm and turn her on.

She always loved the moment in their lazy, exploratory kisses where with a little hitch of the other one's breath or a nip or a brushing of their chests together, the intent changed, kicking passion into high gear. That was a feeling she loved, that no-going-back sense of freedom and wildness, the leap off the diving board into sensation.

That happened when Ryder slipped his hand under her sweater and skimmed his fingers over her nipple.

It was a light, simple touch, yet she felt it from her toes to her inner thighs to her breasts to her lips, and she groaned. Her breasts were heavy, aching, begging to be touched further, harder. Stepping back, she yanked her sweater off over her head and tossed it to the floor.

"Oh, yeah?" Ryder said, his eyes darkening. "You're ready to go there?"

Duh. They were in a room together for thirty seconds and she was ready. "Yes. So suck my nipples, damn it." Just to make sure he understood she was serious about both of them getting naked ASAP, Suzanne popped the button on his khaki pants.

Ryder hated wearing khakis, but at events like this, he needed to be a little more turned out than in just jeans. She would never admit it out loud, but the suburban staple of the adult male got her hot. It was like the challenge of seeing if she could ruffle the feathers of a man determined to behave. At the moment, there was zero challenge though, because Ryder looked ready to get down and dirty as he bent over her breasts.

"Do you know that you have perfect breasts?" he said, hands cupping them as he pressed kisses on her chest.

"No, I wasn't aware of that." Though Suzanne had no issues with them herself. They were decent breasts, a good size and maintaining their perky position quite well, thank you very much. What she really loved about them, though, was that they had always responded to stimulation.

Stimulation that Ryder was providing at the moment with both his tongue, stroking across the top of her breasts, and his fingers, plucking lightly at her nipples. Suzanne let her eyes drift closed, her own fingers idle on his undone pants. She just wanted a moment to enjoy the feelings he brought out in her.

But within a minute or two that enjoyment shifted to restlessness as Ryder teased over her breasts again and again and the flutter low in her belly turned aching and urgent. Suzanne reached behind her and popped her bra loose, but Ryder didn't take the bait. Letting her bra dangle off her arms, he stepped back and looked at her with shiny lips and dark, lusty eyes.

"Are you going to just look or are you going to do something?" she asked.

Ryder made a soft hiss of exasperation. "What I ought to do is spank you."

"Promise?"

He laughed softly and reached out and hooked his index finger in her disheveled bra and pulled it forward so it dropped off her arms and to the floor. "On the bed, smart-ass."

As if she was just going to do what he ordered her to. He knew that perfectly well, which was why he did it. The game of pressing for control, of taunting each other sexually, turned them both on.

Suzanne raised her arms to dig her fingers into her hair on the pretense of tossing it back off her face. Then she strolled toward the bed, shooting him a look over her shoulder. "Are you coming?"

"Soon enough, babe." As he walked toward her, Ryder pulled off his button-up shirt.

Pausing by the table where the spread of dessert Ryder had mentioned was laid out, Suzanne waited until he was almost on top of her. Then, digging her fingers into the whipped cream, she whirled and smeared it across his lips.

Ryder's eyes widened in shock as she laughed, licking the whipped cream off her fingers. "Mmm, good." Wrapping her arms around his bare back, she flicked her tongue across his lips. "Really good."

So good, in fact, that she ate at his lips and the cool, creamy taste, totally turned on by the mixture of the sweet taste of the whipped cream and the underlying taste of him, the sensation of kissing through the soft dessert to find his firm lips. She heard her own moan as she wrapped her arms tighter and plunged her tongue into his mouth, her breasts brushing against his firm warm pectoral muscles.

She was so into the kiss that she didn't realize he had leaned over to the room service tray himself, until he stepped backward away from her.

"What?" she asked then let out a little shriek as a cloud of whipped cream hit her nipple. "Ryder! That's cold!"

"Don't dish it out if you can't take it," he told her, before leaning over and slowly, methodically, deliciously, and painfully licking the cream off her nipple and breast.

"Oh, God," she moaned, holding his head as the tug and pull spiraled out into all of her body, making her ache everywhere. "Oh, God," she said again, because once just wasn't enough when that much desire was rushing through her.

"Take your jeans off," he urged her as he stood back up.

Suzanne did, but as she was complying and stepping out of them, she watched him studying the bowl of strawberries and the little fondue pot that she presumed had melted chocolate in it. "Don't you dare put melted chocolate on me. It's too hot."

"I'm going to have to. They didn't give us enough whipped cream." Ryder picked up the bottle of champagne and shook it as he reached for the corkscrew. "But I'll put a cold base layer down first."

Uh-oh. Suddenly she realized what that meant and she shrieked, trying to run but getting tangled in her jeans.

The cork popped and Ryder sprayed her with the icy cold liquid, catching her breasts, her belly, and her arm as she backed up, simultaneously sucking in air from the chilly impact and laughing, hands up. "You're a total jerk!"

Ryder just leaned over and licked her shoulder. "Mmm. Good stuff."

"Give me that bottle!" Suzanne yanked it out of his hands, goose bumps rising on her skin from the cold. She dumped the remaining quarter of a bottle onto his head. It was satisfying when it trailed down through his short hair to his forehead, down his nose, and dribbled onto his lips.

Ryder licked them. "Still good stuff."

Then he reached for her, and Suzanne backed up laughing, until she hit the bed. Then suddenly they were on the bed, him on top of her, and they were kissing and licking each other, rolling around on the expensive bed cover, and her laughter was replaced by an elemental groan when his tongue slid down her belly.

"You're sticky and sweet." His finger slipped into her panties. "Bet you're sticky and sweet here, too."

"Why don't you find out?"

"Nah." Ryder reached for the tray. "I'm hungry."

Suzanne shivered as his warm body moved away from her and the wafting air tickled her wet skin. "Eat me."

Duh. Never one for subtle, she removed her panties and swung them around on her finger before tossing them at his back. They missed and fell to the floor.

After ditching his khakis, Ryder swiped the remaining whipped cream out of the glass dish with his finger then brought it between her legs with a challenging look. He expected her to tell him no and to grab his hand and stop him. Instead she just laid back down onto her back and spread her legs in invitation. Like she was going to turn down a dare.

So Ryder smeared the cool cloud of whipped cream onto her clit, sending a jolt of desire through her as the cold hit the heat of her body. When he bent over and lapped it up, Suzanne closed her eyes and moaned. She could feel her inner thighs getting wet, could feel all her muscles tensing and quivering. One lousy lick, and she was strung out already.

Okay, it was more than one lick. It was a lot of long, slow, torturous movements of his tongue, up and down and around until she was bucking on the bed, nails scratching at the bedding.

"I want a strawberry," he murmured.

"Later," she gasped. Was he really that cruel that he'd abandon her for fruit? Even though she dug strawberries herself, she had no need for one right at the moment. Really. No need at all for anything other than his tongue or his finger or his cock . . .

"Ah!" she yelled, totally caught off guard by the sensation of something that was most definitely not his tongue or his finger or his cock pressing inside her. "What the hell are you doing?"

Half sitting up, she watched as he lifted the strawberry

he had just dipped into her up to his mouth and bit it, his eyes so dark they were almost black. "Delicious."

Oh, no he didn't. "Damn, you're dirty," she breathed, as a throb pulsed deep inside her and a rush of moisture between her legs showed her body appreciated the gesture even if she was a little shocked.

He tossed the stem and got another strawberry. This time she knew it was coming and she bit her lips when he played around, pushing it slightly inside her then pulling back, the shape strange and unsatisfying, yet terribly arousing because it was so out of the ordinary. "Oh," she said. "Oh, oh, oh, oh." It was the most stupidly repetitive she'd ever been in her life, but damn, he was killing her.

She needed to be filled, and filled *now*.

But Ryder had different ideas. After popping the second strawberry in his mouth, he reached back and dipped his hand in the chocolate. Not even flinching at the heat, he spread it all over his erection.

Suzanne rolled onto her side. "I suppose you're going to want me to lick that up?"

"That's the general idea."

"I am a girl who loves her chocolate." Suzanne wiggled across the bed on her stomach and flicked her tongue across the head of his penis, taking away a rich taste of chocolate. "Mmm."

He made a strangled sound in the back of his throat, which Suzanne loved. Using a methodical strategy of licking from top to bottom in a straight line, then moving over two inches and repeating, Suzanne worked her way around until she'd swallowed most of the chocolate and Ryder was breathing hard and gripping her shoulders.

Then she took him fully into her mouth, the sweet of the chocolate mixing with the salty of his skin and tasting absolutely decadent, arousing, tantalizing. If naughty were a flavor, this would be it. Her tongue, her hand, her lips were all sticky and slick and she rubbed her belly and her inner thighs over the comforter in the same rhythmic motion of her mouth, sliding into that amazing cocoon of pleasure, where time had no meaning and the only thing that mattered was her on him and him on her.

"I need to fuck you," Ryder said, his voice tight.

Suzanne pulled back, his words a triumph. "That works for me." She started to lay back but he shook his head.

"I don't think the chocolate remnants on me going into you are a good idea . . . not sure what it would do, but it just seems like a bad idea."

And thinking about a bacterial infection in her hoohah was a serious mood killer.

"In the shower," he said, reaching out for her hand and pulling her into a sitting position. "I want you bent over the faucet, the water running down over your tight ass."

Mood restored.

Ryder watched as Suzanne gave him that naughty, sexy smile he loved so much before she leaned over and gave his cock one last lick. "I missed a spot."

Then she stood up and wrapped her arms around him and kissed him, their mouths a blend of strawberry, chocolate, whipped cream, and sex, a hot rich kiss that made him want to get even closer to her, to get inside her. Her skin was sticky from the champagne and the whipped cream as her breasts pressed against his chest, and the sweet tangy scent of their indulgences rose between them.

They were good at this. Everything they did here, in bed, felt right. Ryder smacked her backside. "Hit the showers."

Suzanne was momentarily diverted from their sex play by the luxury of the bathroom, but Ryder directed her attention back to him by sliding his hand down over the front of her curls as he stood behind her. As they both watched in the huge mirror behind the sinks, he stroked inside her, spreading her so they could both see the tight pink bud there.

"So pretty," he told her.

"And so ready to come," she told him.

"Really?" Ryder moved his finger and moved to the front of her, going down on his knees before her. "Let's see if I can make that happen."

It was an interesting angle, eating her from straight on, and Ryder had to readjust technique, but what he loved about it was that Suzanne held the back of his head and ground herself onto him, her gasps and moans getting frantic the more he licked and sucked.

When she came, he held her ass tightly and took in the pulsing contractions of her body around him, satisfied that he had satisfied her. He had turned the shower on to heat up, and steam rose behind her as he settled back on his calves, her skin already turning pink and dewy from the moist room.

Suzanne was breathing hard and wiping her lips, but she moved to the tub and pulled back the shower curtain. Stepping inside, she put her hands on the shower faucet, gripping it as her bottom came up in the air. "I do believe this is what you said you wanted?"

Oh, God, yes, it was what he wanted. Ryder almost tripped over himself getting into the tub behind her, and as he watched the water sluicing down over her gorgeous body, he made sure the chocolate was gone with a few drops of hotel body wash and a swipe of his hand over his erection. Impatiently he rinsed himself off, then gripped Suzanne's ass and drove into her.

They both moaned as their bodies joined, that amazing incomparable feeling of being connected in tight, hot passion. Ryder went in and out with a hard, slapping rhythm, his hips colliding with her ass, his cock held tight by her slick vagina. Her head turned upward, her eyes closed, the water soaking her hair and rolling down her cheeks in little rivers. Her lips were swollen from sucking him and bright pink in the harsh overhead light. Everything about her was sexy, sensual, beautiful. Every angle, every tilt, every arch, every inch, and Ryder came inside her knowing that no woman would ever be as perfect for him as this woman.

SUZANNE lay on the chaise in their room staring out at the Strip, a soft drink on the table next to her, a trashy magazine in her lap. She was wearing nothing but a soft, terry-cloth robe from the closet in the room, her inner thighs sore, and her hair still damp from their shower sex. That had been some good, pounding sex. But then, it was always that way with Ryder. And as a result, she felt lazy and content, like the proverbial cat stretched out for a nap.

He was pacing around the room on the phone, doing an interview, but she had him tuned out, realizing that she'd almost forgotten how good she was at relaxing. Doing nothing felt amazing.

When was the last time she'd just laid around and taken it easy, not worrying about anything? Not since Christ was on a potty chair, she'd swear to it. By the time Ryder hung up the phone and flopped onto the chair next to her, she was on the verge of falling asleep.

"I got tickets to that magic show tonight if you're up for it," he said. "I know you've always wanted to see that."

Suzanne turned a little to face him. The man was being really, really sweet, she'd have to give him that. "That was really nice. Does it mean I have to get off this couch though?"

"I can give you a different kind of magic on that couch, but to see the show, you're probably going to have to get dressed and go to the theater."

Suzanne fiddled with the belt on her robe. "Hmm. I can definitely do that. Later. What time is the show?"

"You're all about later, aren't you?"

"What does that mean?" Not that she cared. She didn't want to fight with Ryder. Not now, not later, not ever again.

"Just that you were teasing with me that word in the bakery. It took me five days to get my later."

She reached out and caressed the scruff on his chin. "Poor thing. I'm sorry."

"I'm glad you're here." He took her hand and kissed her fingertips. "Remember how when we were here last time I took you for a drive around the track? And you were screaming, but you loved it? Man, we had a good time. We had a lot of good times."

Normally she wouldn't stroll down memory lane with him for anything. But today it felt right. Nice to be able to talk about the memories they shared. "Yeah, and you did a burnout to impress me and the crew got pissed that you jacked up the grass for no reason."

He laughed. "I was a little too full of myself in those days. I didn't understand the game."

"I guess neither of us really did." Suzanne hadn't really understood what it would mean to be the wife of a stock car driver, though she had to say she'd adjusted to that as well as could be expected given her upbringing. Talking to people was a skill she was good at and she'd excelled at the social events Ryder's career had required. It was her own insecurities that she had chosen to ignore and those had come back to haunt her.

But he was right. Early on, they'd had good times.

"So we're older and wiser now, huh?"

"Definitely older. The wiser remains to be seen." Suzanne thought about her younger self and how she'd just dived into everything in front of her. Maybe in some cases that hadn't been wise, like say, in the case of marriage, but she'd sure had fun. When was the last time she'd really cut loose? Other than in the front seat of her car with Ryder? Or playing touch football with Ryder and the kids?

Suzanne sat up and swung her legs over the chaise. "Let's go hit the town." There would plenty of time to lie still when she was dead, and he was most definitely a man who knew how to show her a good time.

CHAPTER
FOURTEEN

RYDER had thought he'd fall asleep during the magic show or be wincing from the corniness of it, but he was actually fascinated by the illusions, and he spent most of his time trying to figure out how they were done, what the science behind them was. Suzanne didn't care about the science. She just oohed and awed and enjoyed the thrill of surprise. It was one of the things he loved about her—she just dove into everything she tried, and even watching a pimped-out Vegas show was no different.

It was cold outside so she had worn a coat to the MGM Grand, and it was bunched in her lap. Ryder slipped his hand under the bulk and took hers into his, enjoying the way her smooth smaller hand fit into his. She gave him a quizzical look but she let him.

He just didn't think she understood how much he had loved her, how much he still loved her. How much just being next to her made him happy, content, exhilarated.

He even loved their sparring. It had been an electric and amusing part of their relationship until the snarkiness had become real.

But how was he supposed to tell her? How could he convince her that their marriage deserved a second chance?

The only thing he could think to do was show her a hell of a time in Vegas and take it from there.

After the show, he followed her out of the theater, his hand on the small of her back. "I made arrangements for us to have a private showing of the white tigers at the Mirage. I know you always wanted to see them."

"Wow, that's cool, but now? It's eleven at night. They'll let us do that?" She put her coat on as they headed for the front door.

"It's Vegas, baby. Eleven is like happy hour before the real night begins. And it doesn't hurt that I'm a driver in town for Champions Week." He'd also paid a hefty fee, but she didn't need to know that.

"Ah, that's true." She smiled at him, a pure straight-forward smile. It wasn't seductive or coy or sly, it was just happy. "Thanks. Let's go. I've always wanted to see them."

He was busting his balls to impress her, and so far, it looked like it was working.

Thirty minutes later, Ryder stood back and listened to the habitat worker explain the environment of the famous white tigers to them. "There are only a few dozen left in the world who have this combination of white fur with black stripes, pink paws, and ice-blue eyes. The rarest of all tigers are those who are pure white, missing the black stripes."

The tigers looked bored beyond belief to Ryder, which was a little ironic given they were in America's party city, but Suzanne leaned over the railing and stared at them in fascination. "They're beautiful. So majestic."

That she was.

Ryder ambled behind Suzanne as the trainer led her over to the dolphins who were also housed in the habitat facility. He wasn't sure what tigers and dolphins had in common but they were both living the life free of predators with food handed to them umpteen times a day.

"Here is our changing room," the trainer said, a middle-aged guy in track pants and a golf shirt, his head shaved to level the playing field between bald spot and hair growth. "Go ahead and put on your bathing suits and I'll meet you out here in five."

"Suits?" Suzanne looked blankly at him. "Why?"

"Surprise," Ryder told her, hoping she'd think it was a good one. "You're swimming with the dolphins, babe."

Her face lit up. "Really? But I don't have my bathing suit."

"I had it sent over from our hotel. It should be in the changing room." Again, it had cost him more than he cared to think about to pull this off, but that look on her face was worth every dime. She had told him for years that she'd always wanted to swim with the dolphins. Growing up, she had never even made it to Sea World or an aquarium. There just hadn't been money for those kinds of things, and she hadn't seen her first in-person marine animal until she was in college.

Suzanne jumped up and down in her boots and sweater dress. "Thank you."

And she leaned over and kissed him. Right on the lips,

in front of the trainer and half a dozen dolphins. Oh, yeah. Totally worth four grand.

Ryder followed her into the changing room. The trainer looked like he was going to protest them using the same room, but in the end he just clamped his mouth shut.

"Aren't there male and female changing rooms?" she asked with a grin as she ransacked the bag sitting on the bench in the center of the room.

"Probably. In fact, I'm sure of it."

"Then you should use the little boy's room." Suzanne pulled out her teeny weeny yellow bikini.

Ryder had seen that scrap of nothing in her suitcase and had known that was what he wanted to see her in. "I want to be with you in the little girl's room."

She tossed his trunks at him. "Only if you close your eyes."

"Okay." He could play the game. But he could also peek, which he did right when Suzanne was bending over, giving him a view more intriguing than the Vegas Strip. He definitely had a thing for her ass, he was man enough to admit it.

As she started to turn toward him, he clamped his eyes back shut.

"Were you peeking?"

"No."

"Liar."

"Yes."

Suzanne laughed as he opened his eyes. "Just tie my top, will you?"

Ryder nuzzled the back of her neck as she lifted up her hair. She smelled good, like shower gel and the crispness of the winter wind. As he fumbled with tying the strings, he told her, "I'm much better at undoing these."

"Just pull it tight. I don't want to flash the dolphins."

"That's not the porpoise, is it?" he joked.

"Oh, my God. You are so ridiculous. Freak."

He was giddy, that's what he was. A man in love, thrilled to be spending time with Suzanne.

"A freak in bed." He finished tying her bikini top and undid his black pants, dropping them and his boxer briefs to the floor.

If he happened to bump her backside with his crotch after he was naked, it was a total accident.

Unfortunately, Suzanne wasn't prepared for his not so subtle seduction. His bump sent her off balance and she went stumbling forward.

"Dear Lord, put your clothes on!" But she smiled at him as she regained her balance, and started pulling her hair up into a ponytail.

If she had any idea what that position did to her body in that bikini she would never be cruel enough to suggest he put his clothes on. "Your breasts," he managed in a strangled voice. "They look . . . amazing."

And huge. It had to be something about the tiny triangles making her breasts look bigger, but Suz seemed to be busting out all over.

She cupped them, which wasn't helping his lack of desire to put on swim trunks.

"I know, they seem bigger all of a sudden. It must be PMS and all the ice cream I've been hogging on."

"Whatever it is, keep doing it."

Her eyes dropped to his penis and as she stared at it,

Ryder felt it spring to life from semi-erect to fully locked and loaded.

But she just rolled her eyes. "You're insatiable."

"One of the many reasons you love me."

It was a comment people made all the time. He wasn't fishing, wasn't trying to make a statement. But the second the words were out of his mouth, they both froze, her in a bikini, hands in the air, him standing butt naked on the tile floor.

"Because, you know," he started to say.

But Suzanne held her hand up. "It's fine."

"No, it's not fine," he said, frustrated. They always ignored shit like this, and he didn't want to ignore it any more. "I loved you, Suzanne, as a man loves his wife, and I was happy with you. That means that a part of me will always love you and you're going to have to learn to live with that."

He expected her to bluster, to protest, to call him names. But instead, she just said, "A part of me will always love you, too."

His heart swelled. "Really?"

"Which makes us being here together really stupid and dangerous."

"How is this dangerous?" he asked her, softly, feeling seriously optimistic about their relationship for the first time in years. If they still loved each other, after two whole years apart, and could have this much fun together, they could work through the other bullshit. He knew they could.

It was too much though. He had taken it too far into serious and Suzanne retreated behind flippant. "It will be if I drown you."

Disappointed, Ryder tried to shake it off, bending over to step into his trunks. "Nah. I could take you on land or in water."

Suzanne picked up a fluffy towel and wrapped it around her shoulders. "Last one in gets no oral sex."

Then she took off running.

Damn it. Ryder had one foot in, one foot out. "No fair! I'm not dressed!"

"That's what you get for standing around picking your butt." She shoved open the door laughing.

Ryder gave her chase, but by the time he was sliding to a stop at the edge of the pool, she was already sitting down, feet in the water, putting on her life jacket.

"Cheater." He plopped down next to her.

But he wasn't really annoyed, and seeing her smile, seeing her eyes sparkle like that again, directed at him, was something that Ryder couldn't describe. It was like winning a race and Christmas all rolled into one.

As she rubbed noses with the dolphins and learned to give them commands to jump, splashing the hell out of Ryder, her pure laughter and joy gave him the greatest pleasure he'd had in years.

And when they slid into bed together that night, Suzanne yawning, legs wrapping over his, he cuddled her close to him and vowed to just appreciate. If Suzanne didn't want to be married to him, he would take whatever she was willing to give. He just wanted to enjoy the weekend, and that he was definitely doing.

It was clear that she was exhausted and didn't want another round of sticky sex, something he'd known when she had pulled on pajamas and glopped cream all over her face. He'd known her long enough to recognize she was in sleep mode and the sex shop was closed for the night. But he didn't really mind. He was tired, too, and there was something intimate and pleasurable about cuddling up close with her. This was really a kind of relationship they hadn't shared since the divorce. Presumed divorce.

"Thank you," she said sleepily, her fingers brushing over his chest. "That was cool. Both the show and the animals. I can't believe you remembered I wanted to swim with the dolphins."

"Suz, I remember everything."

She sat up slightly and stared at him. "You do, don't you?" she asked softly.

Ryder looked deep into those amber eyes and said, "I do."

I do remember everything. I do love you. I do want the chance to be a better husband.

He left those unsaid, because he didn't want to ruin the moment.

All Suzanne said was, "I do, too."

Then she closed her eyes and fell asleep, while Ryder spent an hour staring at the ceiling, enjoying the feel of her in his arms.

TY watched the women perusing the dessert buffet at lunch and felt a measure of pride that Imogen was piling her plate up high with zero hesitation. A man respected a woman who made friends with a brownie from time and time and wasn't afraid to admit she liked food. Imogen was big on veggies and whole wheat stuff at home, but here in Vegas, she'd been indulging herself, and Ty was digging it. It showed she was capable of cutting loose and enjoying life.

Suzanne and Tammy were right up there with her, and Ty thought he and Elec were lucky men. Suzanne was a hell of a woman, too, and he would say that Ryder was a lucky man, except he wasn't exactly sure what those two were doing, and he figured this might be his only chance to ask.

"So, uh, how's your week going?" he asked Ryder, digging out the last bite of meat from the crab leg on his plate. The six of them were at one of the famed Vegas buffets and Ty had the stuffed gut to prove it.

Ryder looked at him from across the table like that was a dumb question. "Good. How about yours?"

"Oh, cut the crap, Jefferson, you know I'm asking you about Suzanne. What the hell are you two doing?"

"Well, that's subtle," Elec told Ty.

"What? We've known each other a long time. There's no point in beating around the bush, especially since as soon as Suzanne is done building that sundae over there, she'll be back at the table and I still won't know what's going on."

"When I figure out what's going on, I'll let you know," Ryder told him.

"But, are you two dating? Are you exclusive with each other, or what?"

"We don't talk about it." Ryder tore a hunk of meat off his prime rib and avoided looking at Ty.

"You don't talk about it." Now there was a brilliant plan. "You've had a very volatile history, you know. If you don't talk about where this is going, where it will be going is Uglyville."

Ryder bristled. "You make it sound like we've been violent. Volatile. Please. That's fucked up. We've had words with each other, that's it. What couple who is divorced hasn't done that?"

Now he'd pissed his friend off. That wasn't his intention. He just wanted to make sure that neither he nor Suzanne got hurt all over again.

Before he could figure out what to say, Elec stepped in. "I think the point is, we're just concerned about you and Suzanne, and maybe it's time for you all to talk about things. Maybe not talking is what got you here in the first place."

"Exactly." Ty sat back in triumph. "Oh, shit, here come the girls." He made a throat cutting motion with his hand then smiled at his fiancée. "How did you make out at the dessert buffet?"

"I got way more food than I can ever eat, but everything looked so incredible I couldn't pass it up. You're morally obligated to finish whatever I can't."

Ty swiped a tiny pecan pie cup off of her plate and popped it in his mouth. "No problem."

Tammy sat down next to Elec and said, "You three looked very serious when we walked up. Is everything okay? They didn't change the publicity schedule, did they? I have my day all figured out around it."

"Nah, that didn't change," Elec assured her.

"They were probably talking about me and Ryder, questioning him as to what the hell he and I are doing," Suzanne declared, slapping her plate down on the table and sliding into her chair. "God, I don't even know why I got half this dessert. I'm feeling a little nauseous, I think I ate too much."

Trust Suzanne to just say it like it was.

"You're still on Eastern time, that's all," Ryder told her, avoiding her first comment. "It's like we had dinner last night at midnight and breakfast at noon. Your stomach is rebelling."

"Why should that matter?" she asked him, reaching out to brush a crumb off the corner of his lip. "It's not like my stomach has a watch down there."

As they talked, they cut everyone else out, not intentionally, but they were clearly just enjoying talking to each other, and Ty watched them closely. He'd seen a lot of ugly go down between those two, but damn if they didn't look happy together at the moment. Maybe things had changed. Maybe they had changed.

What the hell did he know anyways? He'd nearly lost Imogen from his own stupid stubbornness.

Imogen squeezed his knee. When he looked at her, she was popping a chocolate covered grape in her mouth. "Don't worry," she whispered. "They'll figure it out."

That remained to be seen, but Ty sure wished them all the best.

SUZANNE had managed to avoid Nikki for two whole days, but her luck ran out as she was crossing the lobby, trying to find something to occupy her time that didn't cost money. So far, her options were window-shopping on the Strip or watching TV in her room. Not exactly how she had wanted to spend her time while Ryder was out doing interviews, but then again, she didn't want to spend it with Nikki either.

Nikki spotted her and waved enthusiastically, running

over on her stiletto heels, her black sequin leggings sparkling in the afternoon sunlight coming from the huge
windows, her giant fur enveloping her. Sometimes Nikki
dressed like a sixteen-year-old cheerleader, other days
like a cougar on the prowl, with no apparent rhyme or
reason as to why she chose either one. Today was clearly
the latter.

"Hey, how is your trip going?" Suzanne asked her, giving in to the inevitable hug and cheek kiss.

"It's great. It's awesome, fantastic!" Nikki gripped her
hands and giggled. "I have the most exciting news. Jonas
and I are eloping tonight!"

The entire lobby of the Wynn spun wildly, and for a
split second Suzanne thought she might actually pass out.
By sheer willpower, she fought down the bile and righted
the room. "What? Why would you do that? I thought you
wanted a big wedding!"

A big wedding that Suzanne had spent the last month
planning. They had a ballroom. They had a dress. A cake.
Tuxes. A freaking white carriage and glass slippers, for
God's sake.

"Oh, I do. But all this is stressing out Jonas. He told
me how romantic it would be to get married while we're
here, just go in, be done, then we're on our honeymoon."

"But you won't be able to be Cinderella then." Suzanne
fought the desperation that was creeping into her voice.
She needed that second half of the fee. She needed it to
pay her bills for the next two or three months, and if Nikki
eloped, she wasn't entitled to that.

Nikki's face fell a little. "I know. I thought about that.
But this way we're married like immediately, and I haven't
signed the prenup yet."

Suzanne felt her eyebrow shoot up. Nikki wasn't as dumb as she looked. Or sounded most of the time.

But neither was Suzanne.

She lowered her voice to one of confidant; a gentle, coaxing tone. "Have you really thought this through? You only have a chance to be a bride once and I think you might look back and regret not having a fairy-tale wedding. Think of the little cakes of you. The glass slipper party favors. The horse-drawn carriage and the diamond tiara. Do you really want to give all that up for some five-minute ceremony with strangers in Vegas?"

Nikki looked thoughtful. "I do really want the little cakes."

"No one else can pull off Cinderella mini-cakes the way you can. Same with the gown. We have white gloves for you, and a cape, and a muff. Never again will you have the chance to wear a muff."

Lips pursed together, Nikki nodded slowly. "Maybe I should think about this. Maybe I should tell Jonas no."

"I think you'll be happier if you do," Suzanne told her, squeezing her hands. "Look, I have a picture of your invitations." She pulled out her phone and showed the ivory and blue vellum invitations to Nikki.

"Those are beautiful."

"Only the best for you. They're going out in the mail on Monday."

"Yeah." Nikki chewed her lip. "I'll talk to you later, Suzanne. I'd better catch Jonas before he buys the Elvis wedding package."

"Okay. I'll see you at the awards ceremony."

As Nikki wandered off, her fur slipping off her shoulders, Suzanne felt both relief and disgust. Part of her sighed in total relief that she had just secured her paycheck, yet she also felt kind of sick to her stomach for manipulating Nikki. The thing was, she knew in the end Nikki did want the big wedding and would be happier having had it, but Nikki's feelings weren't what had motivated her.

Saving her own ass was what had driven her to talk Nikki down off the elopement ledge.

That was something she wasn't exactly proud of, and she stood there in the lobby wondering what the hell she was actually doing with her life.

RYDER only had a couple of free hours, but he intended to take full advantage of them. Not to mention he felt bad for abandoning Suzanne for work stuff, and from the look on her face, she'd been bored while he was gone.

But she seemed to have the same plan as he did, because he'd barely gotten the door closed before she was on him and they were tugging at each other's clothes. He wanted to ask her if she had missed him, but he didn't want to spoil the moment, or have her stop and think, or do anything other than exactly what she was doing.

Ryder plunged his tongue into her mouth, his hands already sliding down to cup her breast. Of course, his hands had nothing on the eagerness of hers. Suzanne already had his pants unbuttoned and unzipped and she went on in, stroking up and down on him.

Desire hit him like going into the wall at the track. "Damn, Suz, were you watching porn while I was gone? If you were, you should do that more often."

Suzanne was already dropping to her knees, and Ryder

fell back against the door of the hotel suite. "I just thought it sucked that we haven't had sex yet today."

"It did suck." Ryder closed his eyes as she closed over his cock. Suzanne was one of the few women he'd encountered who really seemed to dig giving head. One of the many qualities she possessed that he fully appreciated. "And now you're sucking, and shit, that feels good."

Suzanne knew she was being reckless and crazy, but she wanted Ryder. She wanted him in her, on her, taking her. She didn't know what she was doing next year, next week, hell, even tomorrow, and there were a lot of things dancing around her head that scared the shit out of her, but right now, right here, none of that mattered. All that mattered was driving Ryder crazy and letting him do the same to her.

She loved doing this to him, taking him into her mouth while he made those sounds, those grunts and moans that told her he was totally losing control. Right when she thought he might go over the edge, she stood up, shoving her jeans and panties down together as quickly as she could.

Ryder took her shoulders and threw her against the wall, grabbing onto one of her legs and hitching it over his. Her pants were somewhere around her calves, but it didn't matter. He had clearance and he pushed up into her, the angle creating a delicious fullness and pressure.

"Ryder," she managed, then felt all the breath whoosh out of her lungs as he thrust again, and she grabbed on to his shoulders so she didn't fall.

After he licked his finger, his free hand snaked down between them and tweaked her clitoris, and Suzanne embarrassed herself by coming, a sharp unexpected burst of ecstasy.

Ryder's eyes widened, then he pumped harder, hand slapping on the wall behind her for leverage. A minute later, he joined her, and they clung to each other, to the wall, clothes cockeyed and damp, breathing jagged and heavy.

"Now that's what I call a hello," Ryder said.

Suzanne swallowed hard and enjoyed the aftershocks of his penis pulsing in her. "I'm very friendly."

"And I'm very lucky."

Not wanting to analyze that statement, Suzanne still couldn't help but stare into his eyes a little, seeking an answer to a question she didn't even understand.

Just enjoy the moment. That's what she had to do.

Now was not the time to worry about the future. That would slap her in the face on Monday, so there was no point in ruining Saturday worrying about it.

It was what it was and nothing more, even if she had to have billboards made to remind her of that fact.

CHAPTER
FIFTEEN

SUZANNE gave Ryder that look he knew so well. "Since when are you superstitious?" she asked, assessing him.

"Since forever," he told her with excessive embellishment as he helped her out of the cab, feeling reckless and damn pleased with the weekend, his life, and his ex-wife.

"I don't think playing the same slot machine we did six years ago makes one wit of difference. It's just dumb luck."

"Indulge me," he told her, reaching out and kissing the tip of her nose.

Suzanne made a face and swatted at his hand, but she laughed. "I think all this sex is going to your head."

"Speaking of head, that was—"

She cut him off with a shushing sound as they walked through the door of the Bellagio. "We're in public! Knock it off." Then she paused as they entered the lobby. "Wow. Déjà vu. It's kind of weird to be back here for the first time since . . . that night."

Ryder had been to Vegas many times since their wedding and honeymoon, but it had never been the same. That had been a wonderful weekend, rivaled only by this one, and he couldn't help but want to repeat some of it. "How much did we win that night? A thousand bucks?"

"No. It was five hundred. We got massages with it the next day and still had enough for a swanky dinner."

"I could go for a massage." Ryder went up to the window and registered his card. "Blow on this for good luck," he told Suz.

"I'm supposed to blow on a swipe card?" She looked bemused. "Alright." She leaned over and blew on the card in Ryder's hand. "Mama needs a new pair of shoes."

Ryder knew exactly where the slot was they'd won on before. He had passed it several times over the years but had never played it, not without Suz. It was their machine.

"How can you be sure this is the right one?" she asked, sitting on the seat as he stuck his card in.

"I know everything."

"And I know you're full of bull."

"Not about stuff that matters." Well, not most of the time anyway. He had to admit he hadn't known a whole lot when it had come to his marriage. Ryder put his hands on her shoulders because he had developed an obsession with touching her now that he was allowed to again. "Push the button."

She pushed it. "I don't even get these games. I can't even tell if we've won or not."

"We didn't. Push it again." When she hesitated, clearly

trying to interpret the screen, Ryder reached over her and pushed it.

"Hey. Am I doing this or are you?"

"Then move quicker. The slots are about speed. Just keep pushing."

Suzanne glanced up at him and said, "I'm going to push you."

But she was all talk and he knew it. Suzanne started pushing the button faster and they won fifty bucks. "Oh! Did we just win?"

"Yep. You've got the touch."

Ryder watched Suzanne get into gambling, betting higher and double, and whooping when they won something. Her enthusiasm was infectious, and an hour later they were high-fiving.

"Holy shit! We just won five grand!" He eyed the machine and felt a surge of gambling victory. This was definitely their slot.

"Are you freaking kidding me?" Suzanne jumped up and did an impromptu butt-shaking dance that Ryder really appreciated. "How much did we spend?"

"I think we spent about two grand, so we're up three."

She stopped dancing and gaped at him. "We just dumped two thousand dollars into this blinking machine?"

"Yeah. Gotta spend to win."

Suzanne grabbed her heart for a second, then yanked his card out of the machine. "Good Lord in heaven. That's insane. That's a huge amount of money."

It was entertainment was what it was, and Ryder considered himself very fortunate that he could indulge himself now and again. He wasn't a big spender for the most part, and he had a career that paid him well. There was no reason to feel guilty for spending a few thousand dollars on a special weekend. "It's not a big deal."

"I'm having a heart attack, I swear." She handed him the card. "Take that." Her cheeks were flushed and her eyes were a little glassy.

Suddenly unnerved by her reaction, Ryder said, "Maybe we should move on to something else. How about blackjack?"

"How about no. You shouldn't spend any more money. We should be glad we won money and just walk away. Good Lord, two grand . . ."

"Well, what do you want to do then? We can get massages with our winnings."

"Maybe you should just keep the money and not spend it."

"What's the fun in that? It's like free money. It's money that I never had, so we should feel completely justified in spending it." Ryder pulled Suzanne closer to him and kissed her.

After a moment of hesitation, she relaxed in his arms and kissed him back.

"We're here to have fun," he murmured, suddenly knowing he was going to tell her the truth, right there on the casino floor. He couldn't hold it in any longer, couldn't pretend he was feeling less than he was. "Just two crazy kids in love cutting loose in Vegas. What we should do is take our three grand and get rehitched with an Elvis wedding package."

Suzanne stiffened. Pulling back, she stared up at him. "That's not funny."

"It wasn't meant to be funny." He was as serious as the heart attack she'd been claiming to have earlier.

"Why would you say something like that?"

Uh-oh. Suzanne was getting mad and he wasn't even exactly sure why. Trying to tread lightly, he just said, "Because I was trying to get you to relax, to not worry about spending the money, to just enjoy this weekend where we're together. I want to be with you, isn't that obvious? For real be with you."

Oh, my God, there were suddenly tears in her eyes.

Ryder panicked and said, "What? Baby, what's wrong?"

Her lip trembled and she waved her hand wildly to indicate nothing was wrong, yet it clearly was, because now a tear had actually escaped her eye and was trickling down her cheek. Suzanne never cried and it was scaring the hell out of him.

"Let's go . . ." Ryder looked around wildly. They were in a fucking casino, there wasn't a single inch that wasn't blinking and beeping and crawling with gamblers. "Back to our room."

But Suzanne didn't move. She just swiped at her eyes and said, "That was a cruel and stupid thing to say. We've never been two crazy kids in love cutting loose in Vegas. Not even on our honeymoon. And you can't possibly really and truly want to be married to me again."

There was one thing that boiled his blood, raised his blood pressure, had him seeing red, and that was when she told him what his feelings were. Nobody knew his feelings but him, damn it, and he thought for the most part, he was pretty honest when he shared them. She had no idea how much he wanted to be married to her, and that she could dismiss it, just like that, infuriated him.

"That's two different issues. One, if I say I want to be married to you that means I do, and don't tell me otherwise.

Two, I was feeling pretty crazy in love on our honeymoon. I don't know what you were feeling. I kind of thought you were happy, too."

"I was happy. But I was scared. Terrified that you had married me because I was pregnant, plain and simple, and that I wouldn't be able to hold on to you. I was terrified that we would drift apart and that we would end up divorced, my heart broken. And we did, and it was."

"You left," Ryder exploded, despite the fact that an older woman with orange hair shot him a glare from her slot stool a few feet away. "I never wanted this damn divorce. And I didn't marry you because you were pregnant. I married you sooner than I intended because you were pregnant, but I always knew, from the first night we met and made love, that I would marry you."

And that was the whole truth and nothing but the truth.

Suzanne's expression was stricken and she just shook her head. "I need a minute. I'm going back to the room."

"By yourself?"

"Yes." She was already backing away from him.

Ryder's heart sank. They always did this . . . got almost to where they were talking about issues in their relationship and then one or both of them retreated.

"Come on, babe, let's talk about this."

"Just give me half an hour," she said, her voice cracking.

Ryder knew she wanted to cry alone, where he wouldn't see her, and while he didn't understand the why, he understood that it was never wise to push Suzanne. Resigned, he just nodded. "Do you need anything?"

"No. I don't need anything."

Maybe that was the heart of their problem. Suzanne never had needed anything from him.

* * *

SUZANNE fought the tears in the cab as she headed back to the Wynn, disgusted with herself, sick to realize that nothing had changed. Six years and she hadn't learned a goddamn thing. She still wanted to be with Ryder, she still wanted him to sweep her away and make everything alright. She had wanted to believe every word he'd said about how he would have married her, pregnant or not, and for a split second had even thought of taking him up on his wedding-package offer today.

Which said things about her she didn't like because that had been a suck-ass offer. It hadn't been even remotely romantic or sensual or even all that sincere. It had been casual and offhand and impulsive, and yet she had hesitated. Ryder did love her, in some way, she believed that. But Ryder didn't want to have to work too hard at it either. Granted, he had tried this weekend, and he'd done good, but she needed a man who put forth the effort all the time, not just once a year.

But she thought maybe that was something they could work out, or at least talk about.

Yet none of that changed the fact that she still felt insecure, unsuccessful, the weaker link in their partnership, and that she couldn't tolerate. That wasn't his fault, it was just the circumstance of his money, her lack thereof, and it was her problem. She realized that.

What she had done to Nikki had shocked her. If the need to make a buck had caused her to that easily manipulate another person, poor wasn't a street she wanted to live on anymore. That wasn't how her granny and granddad had raised her. They had lacked for cash, but had never compromised their values, and she felt a little sick.

As the cab pulled up in front of the Wynn, Suzanne debated texting Ryder. Maybe it was time to be honest with him, to really lay it all out on the table, all her fears, all her insecurities. Climbing out of the cab, she winced as a blast of cold air hit her. Vegas in December wasn't exactly Palm Beach.

Unfortunately, there was also a group of media personnel she recognized standing right outside the entrance, doing some filming. Most of them had been covering stock car racing for years, and a couple she would even count as casual friends, but none of them were anyone she wanted to talk to at the moment. Except that Joe Blass had spotted her and was waving.

"Hey, Joe," she said as he walked toward her. "How are you?" Not that she really cared at the moment, but she'd do the nice thing and then retreat to her room. Ryder's room. His swanky hotel room.

"I'm great, Suzanne. How about you?"

Suzanne knew Joe fairly well, given that he had covered a lot of the charity events Suzanne had been a part of planning and hostessing in years past, and something about the expression he was wearing right now alarmed her. "Good," she said cautiously. "There's something you want to tell me, isn't there?"

She had no idea what it could be, but it was definitely not that Elton John tickets were up for grabs in the lobby.

Joe sighed, flipping his cigarette into the ashtray by the front door. "You know how the game works, Suzanne, so you remember you have to take it with a grain of salt and just ignore it."

"Ignore what?" This was not reassuring, and her mouth felt hot. There must be buzz about her being in Vegas with Ryder.

"That racing gossip blogger, the one who goes by that stupid name Tuesday Talladega, has a post up about Ryder." Joe shoved his hands in his pockets. "Normally, I wouldn't say anything, it's just a bunch of bullshit gossip, but with everyone in town for the awards ceremony . . . well, I figured you'd want to know what people are saying."

"Thanks, Joe, I appreciate it." Though he hadn't told her what people were saying. Not a good sign at all. "Have a good night."

"Yeah, you, too." Joe waved and moved off.

Suzanne walked into the hotel, glancing around for the business center. Spotting the concierge instead, she asked him to direct her, and five minutes and an impatient elevator ride later, she was in front of a computer looking up Tuesday Talladega's blog.

What she saw there had the words on the screen blurring in front of her angry eyes.

The subject header for the blog entry was *Manwhore Alert: Ryder Jefferson Back in Action*.

Suzanne gripped the mouse tightly and forced herself to keep reading.

Below that was not one, but three pictures of Ryder at various locations around the Wynn hotel, clearly at different times, most definitely with different women.

Number two driver Ryder Jefferson takes girl number four to his favorite hot spot in Las Vegas, the Wynn Hotel, which, of course, is all on the corporate sponsor's dime. Must be nice to have your bimbo du jour at your side at no cost to you, though you'd think even he would try a little harder to at least pretend these are something more than meaningless hook ups with women who make drift-wood look intelligent. Our advice to you, Mr. Jefferson, is to mix it up. With all the hotels in Vegas, surely you can choose a different one for each of your extremely romantic trysts in Sin City.

But that would mean he'd have to foot the bill himself, wouldn't it?

Then below that there was a picture of her with Ryder, arms around each other in the lobby of the hotel. It was taken yesterday, given her outfit.

The nausea hit Suzanne like a cannonball to the gut, and she took short shallow breaths, afraid she was either going to faint or throw up.

The latest woman to accompany him is his ex-wife, Suzanne Jefferson, nee Hickey (I can see why she kept the married name, I mean, dude, Hickey?) in town together for Champions Week. Not known for getting along in the best of times, this sudden tender reunion has a lot of heads scratching and the media scrambling for the details of their prenup. Turns out the alimony ran out in October, which only goes to show you that money and sex do make the world go round and keep our lives as spectators all that much more entertaining.

She's a little bit country, he's a little bit rock 'n' roll, folks, and one of stock car racing's most famous couples is back in action.

Cue the karaoke and the chocolate fountain, and let's

hope this race lasts longer than their first time on the track.

That bitch. That lower-than-a-snake-belly blogging bitch. How dare she say that Suzanne was dating Ryder for his money? That was the last reason in the world she would be with any man.

Then there was Ryder. Where the fuck did he get off taking her to the same goddamn hotel he'd taken other women? The only thing that would be worse would be if he'd taken those sluts to the Bellagio where she and Ryder had honeymooned. If that were the case, then Suzanne would have had to cut off his junk and have fed it to the white tigers.

As it was, she just still might.

Suzanne started to read the comments people had posted in response to the blog, but after seeing people write that she was an idiot and/or a gold digger, she just closed the window on the screen and pushed the chair back. She was no gold digger, but she was an idiot. Tears streaming down her face, she ducked her head and fast-walked to the elevator, praying it would be empty.

It wasn't, and she had to pretend there was something in her eye for the elderly couple gazing at her in concern. When she finally got to the haven of their room, Suzanne went for her empty suitcase and started tossing her clothes out of drawers into it. There was no way on God's green earth she was sticking around to be humiliated any further.

She had known this was a bad idea, yet she'd chosen to ignore her gut, and now look at her. Being mocked by some twit with a made-up name, and thinking that this had been so romantic when Ryder had brought a string of women here previously. Probably even had stayed in the same room, had sex with them in the same bed where he'd loved on her.

"Damn it!" She kicked his suitcase sitting next to hers and resisted the urge to squeeze a tube of toothpaste all over his clothes.

She was in the bathroom, sweeping all her makeup into her cosmetic bag, throat tight from holding back sobs, when Ryder came in.

"Suz? What are you doing?" he asked, coming to stand in the doorway, hands in the front pockets of his jeans.

"I'm leaving. Going back to Charlotte, where I should have stayed in the first place."

"Why? What the hell is the matter? We've been having a good time, I'm pretty damn sure."

Where did she even begin to list all the things that were the matter?

Zipping her makeup bag shut, she turned to him. "I am not going to be just another woman that you brought to this hotel for a weekend screw."

"Why would you even say that?" Ryder knew he was gaping at Suzanne, but there were times he just could not follow her thought processes. "I just suggested we get married!"

"If that was a marriage proposal, it was a shitty one! And I know I'm not the first woman you brought to this hotel, and now so does everybody else thanks to Tuesday Talladega and her damn gossip website."

Ryder's confidence they could work things out, which had already been seriously dented in the last hour, was smashed completely. Uh-oh. "First of all, that Tuesday chick is the modern equivalent of a rag magazine, and no one listens to a word she says. Second, you and I have both dated other people since we've been divorced. That's no secret. You've had a life and lovers and so have I."

"The same hotel, Ryder? That's tacky with a capital T."

"This is where the awards ceremony is! It wasn't any sort of conscious choice. Why does it matter anyway?" Those women hadn't been important to him. They had been diversions, amusement, company for a few of his many lonely nights. Nights he much would have preferred to have spent with Suzanne.

"Was it this room?"

"Huh?" Ryder felt a certain amount of desperation creeping over him. This was going terribly, horribly wrong.

"Did you stay in the same room with them?"

"You mean like a threesome? No, of course not!"

"I didn't mean two at once, you dumb ass, I mean, did you have them share this particular room with you on those three separate trips . . . did you screw those women in the same bed you screwed me?"

"No." He didn't think. Hotel rooms all looked the same. "And that's not fair anyway. I am positive you've had more than one guy share your bed at your condo and we've spent the night there together, and trust me, that is not a happy image for me. I mean, Carl, Suzanne? He didn't have brawn or brains." That idiot Suzanne had dated right after their divorce had been nothing short of totally unworthy of her. "But we were apart for two years, Suz. There's nothing we can do about that but accept it's the past. And as a side note, stop calling me dumb ass. I really hate that."

"Stop being one." She shoved past him and threw her makeup bag into her suitcase. "God, I'm so stupid."

"Why? What is so wrong that we can't talk about it and fix it?" Ryder was truly bewildered. "Maybe my suggestion about getting remarried was too soon, or poorly delivered, I can admit that, but the thing is you don't make it easy for me. Half the time I'm afraid to tell you how I feel, because you tear me a new one, so I hold it in, then blurt it out." He tried to touch her arm but she shook him off. "When you care about a woman as much as I care about you, there's a lot at stake. I never want to mess it up, and yet, that's all we seem to do."

"We're just talking in circles again. The same old arguments that never get us anywhere."

"Maybe we should try talking instead of yelling then running."

Yet Suzanne just zipped her suitcase closed, yanked it off the bed, and pulled up the handle. "I'm leaving."

Ryder's anger dissolved as the enormity of what she was saying hit him and his heart splintered yet again.

"Well, that is what you do best."

Her lips tightened at his parting shot but she didn't say a word. She just rolled her suitcase across the room and left. The door closed with a final and loud click.

"I'M worried about Suzanne," Tamara told Imogen under her breath as they suffered through Nikki's bridal shower together.

"I am, too," Imogen said as she bit into the vegan cupcake that had been served for dessert. "She looks exhausted and she will not even discuss what happened between her and Ryder and it's been a week already."

Tamara had known Suzanne for six years and she was her best friend in the whole world. Watching Suzanne move around the room, her dress loose from having lost weight, her skin wan, and her hair dull, she was genuinely worried about Suz. "She wouldn't really talk about it with me either, just told me to go read that Tuesday Talladega's blog. But Suzanne should know not to let that stuff bother her."

"What stuff? Being humiliated online or discovering that her ex-husband took her to the same hotel as three previous paramours?"

Okay, when Imogen put it like that . . . "I know. It's really hard to be the target of gossip. I've endured my share of mudslinging over the years and Elec had someone accuse him of fathering her child if you recall. It's not fun. But it's part of the business, unfortunately."

Tamara had abandoned her own cupcake after eating half, well aware that she had gained a couple of pounds since her wedding—she liked to call it happy hips. But if she could give five pounds to Suzanne she gladly would, since she had extra and Suzanne was wasting away.

Suzanne was moving around the room, ensuring everything was as it should be for the event, a completely over-the-top fantasy-inspired bridal shower for seventy. Tamara didn't know ninety percent of the women in the room, and she didn't really think she wanted to try. What she really wanted to do was kidnap Suzanne and force her to take a seventy-two-hour nap and eat some pasta and steak.

"Has Elec mentioned if Ryder said anything to him?"

"No, he said Ryder is not saying a word and that he's spending all his time down at the garage checking on his Daytona car."

"Ty said the same thing. He said he confronted Ryder and didn't get any sort of explanation whatsoever."

"So neither one of them are talking. Not good." Tamara saw Suzanne moving in their direction. "Let's grab her and make her sit down at least."

She sprang up and wrapped Suzanne in a hug. "Will you sit down?" she whispered in her ear. "You look like you're going to pass out."

"I'm fine." Suz gave her a tight smile. "Nikki only cried once today and that was when she saw what Jonas was wearing, which kind of made me want to cry, too, so all in all, a successful event."

The dark circles under Suzanne's eyes were the color of Tamara's favorite charcoal gray eye shadow, and she went from concerned to alarmed. "Okay, you know what? When this shindig is over you are coming home with me for the night and we're going to put on comfy pj's and drink wine and relax, do you hear me? I can't remember the last time I heard you make a snarky Suzanne comment and we know that's just not normal."

"I just criticized Jonas's clothes, doesn't that count?"

"No, that was halfhearted." Tamara pushed Suzanne down into her empty chair. "I don't think you've eaten, do you want my cupcake?"

Suzanne's already pale face turned waxy. "No, thanks." She did sip from Tamara's water glass then immediately stood back up, taking a deep breath. "Okay, I will come over after the shower if you don't mind me falling asleep on your couch."

"Not at all. I'll even put a blanket over top of you."

"Thanks." Suzanne gave a small smile then winced when Nikki squealed in delight at something she had unwrapped.

"That's the last gift, and I just want to say something," Nikki said, waving her arms to get the attention of the room. "There has been someone who has totally been there for me, who has kept me sane, and helped me figure out every last little detail of this wedding, and I owe her such a huge thanks. It's not easy to plan a wedding in six weeks and I could not have done it without her."

That was nice, at least Nikki was going to acknowledge Suzanne.

"So a round of applause for my best friend, Sara. You're awesome!"

A blonde popped up to the right of Nikki and smiled and blushed and hugged Nikki. "Is that the girl who slept with Evan Monroe?" Imogen asked, moving next to them, her coat on her arm like she was done with the whole shower and heading home before she got caught in the exit flow.

"Yes," Suzanne said, a grin actually splitting her face. "Evan got in over his head with that one. She's got wedding bells on her mind already."

Yikes. "There is no way in hell I'm letting my brother-in-law marry that girl. And Nikki should have thanked you, not that twig!" Tamara said, annoyed on Suzanne's behalf.

"Yeah, well, Sara's been about as helpful as a back pocket on a shirt, but I have to admire a friendship built entirely on their mutual ability to stroke each other's egos. It's really quite amazing and entertaining." Suzanne glanced around the room. "Now let me find the catering manager so I can sign off and we can get the hell out of here."

SUZANNE wasn't sure going to Tammy's was a good idea, but now that she was spread out on the couch in borrowed fleece pj pants, an afghan over top of her, she was damn glad she had. Imogen was sitting cross-legged in a rocker and Tammy was digging through her wine cabinet.

"What time are the kids getting home from your in-laws?"

"Probably about seven since they took the kids Christmas shopping, and Elec's upstairs on the computer, so we can hang out as long as we like. In fact, I think you should spend the night, Suz. I'll make you a Southern breakfast."

Her friends were clearly worried about her and she was touched. She knew she looked like shit. She felt like shit. And she had a worry weighing on her like no other, in addition to the hurt she was feeling over Ryder and his taking her to his love shack, aka the Wynn Hotel.

"I just might, we'll see."

The family room was cozy and warm and the Christmas tree was glowing in the corner, a blinking star on the top. Tammy had a fancy theme tree in the foyer, while the one here in the family room was colorful and vibrant and a little overdone, showing the kids' hand in it. Hell, and probably Elec's touch. Suzanne hadn't even bothered to put up a tree this year. She wasn't feeling Christmas. She was just feeling crappy.

"What kind of wine do you want? Red or white?"

"I'm not going to have any wine."

"I'll take red," Imogen said, then raised her eyebrows at Suzanne. "No wine, are you sure?"

"I can't because I think I'm pregnant." No better way to say it than to just drop it out there. She thought she was pregnant. There it was. As scary and horrible and bile-producing as it was, it was the truth, and there was nothing she could do about it.

There were twin gasps from Tammy and Imogen, but mostly they just gaped at her for a long drawn-out second. Suzanne understood the feeling. She'd been pretty much feeling bug-eyed and speechless for the last week since she had started to figure out something was not right with her normally regular cycle.

"*What?*" Tammy managed, still hunched over the wine cabinet, her butt in the air and her hair falling over her eyes. "Are you kidding me?"

She wished. Lordy be, how she wished she were joking around.

"How late are you?" Imogen said, her feet dropping to the floor, leaning forward as she pushed up her glasses. "You've probably just gotten yourself off schedule a few days because you've been so busy and stressed. You can even skip a period when you're stressed and not eating well."

"I'm two weeks late, y'all. That's not normal."

"Did you and Ryder use protection? It could just be something hormonal, totally unrelated to pregnancy."

Imogen, God love her, always made sense, but Suzanne knew in her gut that she was knocked up again. It felt the same. Fatigue, tender breasts, nausea that always hovered on the edges of her attention. "I forgot to take my pill one night and took it the next day. Ryder wasn't using a condom, which given his past, I should have made him."

The dog. The totally uncreative hotel chooser, super-sperm Captain Dickhead.

"Well, you need to take a pregnancy test before you jump to any conclusions." Tammy stood up, setting the bottle of wine on the buffet and coming over to the couch. "We can go to the store and get one and you can take it right now, while we hold your hand."

"I have one in my purse. I've been carrying it around for three days. I figured that was sort of like addressing

the problem but not really actually having to deal with it."
Proactive to a certain point, that worked for her.

"Then let's take it now."

"You make it sound as if this is a group effort. I can pee
on the stick by myself, but I did buy a multipack because
it was on sale, so you're welcome to the spare."

"Oh, I know I'm not pregnant," Tammy said. "Elec
can't . . ."

Then she stopped talking and her face flushed pink.

Suzanne was actually momentarily diverted. "Are you
telling me Elec can't get it up?" Jesus, and she thought her
life was shit.

"Of course he can! He can definitely get it up, he gets
it up *a lot*. He is younger than me, remember." Tammy
glanced toward the stairs and dropped her voice. "It's not
something he likes known, and I swear if you say anything to anyone or to him, I will kill you, but he can't have
children. It's really hard for him to know that he'll never
have his own biological kids. That's part of why he loves
mine so much."

"Oh, Tammy, damn, I had no idea." Suzanne swallowed the lump that had suddenly risen in her throat. God,
to not be able to have children? That was something she
couldn't comprehend. It put a whole new spin on her di-
lemma. "I'm so sorry."

"We've talked about adoption," she whispered, but
then waved her hand. "But we're not talking about me.
We're talking about you. Get your butt in the bathroom."

"I was afraid you were going to say that." Suzanne
threw the blanket off of her and sighed. "Fine. Let's get
this over with."

"How will you feel if it's positive?" Imogen asked.

"I'm not sure," she admitted. "I mean, I've always wanted a baby, desperately. But this is far from ideal circumstances. I'm broke and I just applied to law school."

"You applied to law school?" Tammy asked, her face squinching up. "Since when?"

"Since Vegas. I always wanted to go to law school, you know, but I was afraid to take the leap, to get the loans and just do it. And after all this wedding business with Nikki, I just realized it's now or never. I can try to do something I've always wanted to, something that makes a difference in the world, or I can just resign myself to a job I don't really care for. So I figured I would apply and see what happens."

She had needed to do it. It was time to grab the steering wheel and drive her own life instead of just being along for the ride.

"I didn't know you wanted to be a lawyer," Imogen said. "That's an excellent choice for you."

"I didn't know you wanted to be a lawyer either and I've known you for six years. I swear, Suzanne, sometimes you're such a guy."

"What does that mean? I don't spit and I don't have any balls to scratch and I've never claimed romance is an ice-cold beer and a swat on the ass." She wasn't a guy, and she was kind of offended by the comparison.

Tammy laughed. "What I mean is that you do what men do in that you think things through quietly, in your head, and then just announce the conclusion. Most women don't do that. Most women fret and worry and talk it through from all angles over and over with their girlfriends and their partner and finally, sometimes, come to a conclusion. Men work it all through in their head, and you don't even know they're thinking about anything so when they announce it, everyone's left scratching their heads and wondering where that came from. You do the exact same thing."

Her first reaction was to deny it, but as she thought about it, Suzanne realized there was a measure of truth to it. "So? It just means I'm not bugging anyone with my stupid shit."

"But you don't let anyone in, honey, to offer advice or to support you," Tammy said in a soft voice. "We can be here for you more if you'd let us. And Ryder would understand you better if you shared with him once in a while."

Disturbed by the tone of the conversation, Suzanne stood up and went for her purse on the end table. "There's been plenty of sharing between Ryder and I lately. We don't need any more sharing or I'll wind up having triplets." She yanked the pregnancy test out of the bottom of her purse where she had wedged it.

While she sat on the toilet seat in Tammy's powder room waiting for the test to do its thing, she pondered what her friend had said. Since when had working through problems and feelings on your own become a flaw? She had always thought of it as a strength, not a weakness. But maybe there was something to Tammy's point that coming to a conclusion on your own blindsided people.

The truth was, she didn't know what she was doing when it came to relationships. She never had. Her grandparents had been great people and had loved her, but there had always been a part of Suzanne that had resented being abandoned by her mother. So she had kept her emotions in check and hidden in private.

It was easy for her to say whatever she was thinking, unless it was an emotion. That might make her vulnerable, and she wasn't having any of that.

Suzanne glanced at the pregnancy test resting on the vanity, figuring it wouldn't be ready yet.

But it was.

Pregnant.

Her stomach did a flip.

It looked like she was going to have to accept vulnerable and learn to live with emotional, because she was having a baby.

Ryder's baby.

Again.

"What's going on in there?" Tammy pounded on the door.

Forcing herself to stand up on shaky legs, Suzanne swung the door open. "I'm pregnant and I think I'm going to faint." The whole room was starting to spin and she was seeing spots. That wasn't good.

"Oh, Lord!" Tammy reached out and grabbed her arm.

But Suzanne was already sliding down the wall, her legs going out from under her like they were made of clay. She was vaguely aware of Tammy screaming for her husband and Imogen saying something about water, but mostly she was focused on getting the blackness dancing in front of her eyes to recede and her saliva to stop multiplying in her mouth.

When she hit the floor with a thud, sitting hard on her butt, a hand shoved her head between her legs, which didn't help, and only made her jeans cut into her waist.

"I'm fine," she managed weakly, swatting at the hand holding her down. "Let me up."

The blood all rushed into her face and she had a precarious moment where she thought her stomach had mistaken itself for a trampoline, but she held it together and took a deep breath. Her hands were shaking. "Well, that was embarrassing. That was such a girl thing to do."

"News flash, you are a girl." Tammy smoothed her hair back off her forehead.

Suzanne realized her bangs were damp from sweat. Sexy. "I guess there's truth in that. I'm a girl. A stupid, idiotic girl who has learned nothing in the past six years." She started to laugh, feeling more than a little hysterical. "I mean, I got knocked up in a car! How high school is that?"

Imogen tried to hand her water but she waved it away as she dissolved into a high-pitched laugh that occasionally turned into a sob. She sounded crazy, she knew it, but she couldn't stop herself. She felt just a little bit crazy.

Elec came around the corner and said, "What's going on—"

His eyebrows shot up when he saw Suzanne on the floor rocking from her laughter. "Um . . . everything okay?"

"Yes," Tammy said.

"No," Suzanne told him.

"Is there anything I can do?"

"Not unless you're volunteering to be the target for all my man hating."

"Hmm. I think I'll pass." Elec started to back up in the hallway. "Enjoy your girl time." He darted into the kitchen.

"You've terrified my husband."

"Hell, I'm terrifying myself." Suzanne forced herself off the floor, taking the hand Tammy offered.

Tammy reached out and hugged her. "This is fine. We'll figure it all out."

"Thanks." She accepted a hug from Imogen, too. "I know it will be fine. I do believe that a baby is a blessing, I want this baby. I may have to sell everything I own to survive, but I'll manage."

Imogen squeezed her hand. "But you won't have to do anything that drastic. This is Ryder's child, too, and he'll be more than willing to give you child support. Given his income, it will be a substantial amount of money."

Suzanne wrinkled her nose. Why did that feel about as good as going on the dole? "I'm still going to law school. I want to be proud of who I am, not raising a kid on the father's charity."

"This isn't something you need to worry about right now," Tammy told her.

No. What she needed to worry about right now was telling Ryder he was going to be a daddy.

"SO you're telling me there's nothing I can do?" Ryder glared at Bill, his PR rep. They'd been having this argument for a week since he'd gotten back from Vegas, smarting from being dumped by Suzanne and furious that some anonymous online blogger was making him look like a smarmy playboy. But even worse, the blogger had made Suzanne look . . . not good. And that made him see red. Whether she ever spoke to him again or not, he didn't want her thinking he didn't have her back.

"No. Tuesday Talladega has the right to say whatever she wants, and it was the truth. Can you just let it go? Nobody cares if you're sleeping around. You're divorced."

Technically, no. But no one needed to know that. Hell, he hadn't even known that until a month ago. "I don't really care what they're saying about me. But she had no right to drag Suzanne into this."

Bill was in his mid-twenties, a fresh-faced wonder boy straight out of college, with a clean-cut look and a hairline that was already starting to take a step back. "I feel obligated to point out that you dragged the former Mrs. Jefferson into this when you took her to Champions Week with you."

Little know-it-all. Ryder leaned back in his office chair, feeling the walls closing in on him. He hadn't been sleeping well, and he was ragged out. He hated being in the office on a good day, and there had been no good days since Suz had walked out of that suite in Vegas. "You're not obligated to say anything. Mind your own damn business."

But with the confidence of a twenty-four-year-old, Bill just cleared his throat and straightened his navy tie as he stood in front of Ryder's desk. "On the contrary, that's what I'm paid to do. So I'm also obligated to tell you that it's time for you to shave. Your image is rock star driver, not weird mountain man."

Ryder scratched his suddenly full beard and scowled. "There's no rule that says I can't have facial hair. Next you'll be telling me I have to shave my balls."

"Since the cameras don't pan in on your balls, I have no opinion on what you do or don't do to them."

See what he had to put up with? "Let me ask you this since you're so full of opinions—why does it matter to a woman that you might have happened to take her to the same hotel that you had been to with a previous woman? One a lot less important than her, too, I might add."

Ryder was still struggling with that being the root of Suzanne's anger. It just seemed like she was making too big of a deal out of it to him.

Bill coughed. "Am I obligated to be honest here?"

"Yes. You look like the type who eavesdrops on women, so maybe you know something I don't."

Rolling his eyes, Bill said dryly, "Thank you, sir. But really, it's more that I listen to women when they're speaking to *me*. I've never had a girl break up with me, ever. I'm a pretty stellar boyfriend."

"Modest, too. So? What do you think, oh wise one?" Ryder was walking a thin line here, knowing he just might find himself without a PR rep tomorrow, but he was incapable of stopping himself. He needed answers, and Bill seemed to be the only one talking. Ty and Elec hadn't been much help because they both had a potential conflict of interest with their significant others, and there was no way in hell he was going to Evan for advice.

"It's a matter of public relations. You know how you have to make your number one sponsor feel special? How you have to wear their merchandise and mention them at important functions? A woman feels the same way . . . she wants to be special. Like she's definitely number one, not like you plastered her logo on top of someone else's with peel-off plastic."

Huh. Maybe Ryder could see the logic in that. He picked up a pen and tapped it on the desk. Make Suzanne feel special. Make her feel number one.

The question was how the hell did he do that?

He didn't think even Bill of the perfect dating record would have the answer to that.

CHAPTER
SEVENTEEN

SUZANNE paced in her living room, waiting for Ryder to show up. It had been surprisingly easy to get him to agree to come over, even without telling him why. She had just texted him and asked if they could talk and he'd replied right away.

See? She could hear Tammy's voice in her head, telling her that Ryder wanted to be with her. But that was irrelevant. She thought.

Or didn't. She was so damn confused she didn't know if she was coming or going. All she knew for sure was that she was having a baby, and despite the fact that it made her want to throw up in her mouth, she had to tell Ryder. She'd already gone around and around on the when and the how, debating waiting until after Nikki's wedding and until after Christmas, then realizing there was no point in waiting. Nor was there any perfect time to drop a baby bomb on a man.

Besides, she didn't think she could see him at the wedding with this weighing on her. Holding it in for four days had been hard enough and she'd had no interaction with him in that time. God knew she couldn't be blurting it out in the middle of Nikki's reception while the bride and groom cut the cake.

Just tell him. Get it over with.

Hopefully he wouldn't freak out.

She was fairly certain Ryder had never really wanted kids since he'd never suggested they try again after they'd lost their first baby, so she wasn't sure how she was going to react.

When the doorbell rang, she held her churning stomach for a minute before forcing herself to the door. "Hi," she said, her voice a weird squawk. "Thanks for coming over."

"Sure." He gave her a searching look as he stepped into her foyer. "Look, Suzanne, first things first. I'm sorry for that dumb blog. I know that must have been humiliating for you and I never in a million years meant to make you feel bad. I didn't think about being at the Wynn with those other women, because well, you're the most important woman to me. You always have been."

Suzanne blinked. That blog was so two weeks ago. Before she'd learned she had a human embryo riding shotgun with her. "It's okay." She definitely hadn't invited him over to dissect their always complicated relationship yet again. She'd invited him over to complicate it further.

"No, it's really not. I want . . ." Ryder paused, clearly frustrated. "God, I'm like the worst communicator."

But the cutest. Suzanne couldn't help but notice how

hot he looked in his jeans and sweatshirt. It was freezing outside, but he wasn't wearing a coat. "Ryder, listen to me. It's okay."

"No, really, I . . ." Ryder frowned as he studied her. "Are you okay? You look like you've been sick. You've lost weight." He reached out and ran his thumb under her eye. "You're not getting enough sleep. What is it, the flu?"

An overwhelming melancholy swept through her. She missed him.

Shit. It had to be the hormones.

"No." Suzanne took a deep breath and stepped out of his touch. She couldn't think when his fingers were on her. "Ryder."

"Yes?" He looked at her expectantly.

"I'm pregnant," she blurted out. "And I swear to God if you actually ask me if you're the father I will cancel your birth certificate."

Ryder hadn't a clue what Suzanne was going to say, but never in a hundred million years could he have guessed she would say that. He just stared at her for a second, feeling like someone had dumped a bathtub's worth of ice water on his head. "You're pregnant?"

She nodded, her cheeks flushed, eyes glassy. She had definitely lost weight in her hips and arms, and her face was thinner. Yet now that he thought about it, her chest had actually filled out. She was bursting at the seams of her button-up top. "You're pregnant."

That time it wasn't a question and his brain started to regroup from the shock. •

"Yes!"

Ryder felt a grin start to split his face. "Holy shit, we're having a baby." He thought back to the times they'd had sex. "Is this my fault for not using a condom?" He'd never bothered to ask if she was on the pill, he had just assumed she was or she would say something.

"No, it's not your fault. It's mine. I forgot to take my pill that first night. I took it the next morning, so I thought it was fine, but it obviously wasn't." She crossed her arms over her chest.

"So you think you got pregnant that first night?" How was that for a bull's-eye? And he hadn't even been aiming. Ryder grinned. "Well, alright, then. So you're what, like five weeks? Because that night was the night of the camping trip . . ." He tried to count back. Then forward. That would mean she was due in August if he had his math right.

But his thoughts were cut off when Suzanne burst into tears, startling the hell out of him. This was the second time she'd cried on him in as many weeks and it was freaking him out. "What? What's the matter?"

"Our baby was conceived in the front seat of a car! That's just tacky!"

Did it matter? It wasn't like they were going to print it on the kid's birth certificate or anything. Not to mention, it had been a passionate reunion, with pheromones flying. Ryder thought that was kind of an awesome way to be conceived, with your parents totally digging on each other and in love. But he knew better than to say any of that.

"It was probably later in the night, when we were in bed. In fact, I'm sure of it."

She looked at him like that was the stupidest thing he'd ever said, which it probably was, but hell, what was he supposed to say?

"How could you possibly know that?" she asked in irritation.

"Okay, I don't! Any more than you know it was in the car. And it doesn't matter, we're not going to tell anyone that you might have gotten pregnant in the front seat."

"I told Imogen and Tammy."

While his initial reaction was one of hurt that she'd shared their news with her girlfriends first, Ryder knew that was normal for a woman. Besides, they weren't exactly *Leave It to Beaver* at the moment. It wasn't quite the regular way of things when you find out you're having a baby. Love, marriage, baby. For them, it had been more like love, baby, marriage. Divorce, sort of marriage, baby again. Love? He wasn't sure where that fit into the equation anymore.

Suzanne's eyes looked a little wild and her lip was trembling, but the sobs had quieted down. Ryder took her hand. "Come on, babe, let's just take a deep breath and sit down on the couch, alright?"

She nodded. "Alright, you're right. Sitting down is good."

"How have you been feeling?" he asked her as they settled onto her sofa next to each other. "You look tired."

"I've been nauseous and tired. Normal I guess, but needless to say, I've been stressed."

He wanted to reassure her, but he also wanted to proceed with caution. If there were more tears, he wasn't sure he could be trusted not to panic. "I know this is unexpected, but this is a wonderful surprise. I mean, a baby. Our baby. Suz, that makes me really damn happy, and I'll do whatever you need me to."

She looked at her hands in her lap, nails digging into

the denim of her jeans. "You don't really have to do any-thing, you know. Like I said, this was pretty much my fault, and I know that you didn't really want children, so it's fine. Contribute as little or as much as you want, it's all good."

Uh, that really wasn't what he'd expected her to say. Ryder wasn't sure what bit of fiction in there he needed to address first. He'd go with the biggie. "Why in the hell would you say I don't want children? Of course I want children."

"Then why haven't you gotten married and started a family?"

What the fuck? Ryder was starting to wonder if those hormonal changes people talked about had kicked in al-ready because Suzanne was acting nuts. "Because I haven't met anyone I wanted to marry and start a family with. Besides you, that is."

"But our baby and marriage weren't planned."

"So? I told you before that it happened sooner than I expected but I knew I was going to marry you. A baby was a bonus." Ryder pried her hand away from her leg and wrapped his around it. "Suzanne," he told her softly, "when we lost that baby, I was devastated. I wanted that baby with you more than anything."

His chest felt tight just thinking about it. And now that they had a second chance, well, damn, he was starting to understand the tears.

"But . . . but you never said anything. And you never mentioned trying again . . . I thought you didn't want to."

Ryder stared at her flabbergasted. "You thought I didn't want to try again? I was just waiting for you to say some-thing, honey. I was afraid if I brought it up, it would be too soon, that you're weren't ready, because you never said you wanted to."

"Of course I wanted to. I wanted to right away."

"Oh, my God." Ryder took his free hand and ran it through his hair. "Talk about a total lack of communication, damn. That pretty much sums up our marriage, doesn't it?"

"So you're telling me you wanted to try again for a baby?" Suzanne was fiddling with the gold chain around her throat. "You really did?"

"Yes." Seeing that look on her face, knowing what they'd both been through, Ryder had a thousand regrets, a million self-recriminations. But right now all he could do was pull Suzanne into his arms and rest his forehead on hers. "Yes, babe, yes. I can't imagine any other woman as the mother of my child."

Ryder wiped the tears off her cheeks and kissed her trembling lips. He wrapped his arms around her and held her tight. "Jesus, why didn't we ever talk about this?"

"Because we're stubborn and emotionally stunted," she told him with a sniffle, cuddling up against his chest, like she was enjoying being held.

Ryder gave a soft laugh. "Which one am I, stubborn or emotionally stunted?"

"I think we each have a fair amount of both. Let's face it—I have abandonment issues from my mother and your parents were so indulgent anything you did half-ass was always more than good enough."

Well, that was slicing through it with a knife. "I guess that's true on both counts. But we could fix all that by just talking about our feelings."

Suzanne pulled back, wiping her eyes. "That's crazy

talk, Jefferson. Talking about feelings? Lordy, we'll have to reconfigure our whole way of dealing with each other."

"Baby steps, right?" Ryder nudged her knee with his. "Get it, *baby* steps."

She gave a laugh that dissolved into a cough. "You're a dork and I need to blow my nose."

"See? That's genuine emotion right there. We're making progress already."

Suzanne stood up and walked across the room toward the kitchen. "Do you want a drink? A beer? I need some water."

"I'll get it. Why don't you sit back down? You look tired."

She turned and gave him a wry look. "That's like the third time you've said that. I get it, okay? I look like hell in a handbasket. I am well aware of that fact, thank you."

"You don't look like hell, you look tired, and I was offering because I'm nice and I'm concerned about you. Nothing more, nothing less."

Suzanne stared at him then shook her head. "This communicating thing is going to take some getting used to."

Ryder followed her into the kitchen and got himself a beer from the fridge as she filled a glass with water from the tap. "So have you been to the doctor? Do you have a due date?"

A baby. He was reeling. He just couldn't believe it. Like the few days and nights he'd spent with Suzanne hadn't been awesome enough, now they'd created a baby out of that time together. It had his head spinning and his heart inflating.

Suzanne took a sip of her water and tried to wrap her head around all of this. All things considered, his reaction to her news was decent. "I don't go until right after Christmas. Tammy gave me her OB/GYN. I didn't want to go to the same one as last time and have to answer a bunch of questions." Like what they were to each other and how they'd managed to do this again.

She wasn't sure what to think about the things he'd said. He had wanted children. That still sort of blew her mind. She had put up so many walls and had been so sure that he hadn't wanted a family with her that it was hard to relinquish that belief now. It had honestly colored everything she had done in her marriage, and standing here pregnant again, this whole new reality displayed in front of her, she just didn't know how to act.

But it had felt good with Ryder's arms around her. Not for sex, but for intimacy. For holding her, caring for her. It had been real nice.

"Do you think it's a girl or a boy?" he asked as he frowned at his beer bottle, unsuccessful at twisting the cap off.

"I think there's a fifty-fifty chance it's one of those. And that's not a twist top, what are you doing? That's your brand. Bottle opener is in the drawer by the stove."

Ryder looked at the bottle in his hand and shook his head. "I think I'm a little rattled."

"I'm a lot rattled but at least we have eight months to figure out what we're doing. I mean, really, what do I know about being a mother?"

"You'll be a fantastic mother. You care. Deeply. That's what makes a good mother."

Suzanne felt her cheeks burning. Lord, since when did she blush. "I say inappropriate things in front of Hunter and Pete. I let cusswords slip out."

"A little cussing never killed a kid. They hear it in grade school on the bus anyway. You'll be a great mother, I know it." Ryder dug around in the drawer for the bottle opener.

"Thanks," Suzanne said softly. "I appreciate that." She did, because her confidence had really been suffering the last few weeks. She wasn't sure she could do this, and do it right. It felt good to have him backing her up. "And I know you'll be a great father."

"I just wish I could be around more. This job is kind of a bitch when it comes to the schedule."

"I'll bring her to see you on the road if I can. It depends on if I get into school or not." The whole thing suddenly seemed daunting again and Suzanne clutched her water glass.

"She? You think it's a girl?" Ryder looked rapturous at the thought.

"I don't know." She wasn't sure why she said *she*. It had just come out.

Then he frowned. "School? What are you going to school for?"

"I applied to law school." Suzanne stuck her chin up and waited for him to laugh at her.

He just stared blankly at her. "Law school? Why do you want to go to law school?"

"So I can be a lawyer. It's what I always wanted to be."

"It is?" He looked incredulous, his hand pausing in the act of popping his beer cap off. "I didn't know that. But okay."

"Okay?" As if she needed his permission?

"I mean, that's cool. If that's what you want, you should go for it. I think you'd be great at it."

His voice was more distracted than insincere, so she would just take it at face value. She couldn't expect cartwheels for her law school plans right now in the middle of all the other news she'd just dropped on him. "Thanks."

"Speaking of lawyers, I guess I should call ours and cancel our court date."

Suzanne had totally forgotten about their court date since she'd been a little busy having tons of condom-free sex with Ryder, planning Nikki's wedding, and forming a placenta. They were due in court in a week, right after the wedding.

"I admit the timing is bad, but why should we cancel it?"

Hope bloomed in her heart that there, right then, in her terra cotta–colored kitchen he would say he wanted to be married to her still. That love conquered all and they could work it all out and be happy, together, as a family.

The need, the desire, bubbled up inside her so fast she was shocked to realize how much she wanted it. That was all she needed to hear and then she could throw off all her old worries and insecurities and look forward to the future.

"Because if we're legally married we might as well stay that way. It looks bad otherwise. It will cause a lot of gossip, and the thing is I really don't want my child born under those circumstances. Just easier to cancel the court date until we figure all this out, don't you think?" Ryder took a sip of his beer.

That was so far off of what Suzanne had been wishing for, she couldn't believe her heart had managed to bridge that gap so quickly. A sharp sense of betrayal smacked her and she felt her hands start to shake, she was so angry.

Angry at him, for being so cold and unromantic and incapable of really loving her. Angry at herself, for never learning that in the end she needed to take what she got and be satisfied with it.

At least now she wouldn't be alone like she'd always assumed. She'd have her baby. That was more than enough, and later, when she wasn't so furious and disappointed and hurt, yet again, she'd be grateful to him for giving her that.

But right now, she needed him out of her line of vision before she chucked her water glass at him. "Get out," she told him, tears choking her.

He set the beer bottle down on the counter with a clank. "What the hell? *Why?*"

"Just go before I freak out even more than I already am." She had about sixty seconds before she lost it totally.

"What happened to communicating? Talking things through?" Ryder looked pissed and astonished.

Now maybe he'd understand how she felt. "I'll take a rain check."

In a fit that made her jump, Ryder threw the bottle cap at her refrigerator door where it pinged off it and landed on the floor, spinning across the tile. "Goddammit, Suzanne."

Then throwing his hands up in the air, he stomped out, her front door slamming shut behind him.

Suzanne waited for the tears to fall but they seemed to have evaporated.

Just as well.

She knew that fairy tales were fiction and that happily ever after didn't exist for her.

* * *

TY stood next to Elec as they both watched Ryder out on the dance floor doing the sprinkler and wearing some woman's bra on his head like a do-rag.

"Okay, we have to do something, this is embarrassing. And God knows someone will take a picture and we'll see it on that Tuesday chick's blog tomorrow." Even though they were in the corner, leaning on the bar, Ty still had to yell a little to be heard over the pounding dance music. Taking a pull on his beer for fortification, he tried to assess the best way to enter the throng of scantily dressed women gyrating on the dance floor.

Didn't these girls know it was December? They were dressed like it was June in Key West, with tiny skirts and cleavage-baring tank tops. Probably the liquor and the dancing were keeping them warm. Not to mention that several of them seemed to be downright hot for Ryder, which was unnerving Ty. He didn't think that Ryder had the sense to say no at the moment.

"I know. I can't believe how much rum he drank. It was like one minute he was just sipping a drink and the next the bottle was mysteriously empty. He's going to have a hell of a hangover tomorrow."

"He's going to wake up with a pounding head, cotton mouth, and a naked twenty-something whose name he can't remember wrapped around him." Ty shuddered. "God, I'm glad I'm not single anymore. That would have been me a year ago, and now I can't imagine waking up with anyone but Imogen."

"I hear ya. I love being married." Elec used his beer

bottle to point. "My brother, on the other hand, seems just fine single."

Evan was out there, too, doing some kind of grinding dance with a cute brunette. "He did plan this bachelor party for Jonas, so I'guess he's entitled to enjoy it."

"I was impressed with the limo so we don't have to worry about driving. Evan's not usually that organized," Elec said.

"He told me your sister did everything for him."

Elec laughed. "Oh, I bet that thrilled Eve. Where is Jonas, by the way?"

"He's with his friend whose name I can never remember playing one of those gambling machines at the other end of the bar."

"At least he has the sense to stay off the dance floor." Elec set down his beer. "I think it's time to rescue Ryder from himself. He's on the floor now doing the worm."

"Oh, my God." Ty abandoned his own beer and shook his head at the sight of his friend making a total ass out of himself. Imogen had told him that Suzanne and Ryder had been having a rough time of it since Vegas, but that was no excuse for rolling around on a dirty booze-stained floor on your gut.

As they maneuvered through the crowd, Ty could have sworn someone grabbed his ass. He turned and stared down a girl who couldn't have been much more than eighteen. The girl just giggled.

"I'm sorry, I think I accidentally brushed against you," he said.

"No, I grabbed your ass."

Well, that was disturbing. She wasn't even going to

deny it. All his mother's dire warnings about bold and loose girls rose up in his mind and he started to think maybe there'd been some truth in that.

"Let's make out," she added.

"Go home and watch cartoons," Ty told her.

Elec shoved him forward. "Don't even make eye contact. I feel like a hunk of raw meat with the lions all circling."

Good point. Ty reached Ryder, who was back up off the floor, thank God. He didn't even want to contemplate what would happen if he had to bend over to haul Ryder up.

"Hey, guys, wassup?" Ryder slapped an arm around Ty and almost fell over.

"We're heading out, it's one. Time to go home, dancing queen."

"But I'm having fun! I don't want to go." Ryder lifted his drink and gave some kind of party yell that had the girls around him all squealing and cheering.

"Nah, it's time to go."

"Evan said we're going to a strip club. He wants to see Jonas squirm."

That was something Ty had no interest in seeing. "Let's talk about it in the limo. Come on."

"Alright, alright." Ryder turned to the pack around him. "Good night, ladies. It's been real." He started to follow Ty, then stopped. "Oh, whatsyourname. Here's your bra back. I'm not sure why you gifted me with it in the first place, but I liked it."

The woman giggled as Ryder took it off his head, grabbing her arms and shoving them through the holes so that she was loosely wearing her bra on top of her tank.

Ty was losing patience, so he tapped Ryder's arm. "Let's go."

"What's your problem? You're a real drag tonight."

"Yep. A drag, that's me."

It took both of them to get Ryder shoved into the limo, and when Elec went to tell Jonas they were taking Ryder home, Ty climbed in next to his friend and assessed Ryder. "Man, what's going on with you? You don't normally drink like this."

Ryder was trying to find his mouth with his plastic cup and gave up after a few tries. "Just having fun, helping Jonas celebrate. Marriage. Three cheers for that." Ryder raised his cup and sloshed rum over the side of the cup.

Maybe if he questioned Ryder while he was drunk, he'd get the true story, so Ty said, "What the hell happened with you and Suzanne?"

"I don't know." Ryder shrugged. "She hates me. I love her and she hates me."

Drama alert. "She doesn't hate you."

"Yes, she does. I'm good enough to fuck, but that's it, man. Good for nothing else, just a quick lay."

It just got better and better. Ty shifted on the seat, wishing he could be doing anything else other than having this awkward conversation. "That's not true and you know it. Suzanne has been in love with you for years."

"Then why won't she be with me?" Ryder slumped forward and stared into his cup. "We're having a baby, did I tell you that? We're having a baby and she still won't be with me."

"Suzanne's pregnant?" That explained why Imogen was dancing around the subject of Ryder and Suzanne with him. She must not have Suz's permission to tell anyone at this point. Talk about a hot mess. Jesus.

"Yep." Ryder tried to take a sip, again unsuccessfully. "First time we did it and she was on the pill. Do I have super sperm or what?"

He wasn't going to talk about Ryder's sperm. "I guess that was a shocker."

"Yeah, but I was happy, man, I was so happy. I mean, a baby." He lifted his arm to indicate holding a baby. "That's like just awesome. A baby with Suz, the only woman I've ever loved. And she hates me."

Where the hell was a lifeline when you needed one? Ty glanced out the window, but there was no sign of Elec. "Did you tell her you love her? That you want to be with her?"

"Yes." Ryder's sullen answer slurred. "I even asked her to marry me."

"She said no?"

"She told me to get out."

"That sounds like an extreme reaction. How did you ask her?" Ty shot a nervous look at the limo driver, hoping he was far enough away that he wasn't hearing this conversation.

"I said I guess we should cancel the divorce court date."

Ty blinked. "That was your proposal? Dude. Look, I'm not exactly Mr. Romance. I mean, God only knows how I even managed to get Imogen to agree to marry me, but even I know when you propose to a woman you actually have to say, 'I love you, will you marry me?'"

"Well, I meant that."

"But did you say it?"

"I don't know." Ryder wedged his cup between his knees and flopped back against the seat. "I'm miserable, McCordle. I think I'm dying." He hit his chest. "Right here. I'm dead."

Oh, Lord. "Just close your eyes. It's time to sleep."

Elec opened the door and climbed in. "We're all set. Limo's coming back here for the other guys after it drops us off. How is he?" He gestured to Ryder.

"A mess."

Elec eyed Ryder cautiously. "I hope he doesn't throw up."

Ryder was mumbling to himself incoherently, his eyes closed. Ty leaned over and grabbed the drink from between his knees and dumped it out in the parking lot. "You and me both."

Evan popped his head into the open door. "I can't believe you losers are leaving."

"Yeah, well, someone has to take Captain Morgan here home."

"Let this be a cautionary tale," Evan said.

"Against rum? Yeah, I'll agree with that."

"Against women. Nothing but trouble."

"Thanks for that, we'll keep it in mind when we're having sex every night and you're not," Elec said. "Catch you later." He put his boot in his brother's gut and shoved.

Evan stumbled back, laughing. "Be safe, brother."

Elec yanked the door closed. "I don't think we should leave Ryder alone at home. He can sleep on our couch. If he gets sick, Tamara will hear him. She has that freakish maternal ability to wake up when anyone has a fever or the potential to puke."

"Sounds like a plan. I owe Tammy a big thank-you." Ty sighed. "I think I'm too old for this bachelor party crap."

"We'll be planning yours soon enough."

That was so not appealing, Ty was almost scared. "Let's just go fishing and call it good."

"Done."

CHAPTER
EIGHTEEN

SUZANNE wanted to cram hot needles in her ears so she didn't have to listen to Nikki's high-pitched laugh anymore. Slumped over the table at the male revue Nikki had chosen for her bachelorette party, Suzanne glanced at her watch and wondered if she left if Nikki would even notice. With all that male muscle gyrating in front of her, Nikki was appropriately distracted.

Had she ever been that young? Suzanne watched Nikki leaping around, her bride sash shimmering in the disco lights, her fake veil slipping. While Suzanne had known how to have a good time, she'd never been as carefree as Nikki, that's for sure. She'd always had a hard row to hoe, whereas Nikki had never faced a challenge in her life. So while it was understandable, it wasn't any less annoying.

Why was it the pretty little blonde, born upper middle class with every single advantage in life except for brains, got to marry a man who loved her and be happy with even more money? Not that Suzanne wanted to be Nikki, she kind of liked not being a moron, but all the same, why was it that some women just seemed to come up golden time and time again when it came to relationships?

Suzanne sipped her Coke and reminded herself that she was just feeling exceptionally bitter at the moment and that it would pass. So Nikki got to be Cinderella . . . so what?

She didn't want glass shoes anyway. Those suckers had to be hell to dance in.

"I'm not into these shows," Tammy said.

"I don't know." Imogen pushed her glasses up as she closely studied the dancers. "I find it rather fascinating. People watching at its finest."

"I can appreciate a good naked man chest myself, usually. But I feel like rat poop." Suzanne forced herself to sit up straight. "I think I need to go home. Morning sickness is more like all-damn-day sickness."

"I'm sorry, it will pass," Tammy said. "And in a few days this wedding will be over and done with and you can relax."

Hah. Relaxation was nowhere in Suzanne's immediate future that she could tell. She was worried about money, about having another miscarriage, about her law school application. And Ryder. She worried an awful lot about Ryder and how they were going to raise a baby together when she was totally in love with him and couldn't be with him.

"I can't wait to see Nikki's skinny butt going down that aisle," Suzanne said. "I just might cry when it's all said and done. And now, I'm going home."

"If you're leaving, I'm leaving, too," Tammy said.

"Yeah, I'll head out as well. I can only take so much visual stimulation before it becomes overwhelming."

They gathered their purses and coats and headed toward the door, Suzanne waving to Nikki. Tammy was checking her phone, and when she looked up from it she frowned at Suzanne.

"Elec says Ryder is drinking a lot at the bachelor party. He's worried about him."

Suzanne ignored the squeeze her heart gave. "It's a bachelor party, of course he's drinking." Probably hitting on women, too, finding his next weekend date to the Wynn.

"Elec says he's not handling your break-up well."

"With all due respect to Elec, how the hell does he know?" Suzanne winced as the cold winter wind hit her in the face when Imogen pushed the door open. "And I don't want to talk about it."

"Okay, fine. Just ignore the problem indefinitely."

"I love you, Tammy, but don't piss me off."

"You called me out when you didn't agree with my choices when I was dating Geoffrey. And when I broke things off with Elec. So I have the right to call you out when I think you're making a mistake. And not talking to Ryder is a mistake."

They stared each other down in the parking lot, Tammy's eyes full of sympathy. Suzanne felt the tears starting to form. Damn hormones. "Maybe it's a mistake. But the thing is, I cannot deal with it right now. I can't handle the drama or the hurt or any of it. I'm just putting one foot in front of the other and trying to ignore that my heart is broken, okay? So just give me a little while to get a handle on things and accept that Ryder doesn't love me. Then I'll talk to him."

"Sweetheart, that man does so love you. It's there in the way he looks at you, like he thinks you're the most amazing woman who has ever walked the earth." Tammy squeezed her hand. "I would bet on my children's health that he loves you."

Yep, here were the tears. "Do not bet Pete and Hunter's health on that, honey. If Ryder loved me he would want to be married to me, not offer out of obligation."

Three hours later Suzanne was woken up from a restless sleep by her phone ringing. Before she could scramble around and find it, the ringing stopped. Squinting her left eye, Suzanne picked up the phone and glared at the screen. It was two in the morning and it had been Ryder who had called. The chime rang, indicating he'd left a voice mail.

Sitting up, Suzanne pressed the buttons to listen to the voice mail. At first she couldn't understand anything Ryder was saying, given that he was mumbling and his words were slurred. It seemed Elec had been telling the truth about Ryder's hitting the bottle a little too hard.

Rubbing her eyes, she sighed. "Oh, Ryder, we're a disaster, aren't we?"

And then he said it. Warbled and drunk, but heartfelt and unmistakable. "I love you, Suz. I want to be married to you. That's all I want—for you to be my wife. All I've ever wanted."

With trembling fingers, Suzanne saved the message and held the phone in her hand for a second, heart thumping. Then she dialed Ryder back, wanting to hear him say it straight to her, drunk or not. The phone rang and rang but he didn't pick up.

Of course not. With a sigh, Suzanne threw her phone on the pillow next to her and closed her eyes.

If there was one good thing to say about the soul-sucking exhaustion of a first trimester of pregnancy, it was that it would pull her into sleep even when her mind was whirling and her heart was aching.

RYDER woke up with a start, a sudden weight on his back and a chattering voice slicing through his pounding head.

Oh. My. God. He wanted to die. His eyes were paste, his mouth was thick, and every muscle in his body ached like he'd been racked. As some living creature bounced on his back, his stomach gave an anxious flip, bile rising in his throat.

· "Uncle Ryder, what are you doing here?" Hunter asked.

The sad thing was, he had no freaking idea what he was doing there. The last thing he remembered was dancing in a way he should never be allowed to do. Then . . . nothing.

Apparently his friends had deemed him too drunk to leave alone.

"Morning, Hunter," he managed, his voice hoarse.

"Baby girl, you need to get off of Ryder, he has a headache," Elec said, coming into the room, two mugs of coffee in his hands.

"How do you know he has a headache?" Hunter asked, but she did obey her stepfather and climbed off him, much to Ryder's relief.

"Just look at his face, you can tell."

Hunter's head popped up in front of him, making Ryder dizzy and causing a sharp pain behind his eyes.

"You're right, Elec, he looks like cat crap," Hunter declared.

Great. "Thanks, kid."

"Watch your language, young lady," Elec said. "Now go on in and eat your breakfast. Your mama's made eggs and pancakes."

The thought of runny eggs made Ryder's stomach flip. "Oh, God, I'm going to hurl," he muttered, rolling onto his back and putting his hand on his head.

"Please don't. You'll turn me off my breakfast." Elec stuck a mug in his face. "Drink some coffee, you'll feel better."

Ryder forced himself to sit up and take the coffee. After a sip he did feel better and he started to worry. "Did I do anything stupid last night?"

"Besides drinking your weight in rum and dancing with a parade of hot women? No."

Shit. Ryder groaned. "Damn, that was so stupid to drink that much. Where's my wallet and my phone?"

He felt in his pocket, pulled out his wallet, and checked to make sure his credit card was still in there. Alcohol made it quite possible he could have opened a tab and left it at the bar without closing it. Everything was there, and his phone was lying on the floor next to the couch. He sighed in relief. There was nothing worse than losing your cell phone. Okay, there were a lot of things that were way worse, like the current state of his life, but it still was damn annoying.

A thought occurred to him. Worse than losing his phone would have been using it to drunk dial or text. He hit the screen to light it up and groaned when he saw he'd missed a call from Suzanne at two in the morning. Of all the nights for her to call him. He'd been drunk as a skunk and hadn't even heard the phone ring. She hadn't left a voice mail.

Then Ryder thought about it. Would Suzanne really have called him that late? He'd sent her texts since their argument trying to talk to her and she had given him nothing more than clipped responses. Last night had been Nikki's bachelorette party and Suzanne couldn't drink, so odds were if she had called that late, it was because she had needed to vent or because he had called her first. Or sent a stupid text.

Ryder checked his dialed calls and sure enough, he'd called Suzanne two minutes before she'd called him. Great. "Hey, Elec, were you with me when I called Suzanne? Do you, uh, happen to know what I might have said to her?"

Hopefully it was nothing too obnoxious.

"No, I don't recall you using your phone at all. You pretty much passed out in the limo, then we got you in here and dropped you on the couch."

Beautiful. "Thanks for hauling my sorry ass around. According to my phone, I called Suz at 2:02 A.M. and I don't remember doing it. God, I'm such a moron."

"You told me about the baby, you know."

"I did? Of course I did." Ryder sighed. "I am happy about the baby, you know, really happy. But why can't Suzanne and I figure out how to be together?"

"I don't know, Ryder." Elec perched on the edge of his chair, coffee mug in his hands. "But I do know that the two of you love each other and you're having a baby, so I think you should do your best to figure it out."

Hunter came running back into the room in her pit stop

pajamas, her hair flying behind her. "Put your coffee down!" she demanded of Elec.

"Please."

"Please!"

Elec complied and she jumped on his lap, immediately flinging herself backward while he held her so that she was dangling upside down. The thought of being upside down made Ryder want to die immediately and swiftly. "Isn't she going to toss her pancakes?" he asked. She must have shoveled them in at warp speed.

Elec shrugged. "Nah. She has an iron stomach. Don't you, baby girl? You have a gut lined with metal?" He blew a raspberry on her stomach, making her laugh hysterically.

Tammy came wandering in wearing sweatpants and a thermal shirt. "How are you feeling, Ryder?"

"Like you'd expect," he told her. "And no better than I deserve. Thanks for putting me up, I appreciate it."

"No problem."

Pete came in, too, and it suddenly occurred to Ryder that it was Thursday and they shouldn't all be home. "Don't you all have school?" he asked Pete.

"It's the first day of Christmas break," Pete told him.

"I've been off for a week already," Tammy said. "My college students won't be back until January sixteenth, thank goodness."

Well, this wasn't exactly going to be a merry Christmas. "I can't believe Strickland's wedding is Saturday. I'll be glad to be done with that business."

"No kidding." Elec nodded.

"How was the bachelorette party?" Ryder asked Tammy.

"We left at eleven, does that tell you anything?"

"Suz leave with you?"

"Yes."

Ryder winced. He'd called her at two. She had to have been asleep. Had he left a voice mail? He had no clue.

He wasn't sure if he should call her and apologize or not. But there was one thing he was sure of. As he watched Tammy and Elec in their cozy family room with their two pj-wearing, bed-head kids, he wanted the same life for himself.

He wanted that with Suzanne so bad the thought of not having it was driving him to pound rum and make an ass out of himself on the dance floor.

What a disaster.

THERE was no doubting that Suzanne was pregnant because when Nikki's mother opened the door and Suzanne saw Nikki for the first time in her Cinderella wedding gown, she actually teared up, completely touched by how sweet Nikki looked. The bride was smiling, and for a second Suzanne forgot all the tantrums and all the pouting when Nikki waved to her excitedly, her eyes sparkling and her complexion glowing.

"Suzanne! Thank you, thank you, everything is perfect." She enveloped Suzanne in a zero-body-contact hug so she wouldn't wreck her hair or makeup.

"You're welcome. You look beautiful. Jonas is a lucky man." Maybe that was an exaggeration, but it seemed the appropriate thing to say, and hell, Jonas seemed to think he was lucky, so maybe it was the truth. "So the other bridesmaids know to meet us at the hotel at four, right? Maybe I should text all of them."

"It will be fine," Nikki assured her, touching the skirt of her gown over and over, like she couldn't get enough of the voluminous fabric.

Hearing Nikki be zen did Suzanne proud. "The carriage will meet us two blocks from the hotel, so you won't be freezing your buns off. We'll just drive up to the hotel for effect. The limo is here to take us now, so whenever you're ready, we can go."

Nikki looked at herself in the mirror one last time while Suzanne conferred with Nikki's mother and gathered up the bouquet, Nikki's bag of makeup and supplies, and her winter white cape and gloves.

"I know everyone thought I was crazy for getting married so quickly," Nikki said. "And everyone is always saying that marriage is really hard and takes a lot of work."

Suzanne froze with a garment bag over her arm and her purse slapping her in the thigh. She looked at Nikki in the mirror, wondering where this monologue was coming from. "Yeah?" she said, because it seemed like there was a point Nikki hadn't quite gotten around to yet.

"But the thing is, Suzanne, when you know that you love someone, those things don't matter. You have to push all the everyday things and the outside world away, and just enjoy knowing that this is the man who has the chest your head is meant to lie on."

Oh, my God. "That's beautiful, Nikki." And Suzanne had a serious lump in her throat. Why the hell couldn't she and Ryder do that? Honestly? Just enjoy each other.

There was no other man whose chest she belonged on.

"Anyhoo," Nikki said, waving her head. "Did I tell you I got my clit pierced as a wedding gift to Jonas? He's going to be happily surprised tonight." She giggled.

With that, the moment of sage Nikki passed as quickly as it had arrived, and the natural order was restored.

RYDER stood at the front of the ballroom having a crisis. He was wearing a tux, the room was decorated in an explosion of flowers and tulle, and Suzanne was standing at the end of the aisle looking stunningly beautiful.

And it wasn't their wedding. It should be their wedding. Hell, this should have been their wedding six years earlier. He should have given this to Suzanne, the whole pomp and circumstance, the huge party. Getting married was a big goddamn deal and he had never really asked Suzanne if she had been okay with eloping.

He was just standing there aching everywhere, wanting to be with her so bad he was sweating.

"Can you stop with the foot?" Ty murmured next to him.

"Huh?" Ryder watched Suzanne bustling back and forth, checking details and talking to the pianist. She was wearing pink, and even though the dress was a little loose, she looked amazing. As usual.

"Your foot. You're tapping it. It's distracting as hell."

Ryder looked down at his feet. The right one was jiggling up and down. "Sorry." He forced himself to stop.

Jonas said to his right, "Everything is changing, but nothing will be different."

"What?" Ryder looked at him. Jonas looked nervous, his arms continually moving like his jacket was too tight, a sheen of sweat on his upper lip. The normal, black tux had been the right move. Jonas almost looked dapper, aside from the flapping arms and darting eyes.

"My vows. I'm practicing them. Everything is changing, but nothing will be different. I will love you today and tomorrow and always, no matter what obstacles come our way or what happens in our lives. Our life. Today starts our future, where two become one."

Wow. Ryder was stunned, and hell, a little touched. He should have said that to Suzanne. He should have done that. Pledged his love, promised his steadfastness, and guaranteed that no matter what, he would be there for her. When things got tough, he should have forced her to open up to him and he should have tried to change, be a better husband. At the end of the day, it was love that mattered.

Just love.

"Does that sound stupid?" Jonas asked him. "I feel stupid. I look stupid. I sound stupid. God, why is she even marrying me?"

"No, man, it's not stupid at all. It sounds great. And she's marrying you because she loves you." He clapped Jonas on the back. "Congratulations, by the way. I'm really happy for you."

"Thanks." Jonas gave one final tug on his tie. "Oh, shit, it's starting."

Ryder turned and watched the parade of seven hundred bridesmaids coming down the aisle one after the other like Barbie clones in ice-blue bandages. Glancing down the very long row of groomsmen lined up to his left, he thought the guys all looked like uncomfortable penguins waiting to take a dive. Suzanne had disappeared, which left him nothing to look at, so Ryder concentrated on just standing still and not thumping his foot until this was all over.

About an hour later, all the women were finally down

the aisle and had been escorted to their seats by the grooms-men. Ryder could never figure out why every wedding seemed to do this process a little differently, he just knew he wasn't digging that he had to stay standing the whole time per Suzanne's instructions. The maid of honor had taken up position across from him, and the minister, or whoever he was, was standing serenely with his book in his hand, looking like he might drop off into a nap at any given second. His eyes drifted open and closed and he rocked a little on his feet.

Then Jonas made a strangled sound in the back of his throat and Ryder glanced over at him. The big guy had tears in his eyes and Ryder felt touched and awkward at the same time. No man wanted to see his buddy crying, even if it was at his own wedding. Nikki had appeared, and started to move down the aisle, a thin, beautiful girl, noodle arms and upper chest tanned to perfection in her strapless gown, the waist ballooning into the biggest skirt thing Ryder had ever seen in his life. Children could be living under that dress and no one would know.

"She's so fucking beautiful," Jonas choked out, wiping his tears and trying to pretend like he wasn't.

"You're a lucky man," Ryder said, because he didn't know what else to say. The only woman he thought was fucking beautiful was Suzanne, and this was all hitting a little too close to home. He was thinking about the night they'd met, about the instant chemistry they had shared. About the night she'd told him she was pregnant, and the night he'd suggested they run off and get married. But mostly he was thinking about all the ways he could have done better by her.

Then and now.

He should have called her again. He had texted her an apology for calling so late the night of the bachelor party and she'd just replied it was fine. He'd been too much of a wimp to call her again, and he was kicking himself. Jonas was right. When you loved someone, you loved them forever, no matter what, and he was going to do whatever he had to in the hope of convincing Suzanne they belonged together.

CHAPTER NINETEEN

ASKING Suzanne to dance to "Big Butts" at the reception was clearly not the best strategy to meet that goal, but Ryder was running out of options. Suzanne had been dodging him for hours. She'd ducked out of reach every time he'd approached her and had actually shoved a cracker in his mouth at one point when he'd tried to talk to her.

He was getting desperate.

So when Nikki, who had clearly been hitting the skinny bitches, grabbed the mic from the DJ and said everyone in the wedding party had to dance to her favorite party song, including the wedding planner, he had seized the moment.

"Suzanne, you heard what Nikki said." Ryder caught her arm as Suzanne tried to slink off behind the chocolate fountain. "Everyone out there."

"Come on, girls! Show off your booties!" Nikki turned

around and shook her nonexistent ass while a cheer went up from the crowd.

"Do you think I should cut her off?" Suzanne asked, shooting a worried glance at her bridal charge.

"Are you kidding? Nikki's been smiling all day long. She's clearly enjoying herself. Which is what you should be doing, too." Ryder tugged her hand again. "Come on, dance with me."

"You're a nutjob," she said, but she let him drag her onto the dance floor.

To his total amazement, after a few seconds, she relaxed and started to break it down.

"Hot mama, look at you, girl," he told her, enjoying seeing her loosening it.

That earned him a smack on the arm. "At least I can dance. You look like a chicken running from the ax."

"Watch out, or I'll do you like Jonas is doing Nikki." Ryder tipped his head in the bride and groom's direction, where Jonas was pretending to spank Nikki's butt.

Suzanne let out a crack of laughter. "Lordy be. Now that's funny. Let's hope that makes it on the video."

"Better than the hokey pokey, that's for damn sure." It was also a good sign that Suzanne was bantering with him. After she'd kicked him out of her house, he wasn't sure they'd be on speaking terms for weeks. Months. Years.

Which would make it a little difficult to raise a child together.

"Oh, my God, I need to go stop her," Suzanne said, panic mingling with amusement in her voice.

"Why?" Ryder turned to look at the bride. "Holy . . ."

Nikki's breast had popped out of her gown when she'd put her arms up in the air.

"Oh, no, you're good, Jonas has it." The groom danced in front of his wife, shielding her, and whispered in her ear.

Nikki took a second to process his words, but then she looked down and started laughing before shoving her breast back in the dress. They kissed and Jonas took the opportunity to fake spank her again.

"Now that's just beautiful," Suzanne said. "It does a wedding planner proud."

"Love," Ryder agreed.

"I have to say, the ballroom looks damn good." Suzanne glanced around and assessed her work with a smile. "It looks like a fairy-tale wedding, just like Nikki wanted."

Ryder had barely noticed anything other than a high volume of flowers, fluffy bows, and the color blue coming at him in all directions, but what did he know? "You did a great job. With all of this. Who else could have pulled this off?" He meant that sincerely. It took a special talent to put up with Nikki.

The DJ cut the song into a slow song Ryder didn't recognize. "This one's for all those married couples out there. Come on out and dance with the bride and groom."

Suzanne got a stricken look on her face, and when she would have bolted, Ryder grabbed her and pulled her close against him. He was not letting this woman run away from him again.

Glancing around nervously, Suzanne tried to discreetly pull herself out of Ryder's arms, but he had a grip on her like gorilla glue. "Let me go," she hissed, covering her words with a smile in case anyone was looking.

"No."

"What do you mean, no? You're making a mockery out of this dance." Which Suzanne immediately realized was such a prissy-ass thing to say, but she felt embarrassed, like a total fraud. Everyone knew they weren't married.

Or weren't supposed to be married anyway.

"Just dance with me, Suzanne," Ryder murmured, and something about the way he spoke to her stopped her struggling.

Oh, God. His eyes were soft and deep and she suddenly felt like she was drowning in them as Ryder twirled her around. Nikki's words rolled around in her head and her heart started beating double time.

"Why?" she whispered. "Why should I dance with you?"

They weren't talking about dancing and they both knew it.

And then he said it. The words she'd longed to hear even when she hadn't known she'd needed them, the words she'd only heard twice in the last two years, one of which was in a drunken voice mail. "Because I love you. Because I love you so much I'm willing to do whatever it takes to make it go differently this time."

Suzanne swallowed hard, unable to speak.

"Because we should be a married couple, because I never wanted to not be married to you. Because all these men out here dancing with their wives can't possibly love them as much as I love you. Because for me, there is only one woman, and I'm sorry to break it to you, but you're it."

"I . . . I . . ." She had no goddamn clue what to say. For once in her life, Suzanne was well and truly speechless. She wanted to cry, wanted to laugh, wanted to tell Ryder she loved him, too, but her tongue was stuck to the roof of her mouth, and her throat was totally constricted.

"We don't get along," she managed to tell him.

"Yes, we do. That's why we screw up. Because we get along and we're meant to be together and we love each other and we know it. And we're afraid. Afraid to fail."

The music receded and the people around them disappeared as she stared up at him, hearing him, really hearing him. "That's true," she whispered.

"And the thing is, we can't fail. We've already hit the bottom and come out of it. From here on out, if we just love and listen, we can't go wrong, babe."

"Love is all that matters," she told him. "And I do love you. God, I do love you."

His eyes darkened and he let out a shuddery sigh. "You don't know how much I've wanted to hear you say that again."

Then Ryder leaned in close as they swayed to the music and brushed his lips over her cheek. He whispered in her ear, "Would you do me the honor of becoming my wife? 'Til death do us part this time."

Suzanne nodded, knowing that this was right. Her and Ryder. The way it was meant to be. Forever. "Yes," she said, and promptly started crying. Fat, wet, obnoxious tears, her shoulders shaking.

Ryder held her close and let her cry. "Thank you. I'll do better this time, I swear to you. And this time, I owe you a real wedding. What I should have given you the first go-around."

Suzanne fought to get her tears under control and looked up at him. "And I swear to God I will stop being such a man and holding all my feelings in."

"Does that mean you're going to cry all the time?"

"Probably."

"I can live with that." Ryder kissed her forehead. "Did I mention how beautiful you look today? Nikki isn't the only princess here."

And maybe fairy tales did come true.

"Did I ever tell you the difference between a Northern fairy tale and a Southern one?" she asked him, indulging herself and letting her head rest on his shoulder. God, he felt good. Her man. Where her head was meant to lie, right there, on him.

"What's the difference?"

"A Northern one starts 'once upon a time,' while a Southern one starts 'y'all ain't going to believe this shit.'"

Ryder laughed. Then he said, "Believe this."

She shrieked when he startled the hell out of her by dropping her back into a dip straight out of *Dancing with the Stars*. "If you throw my legs over your head, Jefferson, I will kill you," she told him from half upside down.

"That's for later, when we're in private."

Suzanne laughed, breathless as he pulled her back up. "Did you notice everyone around us is doing a conga line? I think the slow dance is over."

Ryder looked down at her with an expression so hot

and sexy she feared it might incinerate her dress. "I didn't notice, because there's no one else in this room but you." He placed his hand gently on her stomach. "I love you, Suzanne Jefferson."

And as the Borden-Strickland wedding reception roared around them, Suzanne only had eyes for her husband.

EPILOGUE

TURN TWO FOR THE JEFFERSONS

by Tuesday Talladega

They may have quit the race early the first time around, but Ryder Jefferson and his ex-wife (well, not really ex-wife, we'll get back to that in a sec) have hit the track together for a second time, tying the knot in Charlotte on Valentine's Day (cue the "awww") for two hundred guests. Sponsor- and media-free, details are sketchy, but sources say the bride wore an empire-waist gown, leading to rumors there's a baby driver on board. The bride's attendants were Tamara Briggs-Monroe, Imogen Wilson, and curiously enough, Nikki Strickland, a newlywed herself, whose Dolce and Gabbana–covered butt has been at every race this season since Daytona. Groomsmen were the Monroe brothers, Ty McCordle, and Jonas Strickland, leaving Evan Monroe without a partner. (Note to Evan: If you need a woman, call me, sweetums.)

While the wedding was a standard chic black tie

affair with a string quartet and a litany of expensive beef dishes given French names, the groom's cake raised a few eyebrows by being a dozen pies instead of an actual cake. Don't you hate it when there's an inside joke you don't get?

But I can tell you this . . . turns out the Jeffersons never legally got divorced and were all set to finalize things just this past December twenty-third. Yet instead here they are throwing a wedding, so I guess somebody was naughty and nice this year. It's enough to make even a hard-core cynic like me give love two thumbs up.

Well, I wish them all the best, blah, blah, blah, and won't hold it against them that my invitation got lost in the mail.

Drop by tomorrow for the latest rumor on Evan Monroe, the partner-free cutie driver, who is facing rough waters with his team owner. On your feet, race fans, the season just got a whole lot more exciting . . .

Turn the page for a special preview of
Erin McCarthy's next Fast Track Novel,

The Chase

Coming March 2011 from Berkley Sensation!

"I bet he's as bad in bed as he is on the track."

Kendall Holbrook looked at her friend Tuesday Jones cautiously as they sat on the boards in pit road watching Evan Monroe lapping the track on a test run. That was one particular driver's sexual prowess she did not want to discuss. "Do you mean bad-good or bad-bad?"

"What?" Tuesday cocked her head and frowned. "There is no bad-good."

"Yes, there is. You could have meant that he's a badass. That kind of bad."

Her friend shook her head, making her dark hair slide forward. "No. No badass. Bad is just bad, as in he sucks. I mean, he can't drive for shit, and any man who can't drive certainly can't f—"

Cutting her friend off, Kendall said, "Okay, I get it!"

"Which is really too bad because he is phenomenally

cute. What a butt! That's not a bad ass. That's a good ass. A delicious ass."

"I never noticed." Liar. She was a huge, jumbo, giant liar. Not only had she noticed Evan's butt, she'd seen it naked a decade earlier when she'd been young and stupid and had thought dating him made an ounce of sense. It hadn't.

But she could definitely say that Evan had not been bad-bad in bed. He had opened her eyes sexually, or technically had rolled them back in her head, the first man—boy, really—to have done that.

"You must be talking about his butt, because you can't deny that you've noticed his driving is less than stellar this season."

Kendall waited until Evan's car roared around the track in front of them. "Oh, that I've noticed. This is the worst season of his career."

Speaking of which, would it be considered evil if she admitted that a small part of her was just a little gleeful that the man who had broken her heart was down on his luck? Nope, she didn't believe it would be. Just ask any woman who had been burned by a two-faced man and she'd be on her side. Besides, it's not like she wanted him to die or anything.

Wait, did she?

No, no, definitely not. She just wanted him to not be the successful golden boy for once.

"I feel sorry for him," Tuesday said. "It's like he's so used to being good, he doesn't know what to do with himself."

"I don't feel sorry for him." God's honest truth there. Kendall had fought and clawed to get where she was, and

Evan had just breezed through life, the son of a racing legend, sponsors falling in his lap. "Have you listened to the man? His ego can stand a hit or two."

"Yeah, but I wouldn't mind comforting him." Tuesday pushed up her sunglasses and gave a naughty grin. "Come here, sweetie, let me comfort you with my hands on your bare butt and your—"

Again, Kendall cut her off because she knew Tuesday had no barriers or concern for the fact that a dozen people were milling all around them. But then again, Tuesday was in the media, and didn't have to answer to the same public relations czars.

Not that image was first and foremost on Kendall's mind. She just didn't want to hear Tuesday's graphic description of fictional sex with Evan. Why, she wasn't sure. It wasn't like it mattered anymore who Evan slept with. It hadn't for ten years. But still. Just still.

"I thought you said he probably sucks in bed."

Tuesday dangled her feet off the wall, her boots scuffing the wall. "Oh, I would just make him lie there while I took whatever I wanted. My submissive sex slave."

"Oh, Lord." Kendall rolled her eyes. "If you think Evan Monroe is down with being submissive, you need to start wearing a helmet."

"Wearing a helmet when? I'm not a driver."

"Wearing a helmet when you're walking because clearly you banged your brains up somehow if you think that man would just lie there and do what you say."

"And how do you know so much about what Evan Monroe would or wouldn't do?"

Kendall couldn't see Tuesday's eyes behind her sunglasses but she recognized that tone. Her friend was suspicious and tenacious in ferreting out secrets. It's what made her an amazing racing journalist and gossip blog writer, known online as Tuesday Talladega.

Striving for nonchalance, she fought the urge to tug on the front of her jacket. "Come on, it's obvious. He's a walking egomaniac alpha male. Like every other driver in the series."

"Mmm-hmm. If I didn't know better, I'd think there was more to this story."

God, she was going to blush. Twenty-eight years old and she was going pink in the cheeks. "No story! And don't you dare write me into your blog, speculating about me, or I will egg your house. I know where you live, you know."

Tuesday just laughed. "Please. You would not. And you know I won't gossip about your personal life. Unless it's really, really good."

"That's reassuring." Kendall had read Tuesday's blog many times. Her friend was snarky and biting and raised questions that got people thinking, and not always in a positive way. She did not want to be on the receiving end of that wicked pen. Or keyboard, as the case may be.

Shifting on her feet, Kendall gave in and yanked at the front of her fire retardant jumpsuit. She was starting to sweat. Glancing at the track, she noticed Evan was pulling in to pit and talking to his crew. His brother, Elec Monroe, was already pulling onto the track in his number 56 car.

"I'm kidding," Tuesday said, waving her hand in dismissal. "I do talk about your career, but I have to. Everyone would notice if I omitted discussing the most intriguing bit of news to hit stock car racing in years. A *female* driver in the cup series, hello, it's a major sound bite. But I'll never trash you, scout's honor. I am a loyal friend."

Tuesday didn't sound offended, but Kendall still felt guilty that she had implied she couldn't trust Tuesday. "I know. You are a good friend, and I'm damn grateful to have you around to keep me sane. But I don't want to be the biggest news to hit stock car racing just because I have a uterus."

"I don't think it's your uterus most men are concerned with. It's your vagina. Va-jay-jay. Your man hole."

Nothing like saying it like it was. Kendall was about to tell Tuesday exactly what she thought of the expression *man hole* when she heard a strangled laugh from behind her. Great, someone had heard them.

"Is this what happens when we let a woman driver into the cup series? Instead of chassis and boiler plate restrictors, we talk uterus and va-jay-jay?"

Oh, freaking fabulous. That wasn't just any someone. That was Evan goddamn Monroe. Right behind her.

**Love Shifts into High Gear in
the First Fast Track Novel**

FROM *USA TODAY* BESTSELLING AUTHOR

ERIN McCARTHY

FLAT-OUT SEXY

The last place widowed single mother Tamara Briggs
wanted to find a man was at the racetrack. Been
there, done that. But rookie driver Elec Monroe sure
does get her heart racing . . .

"Steamy . . . fast-paced and red hot."
—*Publishers Weekly*

M661T0310